ALSO BY MARK CHILDRESS

A World Made of Fire

V
for
Victor

V
for
Victor

a novel by

Mark
Childress

ALFRED A. KNOPF
NEW YORK 1989

THIS IS A BORZOI BOOK
PUBLISHED BY ALFRED A. KNOPF, INC.

Library of Congress Cataloging-in-Publication Data
Childress, Mark.
V for Victor.
1. World War, 1939–1945—Fiction. I. Title.
PS3553.H486V17   1988   813'.54   88-45435
ISBN 0-394-56871-1

FIRST EDITION

FOR MY BROTHERS

V
for
Victor

1942

I

THINK OF a place in the heart of nowhere. A place made of water, the sky, a salt marsh. Not much else. Trees, a boat. A boy of sixteen with a dangerous imagination.

Late on one of the last days in May, when the sun was fat red and just inches above the horizon, Victor looked up from his Hardy Boys book and smelled woodsmoke: his grandmother Willie waiting with supper: green beans burned just right in a cast-iron pot, cornbread in the stove, fish lifted from shimmering oil to drain on torn paper bags.

Stretching his arms, Victor felt strong and fast, beyond his years. He challenged the sun to a race. He bet his life. He could run all the way down the island to Willie's before the sun touched the horizon.

He was empty. The aroma promised to fill him. He grabbed up the book and ran hard. He knew he could win. He knew the path by heart, or thought he did until he mistook a dead-end gully for the shortcut. Plunging into a den of tall weeds, he got tangled and missed seeing the root that snared his ankle, sent him off tumbling down a ditch bang roll thud, and drove the air from his chest.

He rolled over slowly, struggling for breath, and looked up to something above him, something so monumental it took up that side of the sky—a mound—no, a *mountain* of gray oyster shells.

He took one shell in his hand. Rough scars and craters told of things that had tried to get at the pearly interior, where the gray quivering had once lived. Someone or something had tossed the shell here, and then someone else, and a hundred, thousands of someones. . . .

A tribe of long-ago people? A secret and ravenous animal?

Victor had played wild all over his grandmother's island. Could this mountain always have been here? Why had he never found it? Could it be an illusion, like false water on a desert?

He remembered his race just in time to lose it. His bare feet slipped and slid and set up clinking landslides of shells; by the time he reached the top, the last fingernail of the sun was gone in the waves.

He settled crosslegged on the summit, admitting defeat. *Pay-up, pay-up*, said a passing seagull.

From this height, in the pink and cool blue afterglow, he surveyed the vast open bay—twenty miles to the north, the faint gleam of Mobile; twenty miles down, the searchlights of Fort Morgan, at the Gulf's open mouth; all the miles up that opposite shore, instead of the glittering necklace of lights, only darkness. The blackout. The war.

With a blink Victor changed all the water to sand. He invented a desert as big as the bay. No one would recognize the skinny boy perched atop this pile of shells as a sheikh, but he was, and this mountain a high windswept dune. He conjured a beautiful lady in danger, marauders to rescue her from, a saber, a cape, a white horse—

Looking down from their cockpits, the Jap pilots thought they were seeing only an island, an oyster-shell mound. None of them noticed the swiveling eye of the gun until too late, the *pocketa-pock* and the flash, then the sea rising up to seize them.

The Japs turned into Nazis, advance parties creeping by night, green as the trees, smelling of leather. Victor spotted a Messerschmidt high overhead—a whole wing of them, fighters, ME-101s—but the nimble German pilots dodged his tracer bullets.

He ran out of ammo.

The last veil of twilight fell away to reveal the true face of the dark. Pure dark. The color of nothing at all.

Suddenly he felt awkward as a giant in a little boy's storybook. He was too old to play made-up games on this crumbling pile of shells, and besides the sun was long gone, and he ought to go back before Willie had a chance to worry herself any closer to death than she was when he left.

A wet smell of fish came in on the breeze. Darkness hovered above, as if someone had tacked a curtain over the stars.

A few timid glimmers huddled together, low and dim in the east. More drifted in, aimless, wandering in uneasy loops as if trying to find their right places.

Victor shivered: a chill.

The moon. Where was the moon? It was past time. He searched the horizon. Nothing.

He pressed his face to his knees. Maybe the stars gather at dusk and wait for the moon to come show them the way.

He waited.

When he lifted his eyes the sky wore a new veil, deep blue, and a million bright stars. A sliver of light peeked over the edge, away to the south. The moon was too heavy with light. It struggled to rise and then faltered, rested its weight on the horizon, gathered strength.

At last it began a slow upward crawl. A gold arm shimmered out across the water. It pointed at Victor.

Then—a fleeting interruption of the light, a black band slipped over the arm—there and gone in an instant.

Victor blinked. All was silence. He saw nothing but the moon pouring glitter on the water.

He would not be fooled by the calm. This bay opened into the Gulf, which mixed with the oceans of the world, and in all that water there had to be something lurking, a thing you could never explain—a shark, an enemy, a monster, a ghost ship, a terrible mouth that could swallow you whole, a creature so big and dark you would not believe it even in wide-open daylight.

Victor knew monsters from books and from dreams, from the terrified moments before he awoke. Of course he knew there were no monsters. But still he guarded the old fear in his heart like a torch, to keep them at bay.

2

THE MAGNOLIA RIVER meanders for five miles down from its spring, widening, opening, mixing with the salty tide as it approaches Weeks Bay. This wide, shallow lake narrows down to a mouth. The lower jaw of this mouth was Willie's island—a half-mile of marsh grass, a long stretch of thickety woods, a high place of two or three acres well-shaded by live oaks, with Weeks Bay on one side and the big bay, Mobile, on the other.

Hidden among the great trees, Willie's house tottered on pilings as if the next wind might be the one to knock it over. Victor lay on his back on the floor of the side porch, his ear to the radio. He was stuck on the island with Willie, waiting for someone to come. For the sun to go down, for the sun to come up, for the tide to come in or run out. For something to happen within sight of his own eyes.

Waiting for Willie to die.

He was sick of waiting. He was too old to love this place as he did when he was little, and too young to go off anywhere else. The radio was his one friend. It was a Silvertone shaped like a church, with a cool amber diamond dial where the preacher would be. It used to belong to his big brother Joseph, but Joseph went off to the war.

Victor wished he could go off and join up too. Joseph had been off getting ready to go up against Adolf Hitler for nearly a year now, and already he was a hero.

All anybody could talk about: war.

The whole world was mobilizing. At Bon Secour High School they handed out cards with the white silhouettes of enemy airplanes. Victor inspected all the transports lumbering over to Brookley Field or the Naval Air Station at Pensacola, but every one turned out to be one of ours.

He listened to Edward R. Murrow, all somber in London, to Hitler ranting in Berlin. He clipped pictures of Churchill and Goebbels and Tojo and Tokyo Rose from the Mobile *Register*. He memorized every line and censor mark of Joseph's letters home, the code words and in jokes of soldiers. He begged for an Army-style crew cut, but his mother had always acted as if his hair were her personal property, and she refused to permit it.

On its own, Victor's hair whipped up into a tangle of stiff curls, an unsettled sea. His mother said this made him look Greek and attractive, while his father muttered darkly about Creoles (or worse) on her side of the family. Victor didn't much resemble his parents, nor his brothers or sisters, who tended to be redheaded, freckled, built solid. He was gangly, the color of light coffee, dark-haired, not the least bit attractive or Greek, he was sure, with his spatter of pimples, the teeth that slanted in front. His shirt showed his ribs. He was so miserable and ugly and tall that he could not look in a mirror.

His life was passing him by. Here he was dreaming up sea monsters while everyone else in every place in the world was out fighting or dying, mixed up in something exciting or furtive or wrong.

Everything poured from the radio, night after night, a torrent of thrusts and attacks in odd places. Jap advance in the Carolines. Setback for Rommel in North African sands. Victor lounged on the floor, eyes closed, soaking it in—the speeches of men who must surely be great to go on and on without ever repeating themselves.

The Cubs fought the Cards. Smooth clarinets on "The Colgate House Party." Henry Aldrich, boy sleuth, crept toward an ominous barn. Charlie McCarthy shot off his wood mouth . . . and way at the end, a feeble signal from New Orleans, a dozen Negroes shouting Amen, stomping the floor so hard the speaker buzzed in Victor's ear.

At least it drowned out the sound of Willie.

She would not leave her island to die. Every night she went down the list of her ailments, from the freezing pain in her elbow to the sores on her knotted old feet. Nothing she had was bad enough by itself to kill her, but if you believed even part of her list, she was not long for this island.

Victor turned up the volume, so her symptoms blended in with static between stations.

"Per . . . why . . . cardia," she pronounced. "An in-flammation of the cardiac muscu . . . musculature. That one sounds fearful, don't it, honey boy. That's what the blue pills are for. I think he was all wrong on that one. I hadn't felt a thing from my heart. Not since I got back where I belong."

The radio dial was on LOUD. "And now, for your listening pleasure, the vocal stylings of one of the loveliest songbirds to come out of Texas . . . ladies and gentlemen please welcome —Miss Dinah Anderson!"

A splash of applause. Victor imagined her willowing up to the microphone, a pale leggy cowgirl topped off with a corona of yellow hair. "Good evening," she breathed, all husky and low. "I'd like to sing a song for our sweet soldier boys, wherever they may be tonight."

Applause in a velvet-lined room. Forks tinkled against crystal. She began to sing:

> "Skylark
> Have you anything to say to me?
> Won't you tell me where my love can be?
> Is there a meadow in the mist
> Where someone's waiting to be kissed?"

"Now, I don't much care for what they play on that radio," Willie said, lifting her feet to the ottoman, "but right there is pretty."

"Dinah Anderson," Victor wondered aloud. "I bet she's beautiful."

"They never look as good as they sound."

"I bet Joseph could play that song," said Victor.

Willie tilted her head. "Wish I could hear him. That boy can flat sing."

Dinah Anderson held her breath past the final applause. Then: "That's a beautiful song from one beautiful fella. Let's hear a big round for Hoagy." She purred over the appreciative roar. "Now, Tommy, let's play a slow tune for all of our lonesome sailors on their boats."

The trumpets piped up, and she went sliding down the melody. It was a minor key, downbeat and sad.

"I wish I was dead," Victor announced.

"No you don't. Just stop listening. It's the way she sings, it'll break your heart if you let it."

"I wish we were both dead then," he said. "Who would care? Nobody."

"Aw now . . . Swaney would come out to bring us the mail, and he'd find us."

"What if Swaney don't come."

"He'll come," Willie said. "And besides, if he didn't, your daddy will be out here Thursday, and think what he'd say if he found us like that."

Victor smiled. A light came on in his eyes. "I'd already have you sitting up by the boathouse. And I'd be swinging by my neck from the cypress tree."

"He'd tan your hide. Honey boy, throw that pillow up under my feet."

"Wouldn't matter how mad he got. I'd already be dead."

"Hush your mouth . . ."

The way she shivered, Victor knew he'd carried the joke too long. "You need a blanket?"

"No, I'm not so much cold. Here it is nearly June."

The announcer was asking another big hand for the singer. Victor turned him down. "Want me to put you a bath on?" he said. "I'll bring up a bucket."

"No, I'm scared of a chill. You just sit. You're a good boy. I ought to be waiting on you."

"Willie." He stood over her. "Don't you go dying on me now, so it turns out it's all my fault. You hear me?"

"Go on, Victor," she said, and that surprised him; she rarely called him anything but honey boy. "Wasn't a minute ago you had me propped up—propped up and dead as a dog."

"But that's different. I'd be right there beside you."

"You go on." She could not help a smile. "I declare, you are about the most unusual boy on this side of the bay."

He leaned down, brushed her cheek with his lips. "I'm gonna carry the radio out on the porch. Time for the Shadow."

Willie cut her eyes and croaked, *The Shadow knows*," and her loony expression broke him up. The organ notes sounded, the theme. She wandered off to her room, fiddling with her dentures.

Lamont Cranston and Margo, dining in a swanky bistro. "Oh, Lamont, look!" Margo cried. "When that waiter started for the kitchen, the door opened without his touching it!"

Victor could almost hear Lamont's knowing shrug. "Yes. Works by photoelectric ray."

"Oh, what's that?"

"Look at each side of the door, Margo. See those chromium fixtures sticking out of the floor? Lights hidden at the top of them?"

Willie poked her head out, wearing a hairnet and a wicked toothless grin. "I took all my pills. Is it time?"

It was the same every night. She loved whiskey. The whiskey would kill her. Victor was under strict orders to keep her away from the thing she loved most in life. It was hopeless. Since the war started, whiskey was harder to come by than ethyl gasoline, but Willie always had a bottle hidden somewhere. No one knew how she got it.

Victor discovered her hiding place his second night on the island, when he looked up from *The Shore Road Mystery* to see her sneaking past to the kitchen. He followed on tiptoe. She knelt by the chimney of the behemoth wood stove, pried loose a board, and drew out a quart of Old Forester Bonded Bourbon.

"*Ah-ha!*" He leapt at her. "Redhanded! Now Willie, you give that to me!"

Before she recovered herself, Victor snatched the bottle and dangled it over his head, like a prize. From then on he kept it in his duffel bag, doling it out to her one glass at bedtime, if she had behaved and taken her pills.

"I guess it's time," Victor said, getting up from his comfortable spot. He fetched what was left of the quart, shaking it into bubbles. "It's nearly gone."

"Don't knock it around." Willie offered her glass. "Be nice to anything and it'll be nice to you. Except stinging wasp, maybe. They don't give you much of a chance."

Victor poured out the last. "Gone."

"Don't worry, honey boy. There's more where that came from."

"Aw, Willie!"

Without teeth her smile was sublime.

"Where's the stuff? Come on, give it." Victor wiggled his fingers. "Tell me where it is." He stalked to the stove, felt for the loose board.

"It's not there. And you'll never find it this time."

He looked down on her. "You're a mean little woman, you know that? Make me look like a fool. You don't need me to look after you."

"Don't think I was born yesterday," Willie said. "Why don't you hush up and have you a sip? It will cure what ails you, I swear."

"No thank you."

"Suit yourself."

"Well, 'The Shadow's' almost over anyway, you talk so much," Victor said. "I guess it wouldn't hurt me."

Willie went into the other room—"Turn your head the other way," she cried—and returned presently with a shot glass and a quart. She cracked the seal, poured out two amber inches.

Victor tossed it back in one stroke. Oh heat. The heat made him cough. "Mmrgh," he said. "Cough medicine."

"That's what it is," Willie said. "Gives you something better to do than cough. But you got to drink it slow. So you get just a taste on your tongue." She perched on the edge of her bed. A breeze tugged at the heavy black curtain, which was bunched up and pinned to the side. For a long time, the coast marshal dropped by with bribes of red licorice, trying to get her to cover her windows. The way Willie told it, she scoffed at him. She had only the one light bulb; that and the radio ran off an old Buick battery. She'd certainly never spotted a Japanese or a German either one off her shore, she told him, and if he covered over her windows she wouldn't be able to see one if it came.

But then the marshal, a young man from Bay Minette with spectacles and an officious manner, broke out in explanations: It's the law, and punishable by such-and-such fines and not less than such-and-such, and wouldn't she hate to be the one who revealed a ship's outline to a U-boat commander?

Leaves rattled, a sound like rain on the roof. "Willie knows," she told Victor. "I was young once myself, if you can believe it. This place seemed like the most awful, most out of the way place on God's earth to me."

"Yeah, I know what you mean." Victor folded his arms.

"But the more I got to know about it, the more I found out. This river, this whole river's just . . . alive." She took a satisfied swallow. "It's a good place to be. I see all them other places in your eyes. But what you don't know is, where you are *right now* is special. This bay is the one place on earth where there is a jubilee. That's a natural fact, go to the library and read it yourself. You can go all the way around the world and you won't see a jubilee again unless you come back to *here*."

Jubilee! The word sounded the thrill of early early mornings . . . the cry coming into his sleep through the window screen. Before dawn, sometimes, when it was warmest in summer, when the heat killed the wind, when the tide and the moon and water worked out a strange arrangement, the fishes and shrimps and the crabs and the eels and the rays would all swim up from the floor of the bay.

The water no longer held them. They wanted out. They threw themselves into the shallows, even onto the thin strip of sand, wave after wave of the species marching to the shore—big limp bottomfish, lead-colored flounder flapping, gasping, a million shrimp pulsating feebly, and everywhere frantic blue crabs, who alone seemed to sense where this action would lead.

The natural rules were relaxed. The bay surrendered itself.

Only a few creatures would survive until the impulse faded, and move back to their rightful depths. The rest would starve for water in the open air.

No matter what time of night, someone walking along the shore would suddenly bolt for his lantern and dip net and bucket, then for his nearest neighbor, shouting *Jubilee! Jubilee!* as he went. The word spread like fog. *Jubilee!* People emerged from their houses, scuffing drowsily out, coming awake to the miracle spread on the beach. They ran to gather the harvest before it changed its mind.

"But there hasn't been a jubilee," said Victor. "Not since I was little."

"That don't mean a thing," Willie scolded. "You think that's a long time? That's the eye of a gnat, what that is. The jubilee's been here since you or me or anybody else. And it will be here after. It may take its time, but it wouldn't be anything worth remarking unless it did. Why do you think it happens?"

Victor picked at his toes. "I don't know. Daddy says it's the turpentine mills."

Willie turned up her nose. "He also used to say it was blood in the water. Blood of all the dead Negroes in south Alabama, washed down to here, killing the fish."

"That's crazy."

"It is, but so is your daddy. His uncle C.L. always held to the idea that it was because there was too many fish. He said the fish took a count of themselves. They all gathered up in a fish convention, voted which ones to give up."

Victor snorted.

"You laugh, but there's wilder things that turn out true.

There's a whole mess of Indian-type stories about it, but you can't believe nothing to do with Indians. They've been gone too long for anybody to get it straight. I got my own opinions."

"Maybe the fish get tired of swimming," said Victor. "Maybe they just want to go for a walk."

"It's not what they want." Willie jabbed a finger into his arm for emphasis. "It's what they *think* they want." She waved at the window, the bay. "Listen to me. Fish are stupid. They swim up and down the shore of this bay, nothing to do all day long but swim and eat, eat and swim. They get to thinking they're a bunch of ocean fish that somehow got stuck in a lake. Not a one of them ever had sense enough just to swim down to Fort Morgan and go out through the pass. They'd rather jump up on the sand and die."

"That can't be right," Victor said. "Some of them are bound to have swum out."

"Don't you see, that's where fish are like people," said Willie, easing her feet to the ottoman. "They don't learn from one to the next. These ain't the first fish to run into this problem. These are fish that hadn't got any better sense than to try it on the beach because that's the way fish are supposed to do. Dumb as that. They get themselves up on the sand, all right, but it ain't the air they were born to. They can't breathe strange air."

"You don't know about me," Victor said. "I'll get out, and I'll stay out."

"What is it you want out of so bad, honey boy? Your own skin?"

"Sure. Why not. You don't know."

"Oh, I know how you are." She looked at him through the curve of her glass. "Don't put all so much past me. You just pining for Joe. He's all right. They'll send him back soon enough."

"I don't care if he comes back," Victor blurted. "I want to

go! Sometimes I—I could just get in a boat and keep going. I wouldn't stop till I got to China."

"What would you do with yourself over there?"

"Find somebody to fight." Victor blew out the lamp; the glass chimney was so hot he almost broke it, setting it down. "I'm going to bed."

"Be careful what you wish for," she whispered. "You might just get it."

"Good night, Willie."

She dabbed the corner of her mouth with a handkerchief. "I thought you were going to catch us a nice big snapper for tomorrow lunch."

"That's what you thought."

"Look at him, talking about going to China, and he can't stand to clean a fish," she said. "Shoot, *I'm* going to bed."

"Good night, Willie." "The Shadow" was over. Victor turned the radio down, pulled off his dungarees. The springs on the Army cot jingled. He balanced the heavy radio on his chest. The cord cut across his nipple. Now they were playing blue-moon music, songs for the night.

"Willie? Did you ever hear about a whale or anything in the bay?"

She didn't answer.

A grumbling thunder broke in the distance—a movement of air, wind in marsh grass, the slap of the tide at the dock. Mullet burst from the water and smacked down to hear themselves hit.

A shiver seized Victor. Don't die tonight, Willie, he thought. Tonight I don't want you to die ever. Never mind what I thought I wanted before.

Then he told himself: well, it must be the whiskey. He fell asleep hoping he would dream of Miss Dinah Anderson.

3

BLOW OUT your candle, Victor," said his mother, taking a drag off her cigarette. "It's dripping all over the cake."

Victor blew.

His littlest brother, the baby everyone called Peanut, laughed, clapped hands, showed his tooth. He sat in a ring of Sylvesters: six-year-old Doolittle, who adored Victor above all things; Margaret Ann, who was ten and would grow up to make some man a good boss; and Roxanne, fourteen, superior to them all, flopped out on the rug with her fingers in her red hair. When they all gathered in one room, the house near the spring seemed even smaller than Willie's.

Victor knew he should be smiling at their expectant faces, the stack of little packages, but he had an ominous sense of his father hovering at the far edge of the room, like the *Hindenburg* nudging up to its pole. One spark might set him off.

"This one's from Joseph." His mother pushed a tiny box across the table. She looked tired all the time nowadays, dark around the eyes; sometimes she did not get up until noon. "He sent me the money and told me what to get."

Victor plucked at the string. In the box, under a cotton pad, he found a chain with a silvery oval: a medal, a man walking, SAINT CHRISTOPHER embossed on the rim.

"Great." He put it back in the box.

His mother stubbed out the cigarette, breathing smoke through her nose. "It's a medal the Catholics wear. It's supposed to bring you good luck, son. Put it on."

Doolittle tugged at her arm. "Mama, what's a Catholic?"

"Shut up, Doo," said Margaret Ann, glaring at her little brother as if she might need to slap him in a minute.

Their father's impatience expanded in the room. "Let's get on with this thing."

Their mother kept her eyes on the cake, the little stream of hardened wax. "You don't have to be Catholic to hope for good luck," she said. "Victor, what's wrong? He thought you'd like it."

"I said it was great, didn't I?" Victor snatched the medal from the box, twirled it on its chain. "See? I love it. It's great."

His father darkened the air behind him. "Son." One warning, the word.

Victor felt blood in his face. "Daddy, you can't just expect me to sit here and act like there's nothing wrong."

Silence descended. The children drew in their legs by instinct.

Victor's mother shook another cigarette from the pack. Every member of the family watched as she lit it and took the first draw. "What on earth do you mean, Victor," she said.

He spoke past her. "Daddy, I'm sorry, you're going to have to tell her sometime."

"*Son*," said his father.

His mother lifted an eyebrow. "Tell me what?"

"*Victor.*" His father stepped forward, rested his hands on her shoulders.

She jerked free. "I said, tell me *what*."

"Victor and I have an announcement," said his father. "I want everybody to hear it."

The younger children inched back against the furniture. The mother sat stone-still in her chair, as if hands were holding her there. The lamp on the table flickered, brightening all the faces except the old man's. He stood away from the circle, in darkness.

"We all know Willie's been sick," he said. "Yesterday the doctor told us she's even sicker than that. Said her heart's gotten worse, along with everything else. The time has come she shouldn't be down there alone."

He stopped and looked down at his pants cuff, where the baby was tugging. "Margaret Ann," he said, "come take this baby and do something with him."

"But you said we could listen," came the answering whine.

Victor hissed, "Get your butt out of here, Margaret Ann."

Their father swelled up behind them with a terrible growl from the back of his throat. Margaret Ann grabbed the baby, Roxanne grabbed Doolittle's hand, and they quietly fled down the hall.

That left just Victor, his father, his mother, the flammable air in the room.

"Lord, she's not coming here?" his mother was saying in a high, pinched voice. "You think I'm going to step and fetch for her while you're off a month on your boat? You've got two worthless brothers who don't lift a finger for her."

Victor was amazed at this show of mindless courage in the face of the great thundercloud, but he had to stop her. "Mother, you don't under—"

"Keep out of this." She was up on her feet. Her dancing electrical eyes were no longer tired or old. "This is between me and your father."

"You better watch your mouth, Ellen," came the rumble from the dark side of the room. "You don't have to worry about my mama coming up here. She don't want to be here any more than you want her."

"Well that's fine," Victor's mother shot back. "I suppose my house isn't good enough for her. Where's she going, John and Rose's? I wish her good luck getting either one of them to lift a finger . . ."

Victor could not stand it. "Mother, *hush*. Willie's not going anywhere. Daddy's sending me down to the island."

"What do you mean? When?" She fumbled for a cigarette. "Daniel, what is this? You haven't said one word to me!"

"Try to get a word in some time." Victor's father waved him away from the cake. "I was hoping he'd come around to volunteer, but he didn't. He'd rather lay around this house and get waited on hand and foot. Well I'll make him go down there if that's what it takes."

"Daddy—"

His father whirled, a weird smile on his face. "Don't *you* say one more word," he shouted. "You stand *there*. Thanks to you, all this got started." The dark eyes glared as if Victor were a trespasser or a madman, someone to be removed from the premises.

His mother rose up, a wall between them. "Don't you go blaming him! You got more to contend with than him. He's a boy, a boy, Daniel, not a nurse! He doesn't need to be down there with her! Do you think he's just going to quit school?"

"I should have known you'd take his side." His father's voice curdled. "I swear to God. I'm not fit for this earth. It's just about more than I can take, now honey, I'm telling you. That old woman down there, that sick old woman you won't call her name, that old woman is my mother. She had me, she raised me, she looked after us all, times we all should have died. And Pop, yeah, he went off, just like I do, he busted his *balls* like I do, sunup to sundown. Slinging shrimp on that boat so we didn't starve. It made him so tired he died. And now she's about to do the same thing." His fist smashed the table, scattering presents. "I'll be damned before I let her die by herself!"

Victor's mother could not find her matches. Her hands shook. Her face was rigid. "Daniel—"

"I'm not done. Wait till I'm done. I *begged* her to come here. We'd have taken her in and you'd have looked after her without saying one single hard word to her, I guarantee. But she wouldn't come. Didn't want to put you out. I'd go down there myself but you all would starve. So I'm taking the boy. He can go pack his bag. I'm leaving at five and he better be ready. And that's the last thing I'm going to hear about it."

"Suits the *hell* out of me . . ." Victor made sure he was already out of the room when he said it.

"Come back here!" his father roared. "You dare talk that way in front of your—"

"Happy *birth*day!" Victor slammed doors, all the doors down the hall. He was sixteen, too old now to cry, but tears came and choked him and burned.

He squeezed a red welt in his palm with the medallion. Joseph was gone. That was when it all started, the disintegration, the combat at the supper table. Joseph was the peacemaker—red face, bright disposition—and somehow he held them together in the idea that they had a happy home. He could disarm the combatants with one well-aimed crack from his mouth. He had power over them, their first child did. He called them by their first names. "Ellen," he would tell his mother, "why don't you get the shotgun, and I'll hold Daniel down long enough for you to get good aim." Then he would burst out laughing, and that hilarious sound always ended the fight.

Now it was war all the time, war in every place, for no reason at all. The family Victor remembered—maybe it had never existed. Maybe it was something he had dreamed up to fill an empty space.

4

A SOUND?

No, an absence of sound stealing in where the noises should be.

Victor lay with his eyes shut, pretending it was all a dream.

But oh, it was not. He lived it again. It was real. He was himself again, wide awake, sprawled off the end of the cot.

It was too quiet. He could not make out a sound. No gonk-gonking tree frogs. Not the tiniest *chip!* of a cricket. No creatures, no breeze in the live oaks. He strained for the sound of the bay. Silence rang in his ears.

What if the world had strayed off course and smashed into the moon?

He opened his eyes just enough to see moonlight. That meant he was alive, in the quietest part of the night . . . or it could be the island around him was gone, blown to bits by torpedoes—everyone, everything but Victor. The devils have come up from under the sea and blasted the island to dust. This silence is all they have left.

A harsh sputter erupted just past the screen, the backfire of a tiny cicada engine.

Victor sat up, scratching the bites on his ankles. Willie's forty-three starfishes dangled on strings all around, silhouetted against the screen. Picking his way through the clutter of clay pots, he pressed his face to the door. The moon was pasted on the edge of a cloud, the bay glinting through dark trees.

Some sound still missing . . .

Willie.

He turned. A vicious sharp point caught the meat of his shin, sent him hopping, spilling flowerpots, flinging the door open, groping into silence thick as a fog. He felt down the wall to her door. "Willie?" His own whisper startled him. He smelled the sweet of her cold cream. "Willie? You here?"

Moonlight fell in slices through the venetian blinds. At the foot of her bed, a plump little mound shifted with a sigh like a baby asleep.

Victor's toes found the quilts where she'd kicked them. He reached out to pat her shoulder. It was her knee, but he patted anyway.

Somehow she had discovered a way to sleep without wheezing. There was even a smile on her face.

Victor smiled too, leaning down to her cheek. Everyone thought she was dying in March, then April . . . now here it was June, and Willie was alive as ever.

This was practice for when she would die. It might happen any day. It might be a year. When it happens, there will be this cold sweat and terror inside, only colder for being real.

Victor's original plan was to wait until she died, then take off and go and keep going and never come back.

Now he was wondering how long he might have to wait. She seemed better, not worse. She started talking when she woke up and told stories all day and rarely hushed before bedtime. She spent hours in the yard, picking up broken twigs. It might be forever, at this rate . . .

But wait. Stop. Isn't that wishing something to happen to her?

The quilt floated out, settling, assuming her shape. Victor tucked at its edges and stole from the room. A trace of her cold cream clung to his lips.

Tiptoeing back to the porch, he lit the lantern and righted the pots. Fool! This was not his first false alarm. One morning last week he rounded the corner of the house to find Willie slumped on the front steps. He ran to her. She peered up, yawned, asked if he'd seen her good pruning shears.

Victor had never seen anyone dead. He did not know the signs so he saw it around every corner. Actors on the radio made choking noises and thumped to the floor when they died, but surely the symptoms were not so distinct in real life . . .

He tried the radio. Too late for anything but static and thin bands of silence up and down the dial.

He settled down with a bag of Oreos, feeling under the cot for the Joya de Nicaragua cigar box that held all his letters.

Gingerly, since the creases were frayed, he unfolded the V-mail photostat, covered over with the censor's black marks.

Dear Vic,
Howya doing? Last week I was driving a truck full of XXX XXXXXXX back to the XXXXX at XXXXXXXXX XX. This is in a pretty part of XXXXXXX that you would like to see. The little hills are green and smoothe with grass. It was me my buddy Darden from S.C. and a colord private from Ohio. We came around the bend to this XXXXXX that looks kind of like XXXXX XXXXXXXX. There were at least XXXXXXX XXXXXXXXXXX great old big ones, XXXXXXXXX out there, as pretty as you please. When we saw that we knew XXXXX XXXX XX XXXXX. We don't know when but we know. They keep having us practice XXXXXXXXXXXX XXXXX. I asked what a XXXXXXX was anyway and the sgt. said it means like a XXXX it can live in the XXXXX or not. We think probably we will be in XXXXXX for the XXX XX XXXX

and don't you think we will sit off some big sky rockits then. Nows when the XXXXXXXX starts up. I heard about you going down to Willies. I can't believe it. Izzat you Victor or an imposter. Sorry shes sick. Tell her she got to get better before I come back and kiss her. Well I guess you prove something to Daddy all right. You can do it. Better than hanging round the house hearing Mom and Pop I guess. Come to think of it maybe you arent so dumb after all. Peace and quiet and fishin, also any girls? Watch out kid. All kind of wild ones down on that river. Don't let Willie see this letter. I'll send her a postcard from XXXXX. Whhooope!!!
Love
Your bro.
Pfc. Jos. Sylvester US Army IX Corps.

PS Loose lips sink ships as they say

The war seemed a wonderful place to be, full of buddies and girls and guns and excitement. Victor wanted to hear with his own ears a whistling bomb. To see a Nazi die. To write letters someone would have to censor.

He ran his thumb over the walking figure of the saint. A medal is not yours, he told himself, unless you do battle for it.

Soon as Willie is gone . . .

He went over details of his plan. Steal out at night. Retrieve the stash of gasoline he'd accumulated with Willie's ration tickets. (Old Pop's A-Model Ford had rusted in the shed since the bridge blew away in 1923, but the ration board at Foley didn't know that.) Steer by memory and the stars. Pray for a mild, easy swell, head northwest across the bay to Mobile. The recruiters were down by the waterfront. Freddie Spencer said so. All you needed was to pass the physical and make them think you were eighteen. Sign a paper. Swear an oath. Turn your head and cough. Then you were on your way, a soldier, a man, in the world.

Now a stunning sound tore the dense silence with one stroke—a thunderous ripping, like a chasm opening in the floor of the bay, a huge downrush of water.

Victor leaped up, scattering Oreos. His heart thumped the bone in his chest. That was not from a dream.

The windowpanes danced in their frames. The cataclysm echoed on and on, rippling thunder. It was a monster, or something as big, coming to the surface. This side of the ship channel.

The bay was an indistinct line through the trees. Victor shoved through the screen door and ran, never minding the things that stuck his bare feet all the way down the path. Branches swatted his face. He scrambled up the trunk of a live oak spread over the shallows like an unfolded hand, its fingers bent toward shore.

The thunder still resounded inside his head, or maybe it was just his heart pounding. Gunfire? Something bigger. The sound that had broken his dream.

This is no game. This is real.

Victor searched the breadth of the water for some sign of what he had heard—boxcars colliding, a great thundercloud, a warship with guns bristling . . .

But the bay was a glittering blank.

Under moonlight the marsh became a bright silver meadow of bayonet blades, pointed up.

5

THE NIGHT held a chill. It was June. It should not be this cold. Victor waited. The tree bark imprinted his thighs. His toes turned to nubs of ice.

A brisk wind swept over the bay, stirring the limbs under him, bringing clouds from the west.

The strain of watching for it, waiting, the huge distant sound replaying itself in his brain—*you have not imagined this*—*now hear it again*—gave the night hours an elastic quality. Growing drowsy, shifting his perch, Victor at last forced himself to admit that he would not hear it again tonight.

Gone, whatever it was. It broke Victor's dream, broke the face of the bay, and then vanished. A shudder so powerful that the air still seemed to carry its echo. A fleeting darkness between Victor and the moon.

Something out there.

Find it. See what it was. Do not wait. Do not pass GO. Go directly to something fantastic and *real*—

No one else heard it. This was just Victor. He knew what to do. He would go to his plan.

First, upriver for the gasoline.

Uncramping his legs, he shinnied down the tree trunk and stole up the path to the house, keeping watch to all sides.

He moved through the rooms like a thief, finding things in the dark: the lantern, dry matches, some crackers and cheese and the rest of the cookies, two pairs of dry socks. He would leave the radio, the cigar box, the brown suitcase—his comics and seashells, his worn copies of *While the Clock Ticked* and *The Mystery of Cabin Island*.

He should leave Willie a note.

But what could it say?

Dear Willie. Heard a whale (or monster). Gone to catch it (them). Love, Victor.

No . . .

Dear Willie. Never saw one true amazing real thing in my life. Now is my turn. Back soon. Love, Victor.

No note.

He would only go up in the bay. Try for a glimpse of what he heard. If Willie got up early, she would think he was off piddling in the swamp. If not, he'd be back before she knew he was gone.

He slipped out the screen door. The stars gave no light; low fog blew over the river. The path declined through live oaks to the marsh, where a rickety boardwalk ran to the boathouse and the pier angled out the other way. The tide was high and still rising. Water streamed over the pier in low places.

The door croaked and gave in. The boathouse smelled of bait and molding duckweed trapped in the footings of the doors, where the current passed through. Liquid echoes, gulp and splash.

The lamplight fell first in one corner, old Pop's unusual cage, three feet square, with six sides but no windows or doors, no obvious way in or out. According to Willie, he used to keep bad dogs in there.

Two small boats, suspended on ropes, gently bumped each other, swaying over a floor of green water.

Balancing on the boards, Victor yanked at the cords for another set of pulleys, but the heavy door would not budge.

On the seventh try it did; he hauled on the ropes; the wall drew out to darkness and swift-moving fog.

He unwinched the wooden skiff with the two-cylinder motor, jumped in, threw off both lines, and moved the boat hand over hand to the open water.

The wind sent it drifting toward the pier. He took up the paddle and went to work in the other direction. Soon he had the nose turned, headed upstream.

The current began to peter out. Kneeling in the stern, Victor shook the rusted fuel tank: just enough to take him to his hiding place. He coiled the rope and jerked. The ancient motor sputtered to life—popping, blowing blue smoke, nudging the boat ahead over the water. In no time he was flying along in the dark on invisible water.

His eyes grew accustomed enough to see points along shore —the Murphys' boathouse, the lights of the fish camp up Noltie Creek, the log cabin known as the old Johnson place.

A party underway there . . . at this time of night? Lots of lights, cars parked all in the yard, hubbub floating over the river.

The river's shores began to converge. To starboard, a parting of trees signaled the entrance to Mullet Creek. He banked the boat over and slowed.

A flash of silver—a mullet leaping, smacking down an arm's length away.

The propeller thudded on a submerged tree.

Victor cut the gas. His wake left a trail of light sound washing behind him. The prow entered the bend. He groped for the paddle. The leaning cypress tree would be about forty yards ahead, on the left bank, in that mass of darkness right there.

. . . There.

His neck hairs prickled up.

Some sound, a rustle in the underbrush.

A possum in the brush.

No. Listen there.

What?

It's nothing.

Sh-*hh*.

A flicker of light, a match struck.

In the cave formed by the cypress branches touching the water.

Victor's hiding place.

The flame sailed out sideways like a falling star, *spt!* on the water. A pinpoint of orange hovered in the cypress, a lit cigarette. It glowed, then faded. Whoever was smoking it continued calmly.

Victor clutched the paddle. Run? Start the engine and flee? His left hand had just touched the starter cord when a voice cut the dark.

"Don't you go nowhere," it said. "Got a gun and I'm pointin it right at the front of your head."

The boat drifted on its own momentum, bringing Victor into the cavern of limbs.

"Put your hands up where I can see."

Victor obeyed.

Silhouetted against the branches was a man looking down.

"I been waitin for you," he said in a hard, flat voice, flinging the cigarette away.

Victor's fingers closed on the paddle. *Come on, man, come closer.* "I just come here to get what was mine," he said. "I left some gas back there behind that tree . . . had some trouble with my boat yesterday."

"Look like you got some more trouble right now."

"I didn't know I was trespassing," Victor said. "I'll just get my stuff and—"

"Stay where you at."

"Sure. Okay." Victor tightened his grip. *Come on.*

The man stepped down into the boat.

Victor hiked the paddle over his shoulder and got halfway into a good roundhouse swing when hands grabbed it, stopped it, wrenched it away. He toppled back. He saw the man's face but it was not a man, just a boy like Victor, maybe fifteen years old—a wild-looking redheaded boy.

"What are you gonna do," Victor said, "beat me up with the paddle?"

The paddle sailed out, slapped the water flat-faced. "You won't need it," the boy said. "You had your last ride in this boat."

"Listen, I don't know you and you don't know me." Victor made as if to stand, but the boy produced a long-barreled revolver which made him take his seat. "You got me mixed up with somebody."

"Yeah I bet. Noltie sent you up here, didn't he, the son of a bitch. You do his dirty work, huh? You tell that old cripple I'm done with his mess, and if he don't quit burnin and shootin at me, I'm gonna come use this on him!" He waved the gun over his head. "Tell him Butch ain't afraid!" His mouth hung open as if he were amazed at what he had said. He wore dungarees, no shirt and no shoes, a sunburn that glowed in the dark. *Butch* . . . built like a fireplug, low to the ground. When he took off his short-billed cap, stringy hair fell around his shoulders.

Victor watched the gun. "Like I said, I had some trouble and I had to leave that stuff here."

"Where'd you get all of that, anyway. Noltie give that to you? Must have been twenty gallon back there."

Victor decided to gamble. He put out his hand. "My name's Sylvester," he said. "Victor Sylvester. Why don't you point that thing off the other way and listen to me. You got the wrong guy. I don't know anybody named Noltie. Just the creek."

The boy maintained his aim, staring at Victor's hand as if it might burn him. "You tell him I'm done trying to pay him what I owe. It ain't worth it. How the hell am I supposed to run a kettle with y'all taking potshots at me, settin fire to my stuff? Tell me that!"

Victor tried again: "Look, I don't know what you're talking about—"

"That's real sharp, actin dumb. You've done burned two good rigs. Tell him that's all he's gettin from me. He can find somebody else." Butch tucked the gun in his pants and sprang like a cat to the lowest branch of the cypress. When it came, his laugh was the oldest thing about him—a wicked sound, animal.

Before Victor could get to the bow he was back, swinging a gasoline can from each hand. He tossed one to the floor of the boat. The one in his hand made a *thoonk!* like the cork from a jug.

"Hey, wait a minute!" Victor spoke too late. Butch upended the can. Gasoline chugged onto the floor, splashing around Victor's feet on his arm on his shirt, then he stumbled back, fumes filling his face. "Wait! Don't—don't burn it!"

"How come?"

"Cause I'm in it, okay?"

"Get out."

"You can have all the gas, man, go ahead and take it!"

"Already did." The bowline secure in his hand, Butch put a fresh cigarette to his lips. "Want a smoke?"

"No! Are you nuts? Don't—"

"I reckon I am." He struck a match, lit the cigarette, dropped the match—

The *whoooff!* of great lungs exhaling, a line of fire racing across to Victor, who had just time to send the duffel sailing out before him and dive. He struck the water on his side.

When he got his head up, the boat was burning entirely. The hull, the wood swivel chair, the fishing poles in flames and afloat, as if the boat had been built to carry bright fire on the water at night.

When the heat reached that can . . .

He swam wildly away, snagging the duffel in his hand, kicking with the power of fear. He lunged up for air. Butch swung by his arms from a low cypress branch, his face shining with the spectacle.

Hang there, you fool. Victor churned through the water. His hands brushed things that wiggled away. His knees touched down in the muck of the opposite bank. Heaving for air, he turned to watch the boat burn.

Butch was gone.

"You listen to me," Victor screamed, "I'll get you! You better run fast cause I'll be right behind you!"

The fuel went off, a brilliant bomb detonating, illuminating the trees like lightning underwater, a thunder to rattle the weeds.

It blew the transom out of the boat, which sank all at once. Only smoke remained in the trees.

Victor swam back across the creek and picked his way through palmettos to the tarpaulin, lying flat on the ground, where he'd hidden his precious five-gallon cans.

Old Pop's boat—

Victor clutched the tarp. A keen new rage sang in his ears. He had never heard such a sound. It made his hands shake, made him want for something to strangle. He knew suddenly what revenge would taste like, the bitterest apple. He wanted that taste.

Through the trees came a stutter, the roar of a powerful motor. A boat roared away, kicking up wake that crashed down both shores of the creek.

Victor got just a glimpse: a white motorboat. It turned downstream, toward Willie's island, the bay.

6

HE MADE his way downriver, walking where he could, swimming for long stretches, flailing and kicking until he reached another shallow place . . . pulling out, stumbling on. He hid the duffel in a lightning-struck oak. He tripped over cypress knees, swatted mosquitoes.

Just after dawn the wind died. Fog settled over the river, protective and still. The surface turned slick as a window. Victor trudged along the shallows, up to his calves in sucking swamp mud that threatened to drag him on down.

The water shuddered, a school of minnows passing. He felt his body turning to mud.

What right did he have? he stormed to himself. What revenge could be awful enough? In the wild west, if you stole someone's horse and got caught, it was the noose with no questions asked. In a place made of water and swamp, a boat was the same. The punishment ought to be too.

Fuming, muttering these things out loud, Victor stepped over the alligator and three paces past it before his mind registered what his eyes had seen.

A long, bleached body, lizardy silver in the colorless early light. Half in, half out of the water.

A cold hand gripped his stomach. His arms froze in their angle. He quit breathing entirely and stood paralyzed as the mud bubbled over his ankles.

He turned, just his head.

He turned all the way around.

The thing lay on its back. Swollen. Dead.

Victor bent from the waist, peering down to make sure.

But instead of the claws of a reptile, he saw distended arms, the hands of a man. Human fingers, inflated like sausage balloons.

A violent stench filled his head. He turned, choking down a surge of spittle.

He reeled away, bent over, spit on the ground. He fought a second surge, taking deep breaths, tasting the smell in his throat. Deep breaths. His heart threatened to pound its way out of his chest.

When he felt his head clearing, he straightened and began to inch around upwind until he stood on a ledge of firm ground dividing two swampy low places.

The dead man lay about five yards beyond, legs hidden underwater, the rest of him splayed out in a trampled half-moon of marsh grass. From this distance he still looked more like a dead alligator. The skin was mottled blue-silver, the head a dark unrecognizable chunk at the top of the body.

Victor covered his nose and stepped closer. That must have been the head because it still wore gold-rimmed wire spectacles. The lenses were gone.

A dark-crimson bloom spread from the center of the chest. The arms held a peculiar stiff curve away from the body, like the beginning of an embrace. A gold ring on one finger. A rope had been wrapped three times about the waist, heavily knotted; the long end ran off into the water.

Victor gave the rope a tug—no resistance. The end came up frayed. The man had been tethered somewhere.

Victor felt a sudden urge to cover him, at least try to get him out of the water. But what if the part he took hold of came away in his hand?

The wind increased, disturbing a storm of black flies.

Victor took up the rope, put it over his shoulder, leaned into the weight. He sweated and pulled and dug in to his knees, but he could not budge the weight.

Go find someone. Tell someone. Bring someone here.

The tide was falling. The dead man was going nowhere. Victor dropped the rope and took off running through the shallows.

7

HE CROUCHED by the screen, peering in. The camel-back clock on Willie's dresser said quarter past nine, and still Willie snored, lost in dreams.

Dear Willie, he considered. *A wild boy burned old Pop's boat. Had to swim home from Mullet Creek. Found a dead man on the way. Back soon. Love, Victor.*

He crept away from the house. He must be going crazy. She was right: he had wished for something to happen, and bang! here it was! too many things! His whole body trembled, a deep chill that had nothing to do with the temperature or his sodden clothes. Whenever he blinked he saw the dead man's face, the gold spectacles mashed against the face as if they would never come off.

Wake Willie.

Let her sleep.

She will know what to do.

She'll keel over from shock and you'll have two bodies on your hands.

Row the boat to the springs. Get Daddy. Let him handle this. He'll place the call from Moore's Store. You're a kid. You don't know what to do. This thing is bigger than you.

The nearest law was ten miles up the bay, in Fairhope. That would take real transportation.

Say, a fast white motorboat . . .

The boathouse stood wide open.

Victor found the rusted pistol and a half box of bullets in the tool bin. He tucked them away in the rowboat, unwound the winch. This was an open wooden shell painted white, a simple machine for crossing the water. Victor slid the long slender oars into their locks, glided away.

He pulled without thinking, counting the strokes, losing count, losing himself in the work of his muscles, stopping now and then to breathe. He kept squinting ahead into the river's glare—surely *one* fisherman would be out on such a fine morning—but never a soul went by in the long hours it took him to row across Weeks Bay, up the Magnolia River, into Noltie Creek.

This was an unremarkable stream except for the fish camp, which wore its ugliness like an award. A sign meant to proclaim it the SHELLSIDE CAMP was missing part of an S, so it said SHELLᴓIDE. Seven trailers hunkered around a boat landing, on a piece of land stripped of every tree, as if the trailers had spread some disease around them. They were squat and rounded, propped on cinder blocks like gypsy trailers, with stovepipes and peep-holes.

Noltie's wooden shack of a store stood fading. Weather had turned the Coca-Cola thermometer a violent purple. Crickets cheeped in wire cages on the bait cooler.

The only boat at the landing was a ratty bay shrimper. All out of breath, Victor looped his line on the post. Sweat dripped from his fingertips. His shirt stuck to him.

A snaggle-haired reddish woman sat on the stoop with her knees apart. She wore baggy clam-digger shorts and a man's blue workshirt with two buttons missing. Her face rested on the flank of the gasoline pump. "Hey, dahlin," she said in a voice like a hinge coming open. She looked Victor up and then down. Her eyes were insolent, bruised. She might have been thirty or fifty, depending. She grinned. "What's your name, you young thang?"

He cleared his throat. "Victor."

"Shoot, you sweaty! You look like you just come from seeing a ghost! What's the matter?"

"Just—just out of breath," Victor said.

"My name's Dauphine," she said, extending her hand as if he might kiss it. "Named after the Lost Dauphine. I'm kin to him, ha ha."

"Where's Mr. Noltie?"

"He left me in charge. He does that all the time. You don't believe me, run punch that thing." She indicated a black box nailed over the cooler, under a sign that said TALK. "That wire runs under the dirt to his trailer yonder. It runs off a thing. Punch that and see don't he answer."

"Where'd he go?"

"Town. But he left me his keys. You want gas?"

"No. It's a rowboat. No engine."

"Good thing. They ain't any gas," said Dauphine. "You ever been to a fish fry?"

"A what?"

"A fish fry. You know. Where you fry fish. I caught me some gooduns. You ought to come up there with me and let's fry us up some."

Victor was thinking how hard it would be to look in a mirror if the worst parts of your life showed all over your face.

"You don't much care for old Dauphine, do you, boy," she said, closing her knees.

"I'm looking for somebody."

"You're in luck, dahlin. Somebody is who I am."

"No, I'm looking for a fellow named Butch."

Dauphine pulled a hair from her mouth. "You a friend of his?"

"Yeah, sure am. He did me a favor and I got to pay him back."

She studied him. "What kind of favor?"

"That's between me and Butch."

"You ain't the law, are you? Naw, you're too young for the law." She brightened. "Butch likes my fish fries."

I bet he does, Victor said to himself with a shudder.

"You look okay to me. Understand, somebody comes around askin for Butch, I got to be careful."

"How come?"

"I'm his mama," she said.

Victor swallowed. "You are?"

"Bet you didn't think I was old enough to have a boy as bad as him," said Dauphine, with a laugh.

"Mr. Noltie hadn't got a telephone, does he?"

"Hell no," she said. "You got a cigarette?"

"No."

"You should start so you'll have one when somebody asks."
She peered at him. "You gonna stand in that boat all day long,
or come sit here by me?" Hopefully she patted the step beside her.

Victor stayed where he was. He had an idea. "That's a fine
boat Butch is driving these days. Where's he keep it?"

"Ain't his," said Dauphine. "It belongs to Noltie. Some folks
turn bad in a gradual way, but you know, that boy started off
at a young age. Like to got me thowed out of here. Last place
on earth I could go. You'd have thought I took that boat, way
that old man carried on. Him and Butch got some business, I
don't even want to know. I warned 'em both." She rested her
hands on her knees. "It ain't like it's the damn Taj Mahal. Take
a look. Fifteen dollars a month and for what. That's what I
asked him, for what. Told him it was Butch, not me, and
anyway I ain't responsible." She looked over her shoulder at the
largest trailer. Someone moving inside.

"Thought you said he was gone."

"Well I lied," said Dauphine. The box on the post squawked
a sound that must have been her name; she got up and punched
the button. "What!"

Squawk squawk.

"He ain't buyin no gas," she yelled.

Squirk squirk rrrr.

"In a minute!" She turned to Victor. "He don't like folks
hangin around unless they buying something. You want to buy
something?"

"No."

"I got to fix him his lunch. He keeps an eye on folks. Got
him a spyglass. He's watchin you now. Don't you steal nothing."

"I won't. I just came to—"

"You listen here. If you see Butch, you tell him he better

bring that damn boat back, and he owes Noltie eighty-five dollars, and he owes me thirty-three dollars and seventeen cent. He knows what for."

"I don't know where he is," Victor protested. "That's why I'm asking you."

"There's a place on up the head of this creek, way past where the bridge used to be." She talked fast, throwing a glance over her shoulder. "Used to be a house on it. Them boys said they seen him hanging around up there. If you see him, tell him Noltie ain't mad at him really. Tell him come back and pay what he owes, and everything will work out. Tell him Dauphine said he better—"

"*Dauphine!*" said the box.

"You come back." She wiggled two fingers at him. "You come back when it's dark out sometime and let old Dauphine fry you up a fish."

Victor watched her swaggering strut up the hill. He sucked the blister on his thumb. His stomach complained. He tore two strips from a rag and wound them around his hands, wishing he had a bite of that fish she kept talking about.

He lifted his oars and set out past the old rotted pilings of the bridge. A turpentine mill had once thrived here, but it failed and was taken apart by the destitute workers, who built their rickety houses with the lumber.

Compared to these poor little places, Willie's house looked like one of the big summer places by the Hotel. Here a structure leaned forward, threatening to topple on its face; here one was nailed over entirely with automobile license plates; there a houseboat had been dragged on the bank, stripped of its pontoons, and made to stand for a house.

Willie said nothing but garbage ever floated out of Noltie Creek.

Victor rowed on around a tight bend. The woods deepened.

Past noon, and the sun was killing. He dreaded closing his eyes. He might fall asleep at the oars. He might see the dead man.

He mopped his forehead and looked for a place where a house was not.

The camouflage nearly worked. He noticed just a glimmer of white in a bank of green weeds, but the rope gave it away, outlined by the sun, running taut from the sycamore down to the white motorboat.

Victor dipped an oar, moving close. Vines had been knotted together in ropes, draped along the hull.

He climbed to the bank. Up the rise, a stone chimney ruled over a grassy clearing. The luck! A fast boat. Butch nowhere around.

Flinging the vines off, he examined the chrome-and-glass windshield, the steering wheel, plushy upholstered seats. The starter cord was built into the Evinrude's cowling, complete with a recoiling spring. Victor had never been near an engine so fine. No wonder Butch had swiped this boat.

He saw no sign of his gasoline stash; he'd watched at least half of it go up in flames in the night.

He picked at the elaborate knots, his ear bent to listen. He wished he had pencil and paper. *Sorry chum. Tough luck.* Something like that. Then again maybe it was better to let it dawn on him slowly. Let him search down the creek, all the way down the river, and out to the bay. Let him look.

One last tangle and the job was done.

A snapping of branches above—

That wild face, an animal's face, looking straight down at him, an animal crouching to spring.

The big branch cracked, split, gave way. Butch plummeted down in a shower of splinters and moss, landing *whump!* on his back.

Before he drew a breath, Victor was standing astride him, the barrel of old Pop's pistol aimed at his eye. "I guess you're not surprised to see me." He pulled back the hammer. "I told you to run."

"Don't shoot." Butch reached for his cap as if it might protect him. Victor saw the resemblance to Dauphine—the bad teeth and insolent eyes. Butch was a fighting dog, nicked and scratched all over his arms and bare chest, new scars and old.

"I just came for what's mine," Victor said. "A boat for a boat." He nudged his toe into Butch's ribs. "Roll over. Keep your hands on the ground."

Butch started to speak. Victor kicked him. "Shut up. Listen to me. I don't know what's going on with you on this river, but you picked the wrong guy to burn. Found your friend out there on the bank. I'm bringing the law and soon as I'm done showing him, we're coming to find you."

With a good running start, Victor leaped to the motorboat and sent it drifting. The very first pull started it.

Butch poked his head up from the weeds. "Hey! That ain't my boat!"

Now it ain't. Victor pushed the throttle. The boat roared ahead, planing out, gaining speed. He held the gun in one hand and steered with the other.

He left a fast crease in the water. Children waved from the yards.

He turned upriver, describing a wide arc, peering over to make sure the dead man was there in the stretch of gray swamp. Low tide had uncovered his legs.

Victor stood at the wheel. He was alive. Under power. In flight. The wind whipped his hair. He set out down the river full throttle, tossing a great rooster tail of spray behind him, faster than he'd ever gone past the old Johnson place, past the Keatons' and Hamrics' and Collins' Camp, past Noltie Creek, the Murphys', the Donelsons', the Wheatons', the stretch of dead cypress, the endless green woods, then, across the wide shallows of Weeks Bay, he flashed past Willie and her island, her boathouse, her symptoms, her stories, her whiskey, his life, and out onto the great watery plain of Mobile Bay.

He turned north. He was five miles well gone from that place when the motorboat sputtered and ran out of gas.

8

N O O N E can hide in a boat on the wide-open bay, but the land all around, where it touches the water, is made of a thousand concealments.

The head of the bay is the great Mobile delta, with its lost shoreless lakes and snarled woods. The bay spreads and widens out south, like the figure of a lady walking in skirts. At her shoulder is the old city, Mobile. Along her hem, slender sandy peninsulas, the fringe of white beach. Where her foot will come down is a gap of two miles, Fort Morgan, the opening into the Gulf.

At the lady's knee, on the eastern shore, was the only grand thing on the bay, the Hotel. Before the coast marshal blacked out its lights, it was visible from everywhere, a glittering palace set on the great point, among ancient live oaks.

Now, when the sun set, the lush grounds grew dark.

Half a mile to the west, led by a sea anchor in a lucky current, the white motorboat steadily nosed toward shore. Victor stirred, tucked his face in the crook of his elbow. He had stood for hours in the stern, waving his shirt at the specklike shrimp boats to the west, but none ever came near. At last the weight of the sun sat him down on the comfortable seat, curled him up, and lulled him to sleep . . .

He sat up, startled.

Wake up.

Where was—

Out on the water.

Oh God. He had only meant to rest his eyes. Now the sun was gone and his skin was painful to touch. The bay was wide open. The western sky still glowed faint pink. That was the Middle Bay lighthouse squatting on its stilts, not a mile to the northwest, so the Hotel must be . . . right behind him.

The long roof ran through the gnarled tops of trees; no one could black out the shimmer of its tin. Joseph had spent a summer mowing grass there, so Victor knew all about it. The main building wrapped the point, four stories high. If there was a breeze in dead summer anywhere in the state of Alabama, you could feel it there. Rich people sailed in, tied their boats in the yacht basin, sat sipping cocktails in canvas chairs on the lawn that ran down to the bay. The richest of them stayed in pink stucco bungalows scattered about the grounds. When they got ready to leave, Joseph said, they untied their boats and sailed off.

Victor took up the oar. He was within shouting distance of the shore, bobbing toward a stone breakwater.

Along the promenade, people strolled—couples, kids running. The sound of a band floated over the water. Were they playing Dorsey? They were into their swing. Of course. It was Saturday night in the world.

Victor paddled into calmer water, toward a forest of masts. Hard to make headway in this heavy boat with one paddle. Snatches of music drifted on the breeze. He wished he could sneak across that lawn and sit in some dark place and listen, but he had something big to do.

He wouldn't think about Willie. Not yet. "You go on," she would say. "I can tend to myself. I got things of my own to do."

Carved in the northern end of the point, protected by the breakwater, the yacht basin was quiet refuge for motor yachts, expensive race boats, neat skiffs, sailing vessels. Sail chains clanked against masts.

Nudging in beside a green-camouflaged launch, Victor stowed the paddle and jumped to the pier. The boats were tied four deep. He didn't have so much as a nickel for a telephone call, but maybe he could scavenge gasoline to take him to Fairhope, the police, the answers.

He cast an eye over the largest boat, a sleek wooden yacht with a flying bridge. He crept down the dock. Tied sideways it took up four slips. It was bound to be loaded. He slipped up the gangplank.

All the hatches were locked tight. Since the start of the war, even rich people guarded their gas.

Footsteps. Loud boots. Victor sprang to the rail of the yacht. The boots strode by an arm's length away, and stopped in front of the white motorboat.

The man muttered and shook his head. He was tall, slightly stooped, holding a hat in his hand.

Victor came out of hiding.

The man turned. "Is this your boat?"

"Yes sir."

"Well get it out of here." He was perhaps thirty, with translucent whitish-blond hair, wire-rimmed glasses, a sharp beveled line to his jaw. Familiar, somehow. Khaki pants, black leather boots. His eyes were in shadow.

"Sorry. I've got to come across your launch," Victor said.

The man shrank back as he passed. "Are you a guest of the hotel?"

"Yes sir." Victor leg-upped over the transom.

"What's your name?"

He lied before he thought about it: "Charlie. Charlie Smith."

"Charlie, do you see what it says on that sign?" The man pointed.

"No sir. It's dark."

"It says, 'Reserved for Official Vessels Only.' You pay attention or I will have to speak with you again. You can move yours up there."

"Yes sir." Victor led the motorboat by its bowline along the dock. *Check your gas, man, you're low. You need gas.*

As if on cue, the man lifted his fuel tank and shook it. He turned a key. The launch's twin inboards hummed as he idled along the row of elegant boats to a split-shingled shed. "Do you mind giving me a hand up?"

"Oh. Sure." Victor leaned down, grasped the cool hand. The man angled up to the dock. His spectacles caught a glint of the moon.

"Thanks. My name is Roy Glass." He unhooked a big ring of keys from his belt. "Sorry to be rough on you back there, Charlie. But I am on official business. There is a war on, you know." He went to a small door in the shed, opened a sheath lock, and brought out the nozzle for the gasoline pump.

Victor read the sticker on the launch's windscreen. "You're the coast marshal?"

"I am."

Not the same one who came to cover Willie's windows, Victor thought. Enough like him to be that man's brother, but different. Taller, or something. "You the only one in Baldwin County?"

"One other man, at the beach."

"Are you, like, a policeman?" Victor said. "Can you arrest people and all?"

"Why?" Roy Glass was faintly amused. "Do you know someone I need to arrest?"

Victor knew he should tell what he'd found, but something about this man made him think twice. The cold hand. The short fuse. *He'd never believe me.* "Just wondered," he said. "I might want to be one sometime. When I grow up."

"Coast marshal? A fine ambition." With both hands, Glass worked the ratchet handle. Gasoline gurgled into the tank. "Have you been staying long at the Hotel?"

"Just since yesterday."

"How do you like it?"

"It's okay," said Victor. "There's not that much to do."

"Oh, you kids. Such a beautiful place you have here, and still you say nothing to do. You should be up where they're dancing. You should be looking for the girls." He snapped the nozzle off the hose. "Put this back in that cabinet for me?"

"Sure." Victor tucked it among the tools and greasy rags. He took care to sound casual: "Want me to lock it back up?"

"Thanks."

He inserted just the tips of the shackle in the lock, and let it fall *bang!* on the door. "Got it."

Roy Glass took off his hat. The path of his comb was still perfect in his thin hair. "Thanks again. Have a nice visit here."

"Sorry I had you blocked in," Victor said.

"Now you know. Go ahead as I say, go and dance with a girl." Glass climbed in, cast off his line, cranked the engines.

Victor waved as the launch throbbed away, and he kept waving until it was past the breakwater.

The lock fell open in his hand. He ran down the dock and

came back with two cans. *Quick, now.* He set to pumping the ratchet, watching the shadows move.

Somewhere in the trees, a girl laughed—a soft musical peal, like water on stones. Then an answer, a murmur.

The weight of the cans sent Victor on an unsteady curve down the dock. When he stopped to get a new grip, he heard them behind him.

"You cad," the girl said distinctly. "You carnivorous beast." She laughed again, that fluid note.

Victor was down in the motorboat by the time they reached that end of the dock. They wore white, as if they had dressed for moonlight. She came first, high heels skittering, skirt billowing out. She might be the slightest bit tipsy.

The man bent her back, wrapped up in the kiss.

If they turned they would see Victor staring at them, but it was plain they had come here to look at each other with their eyes closed, their mouths pressed together.

A heel came up. Her shoe fell to the dock.

"Ooh Billy, you're wild," she said. "Look what you've done."

"I'll get it." He knelt. "My princess, I have found your slipper."

"Oh Romeo, Romeo," she said, "why hast thou forsaken me?"

"That's not Cinderella," he teased. "That's not even *Romeo and Juliet*."

"Beast!" She swatted him. "Get up!"

He folded her in his arms.

Victor felt a stirring. How full of magic they seemed, all in dazzling white and in love. His hand was the man's hand, stealing up the white skirt; there was warmth and a pulse within that fabric: he felt it.

He could do that. Yes he could. He kept quiet so he could watch and learn how. His stomach was cold.

The man pulled away. "We can't. You get me all bothered, then you won't—"

"Shh. Don't be nasty." She offered her hand. "Let's go hear the music."

But he started the other way, down the dock. "You go. I'll be here when you're through."

She took a hesitant step after him, then changed her mind and walked toward the Hotel, faster and faster, until she was running.

If that had been Victor's hand, his mouth kissing hers that way, he would run after her. But the man lit a cigarette and stood gazing out at the darkened lighthouse.

He must know she'll come back. She'll come back and she'll do what he wants the next time. That must be how it works.

Victor started the engine, a sputter that grew to a roar. He passed down the ranks of boats shifting and bobbing, along the breakwater, out into the bay.

Now the wind came from the north. It blew the music off the other way. The shift was a sign. Changes coming.

The boat skimmed along to the drumbeat of waves on the hull, the steady engine drone. Victor drove like an outlaw, checking over his shoulder, standing up so the wind rushed around him. A chorus of nagging familiar voices told him go home, go back to the island, see after Willie, what about your daddy, but Victor drowned them out with the motor's noise. He had been a good boy all his life. Tonight he was out on his own. All his senses were standing on end.

A bank of dark fog spread over the water from the west.

Two miles to Fairhope. He'd prayed for something to happen, and it had. Officer, I've come to report a dead body. Looks like murder to me. . . .

Half a mile dead ahead, the beam of the lighthouse swept

the bay, a finger of light tracing a great circle, illuminating the fog.

A moan arose, the bluest note from a beast: the foghorn. One long blast and then a pause, as for breath, then two shorter soundings.

The beacon went dark. The motorboat passed through a curtain of heavy mist, into the clear. Victor eased off the throttle.

The lighthouse perched on stilts in the water. Tied at its landing was the green-camouflaged boat. Stairs led to the white-frame octagonal house on top. A lantern danced there, in the window, a yellow pinpoint moving corner to corner. Swinging in someone's hand.

The big beam reappeared and made two swift rotations.

Again the despairing horn, drawn out so long it seemed a dying breath. Echoing blasts. The light disappeared.

Victor had the uneasy feeling that he was eavesdropping on a conversation: the lighthouse talking to the fog.

Light blazed again in the huge lens, outlining a man in a fedora—the coast marshal, Roy Glass. The glare moved beyond him, made a swift circuit, flashed over Victor before he saw it coming—a column of light blinding, revealing him in the instant it swept past, and around.

Glass looked down from the window.

The glare slashed by, went halfway around, and then out.

Victor kicked up the throttle and went fishtailing off to the west at a full-motored roar. When he looked back, the lantern was halfway down the stairs.

He passed into a fog so dense that the motor's deafening racket came from all sides at once. The lighthouse vanished behind him.

The fog seemed too thick, sooty black, a faint odor of burning.

He felt for the switch. The bow lamp lit up green on one side, ruby on the other—a pretty glow, but no help at all in this soup.

His boat hit something

Ran up on something

Victor was flung on his back like a doll.

The pitch of the motor went wild, revving free, propeller out of the water. A strip of the hull peeled away. The boat teetered entirely in air, balanced on the spine of a massive surfacing beast.

His fingernails scrabbled for a hold, and lost. He tumbled into the stern.

The propeller bit into metal. Screamed across the face of something. Something. What he hit. The boat toppled and plunged on its side in the bay. Victor rolled out: the water shocked him: the chill: it was June: it should not be this cold: the motor running: a hissing of snakes in the water.

He lunged up for air, found himself floundering in hollow darkness. The boat had flipped over on top of him, so he was inside, breathing trapped air, the snakes in the motor still hissing.

Maybe it hit his head. Cut it off, cut it off!

He went under, fumbling for the throttle. Wrong side. Which side? Upside down.

Found it. Found the handle and jerked it.

The hissing died.

Victor floated in the pocket of air—stay calm stay calm you hit something stay calm you ran into something maybe hit your head get your breath use your head you're all right you're okay got to flip it back over. Just flip it back over.

Better. Deep breaths.

He took a deeper one, forced himself down, and kicked free of the boat. A rough salty wave slapped his face. The taste of salt startled him. He managed to get his head clear and one hand on the hull.

He heard gurgling, the boat preparing to sink.

He gripped it, propped his foot on the edge, *gave* it as hard as he could, and then *gave* it again, and *again*, trying to turn it.

Don't sink now. Please don't sink. Do not sink. *Do not sink.*

But it went out from under his hands, tipped up at the stern and slid down with the silvery grace of a diver entering the water.

White foam sizzled up.

Victor dove down as if he might catch the boat and drag it up to the surface, turn it over, make everything like it was. Kicking hard with eyes open, he glimpsed the Christmas-colored bow lamp drifting down into infinity. He imagined he followed its gentle spiral all the way to the floor of the bay.

Holy God. Not to drown.

He fought up to the air. A wave seized him. He swam for a seat cushion bobbing ahead of him, but no matter how hard he swam it stayed three waves away.

Somewhere a school bell was ringing. Men shouting.

Can't swim in pants. He writhed out of them. He doubled his strokes and caught up with the cushion—an empty gas can, bobbed to the surface. Least would keep him afloat. He flopped both arms over, cradled it, taking air, rising, falling in waves.

The water was not so cold. Once you. Got used to it. Keep teeth from chattering. Only the shock of hitting it. The shock of. What had he hit?

He had a bellyful of salt water. The insistent bell.

A siren shrieked *whooop!* so close by that Victor lost his grip and slid under a wave. By the time he came up again, the bell had quit ringing.

A wand of yellow light sliced through the fog, scanning this way and that, turning, advancing on him.

It fixed him in its brilliant eye.

The siren whooped twice. The beam wiggled away. Then a hard metal clang, a hatch banging down.

Victor was not at all sure it was good to be found by whatever this was.

The fog grew thicker, and blacker, that pungent burned smell. He heard whistling, steam escaping a kettle. Kicking after the sound, he discovered a sphere, two feet across, floating on the waves, spewing black smoke from two nozzles.

A smoke bomb like Agent X-9 used in the comics. Only ten times bigger, and black as the smoke rushing out.

Someone made this fog.

Victor swam toward where the wind was clearing the air.

A bank of homemade fog. To hide in.

God. What had he hit?

A shape emerged from the murk, the outline of something so long Victor had to keep turning his head to see it whole.

What he hit.

It was huge. It was big as a monster, a whale, the long blackness, the curve of the spine coming up in a fin, oh! but whales don't have fins and they don't have a cluster of spires rising.

Some kind of ship. The same black as the smoke bomb. A featureless deck tapering to the water line, so flat and black it seemed to draw the moonlight and hold it inside. Longer than a coal barge, with a fin-shaped turret rising fifteen feet high, a little platform. No flag. No markings.

A black submarine.

Victor thrashed toward it. He couldn't tell quite where it was. It might be close enough to touch, but it kept receding, enlarging, receding, as if it sensed it lay exposed.

It gave out a diesel grunt and began to move.

If he could pull up on deck, he could bang on those pipes until somebody heard. But there was no handle, no outcropping at all on the flank of the ship. Cold metal skimmed under his palms.

The thing moved faster, chugging ahead. The sea seemed to be rising around it. The waves rose with Victor's hands, feeling up the side to the deck, lapping over the top. He caught hold of a cleat and it dragged him half-drowning a hundred yards before he got his head up and scrambled to the deck.

The deck was black, slippery, with slots for the water to drain. A scar looped crazily across one end. His propeller had made that.

Victor shook so hard his teeth hurt. His pants were gone and his shoes. The water was rising, but then again it was the ship sinking out from under him. Everything sinking. Water swirling his ankles.

He waded toward the fin. "Wait!"

The waves washed his thighs.

The engine surged, drowning his shouts. The thing made a belligerent grunt then the deck tilted sharply, lifting Victor way into the air, slamming him to the deck. There came the great thunderous ripping sound, sharp hissing, a million bubbles. The deck slanted up, up, until he was hanging on with his fingers to the slots in the deck. His stomach fell under him. His shirt snagged something—a cleat.

The giant ship pulled him down. He looked up to the moon. Water closed over his head. It would drown him before he could pull himself loose. He threw all his weight against the shirt, but he could not tear it or get it off. The cleat was wedged crosswise, cold on his breast. He felt as if he were watching someone else being dragged to his death, and there was nothing at all he could do.

He was little. Did he remember or dream it? A beach. Way too little to swim. On a strip of white sand, Willie's island.

The sun blazing straight down.

Won't hurt anything just to put his feet in. So he does. It is lovely and cool.

Victor, where are you, son. She does not move her hands.

Right here, Mommy.

He's only in up to his ankles. This shore is clotted with driftwood, pinecones in the water. A big log drifts by. Victor touches it, puts one hand on it, wraps his arms around it. How nice to float! His feet aren't touching bottom. There she is with her hands on her eyes. Her legs slender white.

The log spins, gently spins, like a merry-go-round going round and around. Victor is holding on tight. When he comes back around he sees them again, smaller. The waves are rocking him. He wants to cry Willie look at me, look at me float! but he's floated so far Mommy will be mad so he kicks his feet to head back in before she sits up finds him gone but he can't seem to kick hard enough. The log spins, spinning. She is a tiny thing way on the far other side of the waves.

Willie is up on the sand, one hand shading her eyes, looking out, shouting for Joseph, Ellen get up come hurry oh baby hang on hang on Victor hang on child, we're coming for you! Don't be scared baby.

And that makes him suddenly scared.

Willie!

I know baby hang on, we're coming for you.

She blurs through his tears.

She runs on old spindly legs. Don't cry, she calls, wading out. Here I come!

Here I come.

Victor shivers with panic. The others watch from the beach,

hopping and pointing. They expect him to drown. His mother is weeping.

Now Willie is there. It takes a great faith for Victor to turn loose the log. She pries his fingers free, wraps his arms around her neck, and swims in, bearing him.

Victor almost drownded. didn't he, Willie.

No he didn't.

But you had to save him.

He was swimming fine. I believe he could have gone to Florida, the way he was going.

9

VICTOR'S MIND swam, kept swimming, and came up from the bottom to a place full of pillows and clouds, colored vapors, an infinite softness, white veils that stirred in a breeze.

At first he could see just vague shapes: furniture, windows, a wide-open door. His eyelids stuck together. The light streaming in glanced whitely off the edges of things, but he could not tell if it was morning or late afternoon. When he moved to rub his eyes a pain sliced from his ribs to the shoulder blade, burning bright heat, as if someone had cracked a board across his back.

The four-poster bed was mounded over with pillows and blankets, swathed in mosquito netting, a bed from a magazine story about famous people on safari. The rest of the room was a shimmering gauze.

Victor brought his knees to his chest, propped himself with his arms, and sat up. This room was as big as Willie's whole house. A thick carpet patterned with flowers stretched to the open French doors. Silky curtains waved into the room.

These white boxer shorts were not his.

He remembered kicking out of his pants. So whoever saved him had dragged him here, stripped him the rest of the way, put these oversized shorts on him, put him to bed. He felt himself blush.

He hobbled down from the bed and opened every one of the drawers in the antique chests, but all he found was an empty laundry bag with a fancy script: The HOTEL.

Last night was the shape of a nightmare. Drowning, half remembered. The long black sinister boat.

What he hit. He knew what it was.

He had no idea how he got here, how he hurt his back. Maybe wrenching free of the shirt. That was when his mind had let go. After that he had just snatches. Someone lifting him. The cold. Was it—Willie?

On the wall by his bed, a big painting, dark colors. Victor moved close to see what it was: sailing vessels and ironclad ships, cannonballs whistling through air, showy fireworks, flags rippling, smoke and confusion. A brass plate proclaimed it THE BATTLE OF MOBILE BAY.

That would be Admiral Farragut out on the prow of the largest ship, damning the torpedoes, pointing full speed ahead.

The ironclads resembled the black submarine, the same seamless, ominous taper. Except they had circular barrels for turrets, and no pipes poking up.

Victor stepped stiffly past the curtains onto the balcony. Morning. He'd been dead to the world a whole night. From three stories up, he could see the bay through the tops of live oaks—deeper blue than the sky, so placid it seemed nothing had ever happened out there.

Below, by a curving walkway, two Negro men labored in a flower bed.

Inside, a knock at the door. He felt suddenly naked in the baggy shorts. He dashed to grab a bed sheet and wind it around himself before the door swung open.

Roy Glass's smile was friendly, his eyes shining behind his spectacles, his face robustly pink. Atop a stack of folded clothing in his arms was his gray felt fedora. "Good morning. I am very relieved to see you out of bed."

"How . . . did I get here?"

"I brought you." Glass closed the door behind him. "Here, put these on. They are some of my own. They're too big for you, but something is better than nothing, right?"

"Right. Thanks." When Victor bent his arm back for the shirt, the pain made him suck in a breath.

"Here. Let me help." Glass lifted the sleeve and whistled. "You're all blue. I would have sent for a doctor last night, but . . . I did not see that." His voice was so carefully modulated it might have come from a radio.

Victor sat gingerly on the rim of a chair, for the trousers. "I guess I got knocked out."

"It looks as if someone beat you up." Glass removed his spectacles and peered at them. "I believe you told me your name is Charlie Smith. Is that right?"

"No. It's Victor," said Victor. "Victor Sylvester."

"Ah. It's always a good idea to tell the truth. So now maybe you will tell me what you were doing at the Hotel last night?"

"I came here for help," Victor said. "I live down near Magnolia Springs. There's something going on down there. I was trying to get to the police, but then—I was out there and—I ran into that thing! Did you see it?"

"Wait, slow down," said Roy Glass. "What was it you ran into?"

"A submarine! Didn't you see it? It was right out there, right past the lighthouse!"

"A submarine," said Roy Glass. "In the bay?"

"Yeah! Right there! You were out there, weren't you? You had to have seen it!"

"A submarine." Glass dropped his smile. He turned a chair backwards, and sat. "That is amazing. It's much too shallow except in the ship channel."

"You had to have seen it. There was smoke . . . they put out a smoke bomb. I heard them talking. I couldn't understand any of it. I think it was German."

Glass stared as if Victor had just announced the explosion of the moon. "Let me understand this, son. Are you saying you ran into a *German* submarine out there in our little bay? A *Nazi* submarine?"

Victor ran his hand through his hair. "Listen, mister. I hit it. It sank my boat. I climbed onto the thing. I heard them. It didn't sound like any talking I ever heard."

Glass got up and went to the door. "Come here. Show me where."

Victor pointed out past the lighthouse. "See, the fog was real thick in there, and then I, I drove through it . . ." He told the whole story as well as he could, the parts that were not mixed up with nightmares, but Glass kept glancing at him instead of where he was pointing.

Birds dashed through the trees. A sloop set off from the marina, moving across the crumpled blue bay.

"See that tanker out there?" Glass said. "That's the ship channel. If a boat of any size were to stray much either way, it would run aground."

"There are deep places," said Victor. "All I know is what I

saw. It was floating on the water. I ran into it. At the stern. I climbed up on *top* of it. It caught my shirt and pulled me under . . ."

"You took a bad bump." Glass inspected him. "I saw you go by. There was a terrible fog. Class four. I was putting on the light. Then I heard a—collision. I went after you. I found you floating in the water. Out of your head."

Victor followed him in. "You didn't see what I hit?"

"No. There was too much fog."

"It wasn't fog. It was smoke."

"How large was this . . . ship?"

"Long as a barge," said Victor. "Longer. It was all black and it had this big fin, or a turret or something, and these pipes coming up out of it."

"Tell me something, Victor. Do you go to the movies a lot?"

"Look, I didn't see this in a movie! You were out there! You had to have seen it!"

Glass wore a look of concern, but one eyebrow was up at a doubtful angle. "I know you ran into something. You say it was a submarine. Maybe it was. The Navy has stepped up patrols since so many merchant ships have been lost in the Gulf these last weeks. It might have been one of their boats strayed off course." He straightened. "Now tell me. Where were you going? Something about the police?"

"Yeah. I guess I should have told you last night, but it's just—I didn't think you'd believe me. I found a dead body. On the bank of the river, down—down near my grandmother's place."

Both eyebrows arched up. "A dead body?"

"A man. I think. It's in pretty bad shape. It's got a rope around it, at the waist."

The breeze banged a French door against the wall. Glass's eyes narrowed. "Where exactly was this?"

"The Magnolia. About ten miles south of here." He described Willie's island. "Upriver about halfway to the spring, in the swamp. I can show you."

"I suppose you have an idea where this . . . dead man came from?"

"Not really." Victor knew he had to talk fast. "This kid set fire to my boat. See, I think he's mixed up with some bad business. Moonshine or something. I'm not sure."

"A *rope*." Glass shook his head. "That is not a detail you would make up, now is it."

"I swear it, mister, it's true!"

"For some reason, Victor—why, I am not sure—I am inclined to listen to you. I did not see a thing out there last night, but you ran into something, for sure. So I'll tell you what. I will be out there tonight. If anything shows its face." He stood. "Now. A corpse in a river is not really my department, but I know a policeman in Fairhope who will be interested."

He stopped, folded his arms. "You are not the type who would send me out on a goose chase, are you? Because if you are, I'd rather you go ahead and tell me. Save me the trouble."

"I'll go show you right now, if you want," Victor said.

"No. You stay here. Tend those bruises. I will go bring him here. We can go down to your river together. I have a boat." Glass flashed a white, even smile. "I feel a bit responsible for you, somehow. Very glad I was out there. We might have another dead man on our hands."

"Me too. Oh, don't get me wrong. I guess you saved my life."

"Maybe you will have a chance to save someone else another time," said Roy Glass. "I'll be back in an hour." The door clicked shut.

Victor wandered to the balcony. What was happening to him? Listen, officer, got this kid down here who says he's seen a German submarine and a dead man. Got that? Yeah, that's right. No, me neither. It does take all kinds. Come get him? Okay.

Under hissing sprinklers, the lawn was impossibly green. The sailboat meandered just off the promenade. The gardeners dug with their trowels. An elderly white-mustached man walked his poodle. A woman went by with a little boy tugging each arm.

All this peace! There ought to be sandbags and guns! There was a U-boat out there! Hadn't anyone seen? What were they all doing last night when Victor collided with it, when it whooped and rang bells and submerged, when Roy Glass dragged him in?

Suddenly he didn't want to wait for Glass, or tell the policeman what he had seen. He wanted to go home and go back to bed, and let it all be a dream. Nearly two days gone from Willie's with no note and no explanation. She was frantic by now.

He found a pen and a cream-colored envelope. He drew the eastern shoreline, the mouth, Weeks Bay, the twists of the river. He put an X where the body would be.

Then he pulled on the oversized blue-canvas shoes, left the map on the dresser, and slipped from the room.

Who could he tell? Who on earth would believe him? He was not quite sure he believed it himself.

But he had seen it. He *had*.

His muscles were all cramped up, aching. He picked his way down the narrow stairs.

Joseph would believe him. Joseph would know what to do. But he was on the other side of the world.

Maybe Willie . . .

If only he'd torn off a piece of the thing.

He started across the lawn. Germans in the bay. That's right, sir, about two hundred yards off the Middle Bay lighthouse.

At least it sounded like Germans. What were they doing inside Mobile Bay? I have no idea, sir, I don't speak German. I know it wasn't English. No sir, no flag. The ship was black. So black I couldn't see it, even standing right there on deck.

An elderly man strolled up—the man he'd seen from the balcony, attached by a leash to the puffball dog. He was a walking postcard: an oversized cotton beret, a flower-print shirt, Bermuda shorts, dark glasses. There was a gregarious look about him, as if he had spent a lot of time laughing.

His poodle took one sniff at Victor and reared on its tiny hind legs, snarling, lunging for an ankle. "Sorry," its master said, reining it in. "Come, dratted beast! Leave him alone!"

"He's ferocious." Victor bared his teeth. The dog struggled and snapped sharp little fangs.

"Down!" The man swept off his beret as if to make a formal bow, but instead he swatted the dog. "This miserable animal belongs to the lady of the house. If it were up to me, I'd chain him to a brick and give him a heave right out there. Sink or swim, that's what I'd say."

"Is he that bad?"

"Incorrigible. When you reduce any species to miniature, you also shrink the mass of its brain."

"He's gator bait, sure enough," said Victor.

"I beg your pardon?"

"Where I come from, you couldn't leave a dog like that out in the yard. The alligators'd get him."

"I'd gladly pay for the service." Sure enough, when the old man smiled, his wrinkles smoothed out. "Where is it you come from, so I can walk him in that direction?"

Victor pointed out south.

"In the swamp?"

"More or less. On a river. The Magnolia."

"Ah yes. I've seen it on the chart." The old man extended a

leathery hand. "The name's Gilliam, Edgar Gilliam. Tell me, is there a deep-draft channel in your river?"

There was strength in his grip.

"Yes sir," Victor said. "It's not marked, though. You have to kind of feel your way through."

"And the waterfowl?"

"Sir?"

"The birds, man, the birds! I pursue the winged creature wherever there's a deep-draft channel." The dog sniffed at the seawall, barking every time a wave washed in.

"There's plenty of birds, but season doesn't start till October," said Victor.

"Come here, you damned little—sorry." Gilliam seized the dog by its scruff, shook it once. "No, I have no use at all for dead birds. People kill to prove there's something below them on the food chain. It's an inherited stupidity. I like to look at a bird while it still has the means to fly. I'd read that this bay was a good site for the roseate spoonbill, but the most unusual thing I've seen was a great blue heron with an aspirin bottle on its foot."

"You have a big boat?"

"Only when it's on a small body of water." Gilliam pulled the glasses down his nose for a better look at him. "I also have a punt for close-range exploring. I presume you're familiar with the bottom down there."

Now Victor knew how he could get home. "Well yessir—"

"Very well then, that's set. You'll do nicely. But first you must come have a bite of something, meet Madame. She'll have to approve you."

"I can't," said Victor. "I've got to go home."

"I need a guide for the week," said Gilliam. "I'll pay you more than you make in your present employ."

"But my grandmother's down there all by herself."

"So you'll go home and come back in the morning. We'll get an early start. Right? There you go. I'll pay you fifty dollars."

"Fifty dollars!"

"And not one penny more."

This old man had a boat. Maybe he would want to hunt for something bigger than a bird.

He hastened off after the poodle, which had vanished into a huge azalea.

"Listen," said Victor, "I guess I could help you out."

Edgar Gilliam was down on his knees poking in the bush.

"Good show!" he cheered, clambering up, dusting his hands. "Your first job is to fetch the beast."

Victor wriggled up in the branches and came out with the handful of dog. "Only, do you think I could borrow your punt? I'll be back first thing in the morning, like you said. But first . . . she'll be all worried about me."

"I don't see why not," said Edgar Gilliam. "You seem like a trustworthy lad. We'll arrange the whole thing. Come with me."

See about Willie, then have an adventure. See the world. Meet people. Make something happen. Victor followed the old man down the perfect lawn.

10

VICTOR'S FATHER tied the last knot in his port trawl, squeezed down in the hold to crank the diesels, and then went to round up his no-good crew from Moore's Store.

They were not much to look at, even less to talk to. A big Negro, Sammy, straight from the potato sheds. He was placid and strong as long as you kept him fed, which was a job. A Creole called Lucius—a high yellow, bit of a drunk, with plenty of kink to his hair and an inflated opinion of himself. Handy with the diesels. Played a mouth harp and knew all the old tunes. Once you got him off liquor he'd work four hours on, three hours sleeping, then back on without ever changing the pace of his hauling and heading. Every shrimp in the bucket brought him that much closer to his next whiskey. The most useless of them was Tiny Jones, a half- or quarter-breed, five-two in his cowboy boots—all stubble and lip.

On return, each of these men would get a fraction of the profits; this kept them off the booze and in line. Daniel wished he could run his home half as well.

With the war on, it made no sense trying to hire somebody with brains to help you on a boat. If you found an able, thinking man who wasn't too old to join up, chances were good there was trouble about him. Hire somebody who's a little slow and out of a job, someone who'll do things your way.

Daniel counted out bills for the ice driver, who was also inspecting his crew.

"Lucius!"

"Yay, Cap."

"Listen that rattle. Run down and take a look. Sounds like one of them brackets come loose from the exhaust chimney."

"Got it." Lucius slipped something into Tiny Jones's hand, and disappeared into the hold.

"Tiny."

"Yo."

"Bring me that."

Tiny looked surprised to discover a pint of whiskey in his hand. "You mean this, Cap?"

"Come on." Daniel held out his hand.

"This ain't mine to give you, Cap. This here is Lucius's."

"I know whose it is. Bring it on." Daniel wiggled his fingers.

Tiny wiped his nose on his arm, and edged closer. "You tell him you took it from me," he said. "I don't want him cuttin me in the middle the night."

"I'll tell him." Daniel squinted down at the mean little face. "You boys remember my rules."

The big black man sat motionless on the rail, eyes closed, peaceful as an alligator on a sunny log.

"You hear me? Hey! You, Sammy!"

"I hear." The effort of speaking opened his eyes.

"Remember my rules."

"I do, Cap."

"I got four box of groceries settin under that shed," Daniel said, "and I want 'em stowed right. Tiny, you give him a hand."

When Lucius came up from the hold, he saw what the captain was holding in his hand. "Aw come on now," he started.

"I'll keep it till we get back in," Daniel said. "You know my rules."

"Well it ain't but a little."

"Yeah, and a little is how much it takes to get you going. Soon as they're done I'm ready to go. You go make sure that man packed the ice right."

Lucius shot a longing look at the pint. At the top of the ladder he said, "Cap, we gone stop at Miss Willie's on the way out?"

"We are."

"Spend the night?"

"Nope. Just drop supplies and head out." Daniel glanced up the rise, through the weeping moss to the porch of his house. The little boy, Doolittle, hovered there, a flash of blond hair in the shadows. No one was allowed down to the dock for good-bye. Daniel would not be embarrassed in front of his crew.

But he waved.

The little hand shot up, and waved back with all its energy.

Daniel stepped into the wheelhouse, stilled the buzz in the glass with his hand.

"All set, Cap."

"Cast her off. Where's that Sammy?"

"Back yonder. Asleep." Tiny Jones stuck a thumb over his shoulder.

"That boy sure likes his nap," said Daniel. "Wake him up and let's go."

It was too hot for anyone to move fast, but soon all the lines were cast off. Daniel opened the *Ellen J* up to full rumble. "Tiny! Get up there and watch out." The boat stirred sideways from the dock. Imperceptibly it began gaining speed. The trees reflected the throb of its engines. Here the Magnolia was so narrow that Daniel could bush-hog both banks if he lowered his outriggers. His wake spread in a V, washing a flock of black-headed ducks from their fallen log.

Tiny Jones flapped his hand to starboard. Daniel slowed for the bend into Devil's Hole. Lucius applied a pole to the bank, trying to manage the big boat through the awkward turn. "More!" he cried.

Then Sammy was in the bow, commandeering the pole, leaning against it. The nose came free and around. Daniel pushed the throttle and they emerged into the wider part of the river.

Sammy went back to his place, settled in, and assumed the expression of someone watching a dream on the insides of his eyes.

Lucius and Tiny leaned against the forward hatch, sharing a cigarette. They knew better than to waste this time: the effortless progress of the boat across smooth water; the delicious leisure before the first net was dropped and the rhythm of the work set in. Daniel had been there himself, on the crew, right up to the day old Pop could no longer captain this boat and went off to New Orleans to die. Daniel remembered the dread of the work and he savored this time, too.

The gentle loops in the river took him back through his life. The houses of town with their neat little lawns running down to the river, the first Creole shanties, the first patch of marsh. The long wastelands of wading cypress and big-piney woods. He pictured the river as it was, summer evenings before the first electric lights. Boys in jonboats would head upriver toward a girl, a dance. Folks who lived along the banks would build bonfires to mark the bends in the river. Daniel was one of those boys. All the girls were pretty. The air felt heavy with life.

That was when he met Ellen, who was lovely and soft by the firelight. It seemed the magnolias had a perfume then, though now they were blooming like mad and had no smell at all.

Daniel wished he could tie up his boat for the night. Let his mama cook him a decent supper. Let the boy find a ball game on that radio. Sit on the porch and listen to it. Count the starfish dangling on strings. Get his mama to tell it again, the starfish jubilee.

But that was dreaming. Things were not that way. Willie hadn't cooked a meal in five years. She'd probably start to tell about the starfish and get halfway through and forget where she was, who he was, what she was talking about.

And then Victor was not exactly the kind of son you could sit with and listen to a game and both of you be able to stand it very long. Born fractious, that boy. Dreamy-headed.

So Daniel would drop off the groceries, check to make sure she was taking her pills, think up some orders for Victor, and put out to sea.

A familiar yellow runabout came through the bend. Daniel stuck a hand out his port window in greeting, but Swaney roared by as if he'd just heard the post office was burning down.

Daniel mulled that for a while.

Around a wide bend, the river opened up. Marshes shimmered in the heat. Seagulls were laughing and diving.

Straining his eyes, Daniel made out the wedge of island a mile in the distance. He took Lucius's pint from his pocket, took a swig, trying to steady his nerves for a smile. It was hard to smile past Willie's decrepitude to the strong, hardy woman who raised him. People you once knew as fine healthy folks turn to withered old scarecrows before your eyes.

The warm wind from the south smelled good. This was season. The shrimp would be out there in millions, looking for Daniel's nets. Used to be no one would eat them but Catholics on Friday. Now, with the war on, meat went to the Army and shrimp had doubled its price three times.

Tiny and Lucius squinted out from the railing.

The flash of the late sun off hot tin: Willie's boathouse. Here the current was strong, picking up, heading straight through the pass for the vast slate of the bay. The wheel came easily around in Daniel's hands.

Lucius waved.

Maybe Victor had come to the dock to greet them. Daniel reached for his field glasses, but they were not on their nail.

There was someone on the dock, sitting down. On the dock. Returning the greeting.

Then Lucius stopped waving.

The whole crew turned around and looked at Daniel.

He saw what they saw.

It was Mama. His mama. Sitting on the dock. Slumped to one side. Her hand up, frozen, waving.

Daniel gripped the spokes. *Willie—* He examined the texture of the wheel sliding under his palm. He thought about breathing, then took in a breath and tasted the sweet mix of diesel and salt air.

Must not hit the dock. Must not lose the grip on the wheel. Slowly, slowly release the spoke, feel for the throttle, ease it on back—do justice, now park the boat right, bring it up bring it up, holler Tiny to man the bowline and Sammy to get to the stern.

Oh do justice. You know how to bring in a boat to this dock.

Willie is sitting on the dock. What does that tell you. Asleep maybe she's only asleep. Somehow come down to the dock to wait for you. Passed out. But there is no bottle.

Where is Victor.

Where is that son of a bitch.

That little son of a bitch. Find him and kill him. He deserves to believe it, to really fear it, to be sure it is coming this time.

"Cap." One of the men calling. "Cap."

Oh Willie.

Steady, hands. Do what you do.

Oh great God.

The bowline sails out. Daniel's eyes will not follow the arc to the dock. He cannot look at her.

Lucius leaps, starts across—

"*Lucius!*"

—stops.

"Come back here!"

Now just calm yourself, step away from the wheel to the deck, keep your balance, steady.

"I think somethin's wrong with her, Cap."

A shadow: Sammy looming behind.

Daniel says, "I'll go see." It is not his own voice. He hears his voice way inside him, sobbing, so deep it cannot escape.

Turning away from his men, he swings a leg over the rail. The tide laps over the bottom step.

Willie rests against the wall. Eyes closed. Her hair loose in a tangle on her shoulders, the same silver as the young tips of marsh grass. One hand clutching a handkerchief, the other raised in greeting. Legs folded under. No expression at all on her face.

"Mama," he says, kneeling, "*Mama*, oh God . . ."

The hand he seizes is cold. She will never wake up. He does not have a daddy, and now it is true, he does not have a mama. He is an old man. He is going to die.

Big Sammy is kneeling beside him. "She gone, Captain," he says over and over, a chant, or maybe he said it just once and the echo is sounding again.

He knows Sammy is there for a reason, just as there is some reason his mama has come down to this dock to die.

Sammy bends down, collecting Willie in his own big arms. He carries her up to the house because he knows that is where she belongs.

II

EDGAR GILLIAM'S manservant Charles slipped down a rope ladder into the punt. He checked the fuel, secured the lines, brushed the driver's chair with a whisk broom. "I assume you're familiar with the operation of an outboard motor," he called.

"Oh sure . . ." Victor stood on the deck of *Constance*, the finest and richest, most elegant boat he had ever seen. Last night, when he looked around the marina for fuel, he had noticed only her size and the height of her flying bridge. Now he admired the intricate herringbone-pattern plank deck, the gleaming brass fittings, the gear cabinets with porpoises carved in the doors. At intervals along the railing were mounted special life rings, with the boat's name embossed in crimson and gold.

"This is Mr. Gilliam's personal craft," said Charles, interrupting Victor's reverie. "May I ask you to please bring it back in one piece."

"Don't worry, I grew up in boats." Never mind my run of luck these past few days, Victor said to himself, turning to find a dark woman at his elbow. She introduced herself as Sarah and handed him a white cardboard box tied with string. "For later," she said.

"For me? You guys think of everything."

She inclined her head, hurried in.

Victor cradled the box, picking his way down the ladder. The punt was about the same size as old Pop's rowboat, but so gleamingly lacquered and varnished it looked as if it could glide through the water without getting wet.

Charles started the motor. "We'll see you in the morning, sir," he said, then was gone up and over the rail.

Victor pulled a switch. The running lights twinkled on. He puttered along the polished length of the *Constance*, down the bobbing sterns of the other yachts, down the breakwater.

It was evening now. The bay stretched like a great sheet of silk settling onto a bed. Beyond the hotel, piers ran from the old summer homes out over the bay. Most of them had a pier house or a handmade lean-to at the end, so a family could sit out on summer nights. Shrieking boys raced up and down, ignored by their parents, who sat drinking beer and watching the water. Smaller children dangled crab bait on long strings off the ends of the piers.

Victor sped by close enough to hear one of them screech when a crab caught his finger.

The summer homes gave way to armies of drowned trees marching along the edge of the water, darker woods beyond, with only a shattered trunk or a glimpse of white sand to interrupt the miles. Lights winked, way out on the water: bay shrimpers dragging their nets, crossing each other's lines.

Victor sang songs to himself.

The coast angled out. A sea of marsh grass opened up to the mouth of the river. Across the expanse, he saw the subtle rise of Willie's island.

He swung the tiller to avoid the sandbar on the channel's north side. He had never intended to stay gone so long. He hurried the punt through the open mouth, straining to see into places where there was no light.

But there was a light at the dock. A white light. On the deck of a big, winged boat tied at Willie's landing.

A shrimp boat. When Victor recognized the outriggers, the peculiar snubbed nose, he cut the engine and slowed to a crawl.

His mind flew in a dozen directions. This was close enough. Turn around now. He had found out what he came for: somebody: come out to see about her.

It warmed a path down his neck, the thought of that somebody hot on the scene at the moment Victor deserted his post.

No one was on deck. The light came from one bulb hanging on an outrigger.

Dipping his paddle, Victor moved past the dock.

He could land quietly, slip up to the house, make sure everything was okay, and flee, flee.

The island was dark. It hid everything. The stars were no

help. The frogs were tuned up, their orchestras rounding the night. Victor worked toward the overhanging trees.

An owl called, a circus of cackling and hooting that ended in a cool, weird purr. The frogs hushed. The owl lived in the biggest water oak, up top. Its laughter kept Victor awake on hot nights. Now it sounded a signal, a warning—

Don't get carried away. It's only an owl.

The punt nudged into a stand of reeds. One step and Victor was on the island, or in it; the pillowy mud sucked his foot to the knee. He caught himself on the transom and worked the boat through the cane jungle to a place on shore where the ground held.

He found the path just where it should be.

His ears were burning at the thought of what he had done. Going off. Leaving Willie. No telling how long his daddy had waited for him.

A light bulb in the kitchen. A lantern on the porch. Victor hovered in the shadow of the pump house. The porch faced away from him, out to the bay. Whoever was on it could not see him coming up that side of the house.

Under a window he paused, listening. No sounds. Raising his head an inch, he saw a slice of the kitchen and the room beyond. No one there. Duck down.

They must be on the porch. Careful.

Careful.

Victor lowered himself to all fours, pressed down low to the ground, inched forward. Someone. Two or three. Through the tangle of vines, he saw white rubber boots. His father's crew.

His father strode in among them. The light hid his face. "Y'all hear a boat?"

No one answered.

A rumble, dark thunder: "I said, did a one of you men hear a boat?"

"No sir, Cap," said a voice.

"Lucius, take him and see what it was."

Two of them rushed for the door as if they had heard a starting-line gun.

Victor breathed, peering up from the sand. Now only one pair of boots on the porch. His father was inside the house.

Where's Willie?

Something wrong. They were looking for him. His father's voice grave with anger.

Flee. Get to the punt and keep going.

He crawled back the way he had come. Don't get caught. Not now. Don't run.

Run!

Halfway across the yard his father stepped out of a shadow and took Victor by the arm.

Victor did not know the man in the face. A stranger. His father. A picture of rage. Rage was eating him up, washing the frozen planes of his face, igniting his eyes. It rendered him speechless and twisted his face. Victor was astonished how quickly he'd come over the yard. He was not even breathing. He took a most powerful grip, his knuckle ring digging into the flesh.

"Ow! That hurts!"

The eyes loomed to say, *Does it hurt? Not enough*. The vise tightened. His father's head jerked. A word tried to get out and got stuck in his throat.

"Daddy. What's wrong?"

This time a word came out—something like "here"—Victor found himself dragged stumbling over the yard, through a bush, around the corner of the porch, up the steps. Shoved through the door. He fell hard on his back. A long needle of pain ran in.

Victor lay at the feet of a big black man, who sat with his hands on his knees, eyes closed, as if nothing could ever wake him.

Then his father was on him, lifting him by his shoulders. He jerked Victor up straight, took him by both arms, bent them back, got behind him and held him that way, kicked the backs of his knees, sent him staggering ahead, then snatched him back up to his feet. One good thrust sent him through the doorway into Willie's room, careening *smash!* off the dresser.

Victor lay curled on his side. One hand flopped to his face, came away smeared with blood. His father filled the door. He heard himself sobbing, "Jesus, Daddy, I'm bleeding!"

He saw the face plain, the stranger, the monster, bent and enraged, not the least glimmer of recognition or mercy in those killing eyes.

Victor dragged himself away. His head whistled. White sparks danced in the air. His mouth was busted open. He pulled up on the window, turned to defend himself, and there was Willie on her bed.

Her skin had a floury sheen. When she died all her wrinkles came out. They were dozens and dozens, folds within folds, a map of an old crowded place slowly losing its roads, its borders, its furrows and hills, fading until it was blank as a map of the sea.

She lay between Victor and his father. She was dead and he knew his father would not come across her to get him.

His head drifted to one side. "Willie."

A piece of himself broke off.

She looked cold in only her white nightgown, the sheet pulled to her waist, her hands clenched, lips apart. Victor reached for the sheet. His father swelled in the door.

Her hair had been brushed out, whiter than the pillow. A jar of cold cream sat open, splashes of powder around. Daniel lurched into the room. He dragged the sheet over her face.

"Oh, Daddy, oh please don't hurt me—"

His father took a corner of the sheet in his big hands, ripped it, tore the corner with his teeth.

"It wasn't my fault, Daddy, she was dying! You know that, now please . . ."

His father advanced, wrapping each fist in one end of the cloth. Victor clung to the wall, saying please and weeping just like when he was a child and he knew it was coming and oh, it was coming and please I take it back I didn't mean it I won't do it again ever Daddy, I won't—

He was lost.

His father slammed him into the wall. The cloth came around his face, over his eyes, cinched tight and binding. His arms bent back again. Pushed, falling over furniture, through a door and into a chair and another door.

Scraping chairs. Someone kicked a door and it squealed. Victor fell down the steps. He was jerked to his feet.

He would be killed. His own father would kill him. His father was out of his mind. He must have veered off forever when he found her.

An arm locked him, forced him on, over roots, down a slope. Victor fell, but he scrambled up quick to keep from being snatched again. He was wondering how he would die.

"Listen, Cap," someone said, "let him go."

A hiss exploded.

They were on the dock now. Well then he would be drowned. Taken out on the boat and shot dead and dumped over. So no one could find his body.

The blood tasted sweet in his mouth. He quit resisting. The arm had him. His face met a wall. He was in the boathouse. He knew not to move.

"Don't hurt me—"

From behind came a thud, then a great metal clanking and

groaning, as if the boathouse were being ripped apart beam by beam. Rough hands marched him up two steps, against another wall. The banging resumed, and finished with a massive weight clanging down.

His father walked away.

Lapping water . . .

Victor tore the rag from his face.

Think now.

You're all right you're bleeding to death.

Think now.

Where is this?

Boathouse. The boathouse.

But where? It's so dark.

You're okay you're not dead.

Oh God Willie.

Boards all around boards with spaces between, just the merest light showing. A floor, wall, and ceiling of boards with thin spaces between. A heavy wire grate. A cage. No way in or out. "Willie," he cried just to hear her old name.

12

HONEY BOY, if you'll hush up and pull down that window, I'll let you in on a little secret. Wasn't always the way you see me, with the liverdy spots on my legs and my teeth in a jar on the table. For shame, to let a boy see me like that, but how else will he know what is happening when old age starts in on him? Give and take, live and learn, what I say. Looka here. See this place? Fell off my granddaddy's canoe when I was five and got this climbing out on a rock. This here is the time your uncle Chester brought the monkey back with him from Mexico. That thing bit me like I was a banana. You see this? This is where your daddy was trying to brand the kittens one time, see, he'd seen 'em branding cattle in the Tom Mix picture, he made up his mind that was just what he needed to keep track of Blackie's new litter. That's what I got taking that red-hot poker out of his hand. One of those kittens never did come back. I think of this mole, and I picture your granddaddy when he was young, young and fine. Fine as you. That's where he kissed me as soon as he asked me to marry him. Kissed me right on that mole. Any man that will kiss me on my mole, I said, you're the man for me.

Wait, I'm getting to that. I'm not telling this to hear you tell me how to tell it.

I married that man, yes I did, I'll admit it to anybody that wants to hear it, and be proud of it all over again. You might say he sung a good tune. Or at least a tune I could dance to. You don't think there was dancing back then but there was. There was everything back then that there is today, and more of it, too. More high times. More fish in the water. More watermelons in August. More dancing.

He said to me Willie, you come live with me and I'll build us a house in a place out where nobody goes. Just us both. You and me and the fishes. Well brother, I bought it, I paid him in cash. I was head over heels and just thinking about it makes me dizzy right now.

Honey boy, turn down that lamp. You trying to put me in mind of the heavenly light? Never mind. I'll get to it myself.

We came out to this island. It wasn't an island back then but that's another story. Now I'm asking you to pretend you remember how pretty-looking I was. I got pictures to prove it.

Came down the river in a catboat, wasn't hardly a house between here and the springs then, he brought me down here to this house on a cold winter day, and he told me to see what I could gather up in the way of firewood so I could stay warm, while he went off to start catching fish. And he did, and I did, and that's how things went on for the longest time. That man caught more fish than Jesus could turn into bread. He'd go out on the water and stay there, and leave me alone, leave me just to look in the mirror and admire myself. You know, folks can live out a life, day by day, and spend every one of them wishing this day would get over, so they could get on with tomorrow. If you don't know what I mean, honey, you will. I got to thinking about how many other men there was in the world, besides him.

When it happens to a woman, likely as not she'll get on one kind of a jag or another, and I got on a jag for crying, so that every time that man came home, whether it'd been a day or three weeks since he'd seen me, I'd be setting there at the kitchen table with my head on my hand, just a bawling. Now you might imagine that this give him cause for alarm. He and I had got on pretty well up to then, according to him. But he decided he would be concerned. Honeybunch, he called me. Honeybunch, why is the sight of your crying eyes the thing I see first when I walk in my door? That's exactly what he asked me.

I'm better than you, I told him, never should have married you, don't want to look at your face anymore, you horrible worm-eating man. I mean, I was awful to him.

He just said, honeybunch, what can I get for you?

I didn't want a damned thing, and I told him just that.

He kept after me. Honey, what's that frown on your face? Is it something you need? I'll go get it. Just tell me what it is.

A starfish, I told him. Go get me a starfish.

A starfish?

That's right. You heard me. If you ever cared a thing about me you'd go find me a starfish.

He looked right down at me, and you got to trust me, that man never cracked the first smile. He turned around and went out the door. I thought I had lost him for good. He got on his boat and lit out for the Gulf and stayed gone. I went ahead and packed up my little things, in case somebody I knew should come by in a boat, I could go on and leave.

But I went to sleep one night, it had been a week, a harvest moon, I remember, it was in that window yonder, so bright I could see it with my eyes closed. I was somewhere in there between sleeping and not, you know, where you're floating along. I heard that man's boots on the porch. I rolled over, not all the way, not so he'd think I was glad to see him, and I said well? Did you get it?

Willie, you better get up and come out on the porch. All he said. I thought somebody was dead. I got out of bed and went out there, and he said, you got to come down to the bay, here, with me. I said why are you scaring me this way, he said, just come on with me. Well, he led me right down to the water, and he asked me what did I see. His eyes were big. He was pointing out where he tied up his boat.

And well I saw it was something in the water, but I couldn't say what, but whatever it was there was millions of it, it was some kind of jubilee, that's for sure. He swashed his hand around and brought one up out of the water. He lit a lamp and showed me. The water was busting with them. They were everywhere. It looked like there was one for every last star in the sky. That man, your granddaddy, he put his arms around me, you know? He held me real close like we did in those days. He said, honeybunch, I swear I looked all up the beach from here to St. Petersburg, Florida, and I never saw a single one. Said, I finally decided you'd have to take your chances with just me, and if what I could get you wasn't good enough, well, that was that. I headed on back. When I got here tonight, tied up my boat, I just looked around and they were here.

That's what he said. *They were here.* They came all the way here just for us. They heard what you needed, they knew how bad I wanted to get it for you, and they every one came.

Well. I couldn't help but love that man. I told him, kill me and lay me down here, because something like this only happens to you in your life once. If you're lucky. I took as many of those starfishes as I could carry, and I've got 'em, every one. That's some of 'em, hanging right there on those strings.

Yes, of course it is. Every last word of it. Ever since that night, I've been ready to drop in my tracks anytime. I've seen my one thing for this life.

That man could make me see starfishes where there wasn't a one. It ain't changed a bit since he died. As long as you known somebody who one time made you see things that wasn't there, you can go on and die and know you didn't miss a thing. Do you hear what I say?

13

VICTOR'S EARS sang, the smart from the last blow. Never mind that Willie was old, that she had been dying for months, that something on the doctor's list had finally crossed her out. She died alone: it was Victor's fault: it would stay his fault from now on.

What was it she told him? Almost the last thing. Be careful what you wish for . . .

A spark shot through his mind: *I wish he'd killed me so he'd know how it felt* and then *no, I wish he was dead*. Just thinking that made it a fearful live picture in his brain, his father's face slack in that awful sleep, the family solemn around the bedstead. Victor's mother might be sorry. The younger children would cry. But not Victor. He would be free. All the battered and hurt little creatures inside him would be out of their cages.

He was not crying now. A little shudder when he took a breath, but that was all. The blood from his lip would not stop. A large knot had grown on his temple; that side of his face was swelling.

The cage was so small he could not stand up or stretch out, even at an angle. He felt with his hands to each corner, and over his head.

Heavy footfalls on the dock—two or three men moving with purpose the length of the boathouse and out to the end. Victor struggled against the urge to cry out.

The door swung in.

Victor's stomach froze. He pressed to the wire, straining to see.

"Where you, boy?" A hoarse whisper. Not his daddy. The door closed. "You in here somewhere?"

Victor held his breath.

"You all right? Where you at?" A solid thud, flesh against metal, and the whisper exploded in raving—"Ow Jesus god-damn it!" A crash of machinery. Whoever it was fell hard on the ledge just outside the cage.

"Who is that?" Victor whispered.

"I believe I have done broke my foot."

"Who are you?"

"Lucius. I crew for your daddy. Jeez Louise, that one *hurt*."

Victor spoke fast. "You got to get me out of here. He'll kill me."

A whiskery face came to the grate. Victor smelled liquor.

"How bad did he beat up on you?"

"I'm bleeding. My mouth."

"I think he's 'bout finished with you." Lucius grunted, pulling off his boot. "He's up there with her. She was sittin yonder on the dock when we come up. Dead as anything. Cap kind of cracked."

"Yeah. I know."

Lucius made a painful noise, standing. "Least he didn't kill you. Listen. We're sposed to carry her down and back to town. Seem to me the best thing is you just stay here. I'll send somebody back for you."

"Don't leave," Victor begged. "Look and see if there isn't a pulley or something up there."

"If he caught me lettin you out, he'd kill me too."

"You can't just leave me in here!"

"I'll send somebody back. Now I got to go."

"But you got to help me!"

"Boy, why you think I'm here? Now I'm gone. Here. Take this." Lucius shoved something through the open inch at the bottom of the cage. "That'll help."

Victor picked up a skinny bottle.

"Just drink it," said Lucius. "Rub some on your cut place. I got to go." He hobbled toward the door. The light showed again. He closed it behind him.

Victor unscrewed the cap. Bourbon. The heat of it swarmed down his throat.

Beyond the tin wall there was shouting. The men shuffled unsteadily onto the dock, as if balancing a dire load.

Victor put his head on his knee. There was no longer much blood coming into his mouth.

A stumble, half-step—someone's knee struck the dock—and then shouting, *whoa!* and *look out!*

Victor held his breath for a splash that did not come.

"Goddamn it, be careful!" his father rumbled, quickly answered by murmured apologies. "Watch it, Tiny! Watch your foot!"

Feet scuffled, back in control. A diesel caught up, then the other. Together they smothered all other sound. The steel grate vibrated. Propeller wash swirled through the boathouse.

Victor clawed at the grate, screaming, "I didn't kill her! Come back here! Daddy! It wasn't my fault!"

The diesels surged and moved off.

Victor yelled every foul word that came to his mind. Every word he'd stored up. None of them came anywhere close to his father, but he found a powerful freedom in letting them fly.

14

THE SPRING that Mrs. Wagner introduced his second grade class to the multiplication tables, Victor came down with a fever. It felled him like an ax, on his way home from school. He fell down on the sidewalk and could not get up. His father came running, carried him to the house, to the dark back bedroom.

For four nights his fever ascended. No one knew how high

it went. As far as anyone knew it peaked at one hundred and four. In his delirium, Victor decided that if the fever went any higher he would die, so he sneaked the thermometer out of his mouth and dipped it in the water glass.

He was seized by drastic chills, fits of shivering, sweating, passing in and out of this world.

The wallpaper in his parents' room was patterned with diagonal rows of printed gold medallions, marching in unchanging rows. The grid took on a horrific regularity in Victor's overheated mind. The medallions turned into numbers. The numbers sprang to life. He counted the row up and then the row down, and the other rows running across—five times five, twenty-five, six times six, thirty-six . . . endless combinations of numbers, contorting and swelling. They waddled like hulking huge beasts, then suddenly shrank down slender, razor-sharp, wicked. They shouted their names in his ears.

Out of his mind again, he found himself counting the diamond-shaped spaces in the steel grate, but at first the numbers brought a strange kind of comfort: nineteen up, twenty-seven across, six sides to the cage . . .

Then the old terror welled inside him—*Stop! Get your mind away! Be strong.*

He heard scuttling crabs and the insects and frogs and mullet splashing. They mocked him with the noise of their lives. They were free. He was their prisoner. He felt the rise and fall of his blood, a rocking sensation.

He started up, banged his head on the grate. "Who's there!"

From just over his head came an answer: "Howdy, stranger."

Victor shrank to a corner.

"It's your old best buddy, remember? Somebody's *always* gettin the last laugh on you." Butch hunkered on the grate overhead, waving a lighted Zippo, peering down with a malicious grin. "Looks like they put the bad dog in his cage!"

Victor squinted up. "What are you doing here? Look, we got no fight with each other."

"I got word you was having some trouble. What'd you do, kill the old lady?"

"Go to hell," Victor snapped.

"Woo," said Butch, "bad dog! Bad dog!"

Victor lunged against the cage. "Go to *hell* I said!"

"Arf, arf! Down, Sandy!" Butch kicked at the boards and sat back laughing. The lighter snapped shut. He climbed down from the cage and went out.

Victor smashed his shoulder against the top and the sides, but the cage would not budge.

Then Butch was back, dragging something behind him— a long scraggly pine limb with a fan of dry needles at one end. He broke off twigs and began shoving them under the cage.

"Hey, what are you—what are you doing?"

"Buildin a fire," came the toneless reply. "I'm a little chilly. How 'bout you?" Now he was wadding up old paper, stuffing it in the cracks.

Victor poked it out with his fingers. "Quit! You're crazy! I didn't hurt you!"

"You messed with me," Butch said. "Shouldn't have done that."

"Well you blew up my granddaddy's boat! We're even!"

Butch got to his knees. "I don't like being even." He flicked the Zippo. "I like to be way out in front. Now tell me where you hid Noltie's boat."

"Hey, stop! You got to listen to me!"

"Gonna have barbecued dog." Butch bent over his work.

Victor knew he would never get anywhere begging. "You're too late," he said.

The needles were green and wouldn't catch. Butch swore and

began searching around for some other fuel. "What's that you say, Sandy? Didn't hear you."

"The boat," Victor said. "You're too late. It sank halfway across the bay and you'll never find it."

Butch stared down at the guttering flame. "You're a liar," he said.

"No, I'm just a thief. Just like you. It took less time to sink than it took me to steal it from you."

Butch smacked the cage with his fist. "I oughta kill you, you—"

"Go on and try it. You won't be the first one tonight."

"What'd you do with it? You better tell or I swear, I'll . . ." Butch looked around for something more terrible to do than he could think of himself. "You got it hid! Tell me where!"

"Let me out and I will."

The flame fluttered again. Butch moved close to the cage. "What's that yonder?"

"What?"

"That bottle. That whiskey?"

"Yeah."

"Give it to me. Slide it under."

Victor did as he said. "Go on, help yourself."

Butch took a big slug. "Yahhh . . ."

"Get all you want," Victor told him.

"Who put you in there, Sandy?"

"My old man."

"Looks like he made you uglier than you already was."

"I guess so." Victor covered his face with his hand. "He beat the hell out of me."

"How'd he get you in there? I don't see no way in."

"There's a rope or a pulley or something. I think the top comes up somehow."

Butch's fingers came through the grille. "I just leave the old dog in his cage, I believe. Go find that damn boat on my own."

"Good luck," said Victor. "Look around. Look from here to Mobile. You won't find it. It's sunk. Get me out of here and I'll tell you what happened. You won't believe it."

This was not part of any plan of Victor's, but it seemed a chance and he took it. He was in a cage: Butch was not: not a thing on earth to lose by trying. He pressed his hands on the wire. "You and me already settled with each other. A boat for a boat, like I said. Now we got something bigger to worry about. It's bigger than anything you ever saw."

"Yeah, what's that?"

"Let me out and I'll show you. I will. Listen. You need me. I found that dead man. You know who killed him, right? What is it, some kind of whiskey business? You running a still for Noltie? Is that it? I don't care about that."

"I don't know what you talking about. A dead man?"

"Halfway between here and the springs. He'd been shot in the heart. Tied up with a rope. You don't know about that?"

"Naw, man, I make shine and run bond whiskey for Noltie, but I never . . ." Victor's hope soared as Butch got up from the floor and began pacing side to side, like a cat. "See, somebody's been burning me out," he said. "I thought it was you, count of all that gasoline. That was how they done it. Burned two perfect good rigs and poured out five new cases of bond on the ground. When you come for that gas, I thought Noltie had sent you." He stopped and peered into the cage. "But I went to tell him what I done to you, to tell him I'd do worse if he didn't quit, and it ain't Noltie. He never even heard of you."

"I told you."

"He wants to go back to business, forgive and forget, just bring back the boat . . . but there's something going on."

Victor said, "That's just the start. Let me out. I'll tell you all about it." He whispered the words through the grate: "It's Germans."

Butch stopped pacing. "What?"

"The Germans. They're out there."

Butch's mouth fell open. "The *who?*"

"The Nazis. The Krauts. They're out in the bay. Night before last. A submarine. A U-boat, man, I ran smack into it."

"Aw bullshit."

"It's the truth," Victor said. "I was driving that boat off Point Clear. I hit it. I ran up *on* it. I climbed on it while it was sinking. It sunk your boat. I nearly got drowned."

Butch snorted, drumming his hands on the cage. "And I reckon ol' Hitler was driving it too."

"Let me out. Let me out and I'll prove it to you. I'll show you the dead man. We'll go to Point Clear. I met this old guy up there. He's rich. He's got this great big boat. I think he'll help us. We can find that thing."

Butch took a pull on the bottle, scratching his chin. He looked as if a bath or a shave might kill him. He probably hadn't changed his clothes since the first time he put them on. He wore something that had once been a man's white dress shirt, with the sleeves ripped off at the shoulders. "This stuff ain't bad," he said, smacking his lips. "Did they have on their helmets?"

"Who?"

"The Krauts."

"I couldn't see."

"How you know it was them?"

"I heard 'em talking."

"How do they sound?"

"Like on the radio." Victor softened his tone. "Listen, why

can't you help me get out? You won't be sorry. I'll pay you back. We can find that thing, and, and I bet when we do, I bet we'll get a big reward."

"That's baloney."

Victor embroidered as he went. "We could use you when we go after it. We'll need all the help we can get. That man's rich as God. He loaned me a boat. We can go up there now. He said he'd pay us."

"Did he get a look at the Krauts?"

"No, uh-uh. Just me."

"And this guy says he's gonna help you look?"

"Look, Butch. Something like this doesn't just happen all the time. I got to be careful, you know what they say, loose lips sink ships and all that. But I think we can trust him. He's not bad for an old guy."

"I don't think it was Krauts," said Butch, "and even if it was, I don't think you saw them. If you didn't see their helmets. They all wear the same helmets."

"See," Victor put in, "that's the kind of stuff you'd be good at. Telling their helmets. There's a lamp over there. Why don't you shine it up here and see if you can see the rope?"

Butch stood back from the cage, pondering. He looked as if he wanted to believe. "You know, Noltie said there was forty-some ships sunk just last month, right out in the Gulf."

"I'm telling you, man. I know what I saw."

"Say he lent you a boat? Where's it at?"

"Oh no," said Victor. "Get me out of here. Then I'll show you everything."

Butch came back with the lantern.

"See, there's a ring." Victor's spirits soared; he could already feel how it would feel to stretch his arms. "I bet you tie a rope on right there and pull it up."

Butch rummaged, fiddled, considered, finally located a pulley mounted in a roof beam. Victor coached from inside. "Now tie that here and run the other end down through that loop."

"Down, boy," said Butch. Before long he had the rope rigged and tied fast on the winch pole. He set the lantern on the floor and started pulling. A scraping groan filled the boathouse.

Victor shoved up with his hands. "Pull harder!" The massive steel frame detached and raised just an inch, like the lid of a giant kettle. "That's it! Keep pulling!"

Butch grunted and cussed, but he leaned into it. When the space was wide enough, Victor wiggled out. The pain flooded back. He sank to his knees, breathing, giving in to a surge of gratitude. "Let me tell you, I owe you for this. I mean it. Who knows how long I could have stayed in there before somebody came."

"Damn, Sandy, you look bad." Butch held the light near his face. "Why'd he do that to you?"

Victor looked at his feet. "My name's not Sandy. It's Victor."

"Sandy suits you better," said Butch. "Man, he put a whelp on your head."

"He got here while I was gone and he found her. She was dead. It made him so mad . . . when I got here, he caught me and—"

"You must be sissy to let him beat on you like that."

Victor got to his feet. He had no strength to fight. It took everything not to show how much it hurt just to stand. "That was it. That was the last time. He won't hit me again." The words sent a cold wind rushing through him. "I'll kill him before I let him hit me again."

He saw his father's fist coming, the whole vivid landscape of rage on a paunchy, battered old man. Victor had gone off and committed the crime of all time. Bigger than the Lindbergh baby. Bigger than anything Hitler had done yet.

He could beat something bigger than his father.

"You wouldn't have to kill him," said Butch. "You could burn him out."

"No. I'm finished with him," Victor said.

Butch strode down the dock. "I bet the old lady left something to eat in that house."

"No. There ain't anything there. We're not going up there. We're not eating her food."

"She's dead," said Butch. "She ain't hungry."

"You listen to me," Victor started, but the place that was Willie was too big to explain, and too empty now. "There's some food in the boat. You can eat that."

"Look who's givin orders."

"Come on." Victor walked straight ahead to the cane patch. He did not want this boy to see his face. Soon the sun would come up. They would bury Willie. He did not want to see that. Willie would hate it in town. She loved the island. She was here, right here somewhere, out under the oyster-shell mound, maybe, or in the air. They could put her body on a boat and take it upstream, but they could not take Willie out of this place.

15

T H E G L I M M E R of sunrise advanced in the clouds. Victor pushed the punt from the reeds. He did not look back at the house. By now it should have vanished.

In the bow, Butch tore the string from the box and set into

breakfast—a chicken leg in one hand, a sandwich in the other. "Where'd you get this stuff?" he said around a mouthful. "Ain't seen a piece of roast beef this big ever."

"The old man had his servant fix it. He's got servants all over the place." Victor watched him eat. He did not care about food. His mouth ached and anyway it had been so long since his last whole meal, since his last good night's sleep, that he'd almost forgotten why he used to do those things.

He started the motor and set the tiller upriver. The windless dawn polished Weeks Bay like a sheet of pink glass, the little boat trailing a refracted V across the surface.

"Listen," said Victor, "who told you I was in trouble, anyway?"

"Looffuf."

"Who . . . ?"

Butch swallowed. "Lucius. Come to get a pint. Said he give his to you. He was in one hell of a hurry. He told me how they found the old lady."

"Is he in business with you?"

"Who, Lucius?" Butch tossed a leg bone over the side, and looked sorry to see it go. "Naw, he was one of my best customers, him and her both. Both regular as clocks."

"Him and who?"

Butch ate the next sandwich in three bites. "The old lady," he said, chewing. "Your grandma. Wild Willie."

"Wild . . . what are you talking about?" Victor clutched the tiller. "How do you know her name?"

"Name, hell, Sandy, I known that old lady about as good as you did, I reckon." Butch dug in the box and came up with the last chicken leg. "Did you think it was old Jack Daniel bringing her bottle out to her?"

Victor cut over hard to avoid a floating log. "You don't mean it was—you!"

"One quart Old Forester, ever second Tuesday," said Butch, catching himself with one hand. "Watch where you're going there, Sandy. Don't look so surprised. I took over for Noltie when he got his legs shot. We got business all over the place."

Well. That was a fine joke. All these years everyone had suspected Swaney the mailman, and here was Willie's bootlegger straight out of Noltie Creek.

"That was her boat you burned," Victor said.

"Sorry to hear that, Sandy. Shoulda told me before I burned it. I liked that old lady just fine. She used to give me stuff to eat when *my* old lady was off on a goner."

"I ran into your old lady," said Victor. "I see what you mean." Heading up the narrowing river, he tried to picture Willie ministering to little wild redheaded Butch. She'd had secrets on secrets, a whole life that Victor could only imagine.

"What was it you called her . . . ?"

"Wild Willie? That's Noltie. Says she's wild as any fish in the sea. Or used to be, before she got old. He says she used to stand down on the dock and sing hymns at the fish." Butch made a face. "They all crazy down here."

"But I've never seen you around. Not once."

"You hadn't looked. I seen you plenty. I used to stand down there at the big mouth and look over at all y'all brothers and sisters playin on your big fancy island. Had to wait for y'all to leave till I could row over and eat what you left over."

Sure. Victor remembered. Those long lazy afternoons of kick the can and dodgeball with Joseph and Roxanne and the cousins, there always seemed to be a clutch of raggedy children fishing on the bank across the channel. . . . But the Sylvesters weren't *rich*. Not ever. They wore each other's worn-out clothes and overheard fights about money, late on too many nights.

Still. There always was plenty to eat.

The punt passed through the wide stretch of river at the old

Johnson cabin. "Right out there," Butch said, pointing into the woods, "that was where I had my first kettle. They burnt it and wrote me a note in the dirt, said I'd be the next to get burned."

"What'd you do?"

"Set up a new one yonder. Same thing. Only they found my cases that time. And didn't see fit to leave me no note. I was standin there cussin about it and damned if somebody didn't take a bead on me from across the river with some kind of rifle that took out a big hunk of tree."

Victor stood up halfway to see over Butch. No, that wasn't the right swamp. He had memorized landmarks so he could find it again: a certain bent pine tree, the sandy stretch between patches of marsh grass.

Butch shook the crumbs down to the corner of the box, pinched them onto his tongue, licked his fingers.

"Okay, here we go," Victor said, peering ahead. "Right up here."

Butch turned to see for himself. "I don't see nothing."

"Should be . . . in there." Victor saw the pine, the sand, the tide as low as he'd expected, but—

"He's gone."

Butch rolled his eyes. "Guess he wadn't as dead as you thought."

"Oh, he was dead all right. He didn't take off by himself." Victor switched off the motor, aimed the boat up on the sand a few feet from the shallow indentation, the trail of something dragged down into the water. "Look, that's where I found him. I tried to move him but he weighed too much. There was a rope . . ."

He followed the line from Butch's finger to the pine tree, up the curving trunk to the first branch—the rope hanging there, soggy, gray, one end frayed, twisted into the crude but unmistakable form of a noose.

"Who else did you tell, Sandy?" Butch's voice was almost gentle, or fearful.

"Just—this guy at the hotel. The coast marshal. He was gonna get a policeman and bring him down here. I drew 'em a map. They must have took him . . ."

"That don't look like what a cop would do." Butch was still pointing. "Somethin awful funny about all this, you know?"

"Yeah. Only why ain't I laughing," said Victor.

They climbed in the punt and set out downriver.

S L I C K little boat," Butch said as it bounced and careened on the choppy bay. "How rich you say this man is?"

"I'm not sure." Victor had to shout into the stiff morning breeze. "You take a look at this yatchet of his, and you'll see what I mean."

"What's a yatchet?"

"A big boat. For rich people. You know."

"What's he got we can take?"

Victor straightened. This boy was one big domino row of surprises. "I . . . I don't know. I wasn't exactly planning to rob him. You always steal from somebody or burn 'em out the first time you meet 'em?"

"I have, here lately." Butch licked a finger, and held it up. "It just seem to happen that way."

"Listen," Victor called. "You have anything to do with that school in Bon Secour?"

"So what if I did."

"Just wondering." Victor steered wide of the sandbar. "Why you did it."

Butch pulled a red hair from his mouth. "They was trying to make me go there."

"Oh."

"Soon as it burned, they quit trying."

"I bet." They bounded over a white-curling wave. Victor kept his eye on the fuel gauge rocking ever closer to empty. It was one thing to run out all by yourself in a boat, and another with Butch to keep you company. Victor would never have guessed he'd be sharing a boat with an untamed red-faced wild boy, but it was starting to seem they had more things in common than not. On the run, both of them. In an ocean of trouble. Cut off from whoever they used to be.

Butch sat facing the wind as if setting out in search of dead men and submarines was something he did every day of the week. He had a wildness that Victor wished he could capture for himself. He didn't care about anyone else. He would never let himself get beat up. It would always be better to have him on your side.

16

THE SERVANT Charles peered from the dock with a long narrow look down his nose at Butch. "Mr. Gilliam did not mention that there would be two."

"Howdy," said Victor. "This here is Butch."

"Indeed." When Charles saw Victor's bruises, the cut, the eye, the dried blood, he drew himself up to a height of indignation. "I'm sorry, sir, but your appearance is quite unacceptable," he said, tying the bowline with pasty hands. He looked as if he'd spent his whole life indoors, eating unhealthy food.

Butch was busy ogling the floating wealth in the Hotel's little harbor. "Man, get a look at these tubs," he said. "They look like a bunch of cakes floating. Which one is it?"

"That one. On the end."

"The big one?"

"I told you."

Butch whistled, stuck his hands in his pockets.

Charles waved them away from the punt. "Quite sorry," he quavered, "but I can't announce you until something is done about the way you look. The Gilliams simply do not associate with brawlers and bums."

Butch whirled. "What'd he call me?"

"A bum," Victor said. "Never mind. Listen, Charlie, I'm sorry if it hurts you to look at my face, but I can't help it. I . . . ran into a brick wall. You don't want us, we'll go. We only came to bring back your boat."

Edgar Gilliam strode down the dock, tapping his walking stick before him. He wore a white Panama hat and an elegant sky-blue suit that flowed as he walked. "And what have we here?" he boomed. "A detachment from the motley brigade!" He leaned over to touch the edge of Victor's eye. "It's a lovely morning, lad, but I imagine you're only seeing about half of it."

"I got in a little trouble."

"I'll say," said the old man. "Someone didn't care for the way you look?"

"Mr. Jeeves here, for one," Victor said.

Charles spoke up from the punt. "Sir, I tried to tell them—"

"Never mind, Charles. This lad is now in our employ. You're to treat him as a member of the family."

"Yes sir." Charles's face froze. He glared at the boys and disappeared over the rail of the big boat.

"Lad, who's your friend? We haven't been introduced."

"This is Butch. He . . . he got me out of a tight spot last night. I told him about you. He knows all about the river down there, all kinds of birds and stuff, don't you, Butch."

"Yeah, I'm a expert."

". . . So anyway I figured he could help us."

Edgar maintained his friendly smile as he looked them over. "Well, heaven knows there's room. My original offer still stands. Fifty dollars. You'll have to work that out between you. Now you'll come with me, clean yourselves up, let Madame have her look at you. Then we'll be on our way. Right? Here we go." He set off at an impatient pace.

The long lawn stretched out in the shade of live oaks. Brightly dressed people sat lounging in chairs where the morning sunlight fell through the branches. Negroes in white coats moved among them, balancing trays of coffee and pastries.

"Makes me wanna cut down a tree or take a dump on the grass or somethin," said Butch.

"Shush," Victor said, hiding his smile in his hand. "You'll blow the whole thing."

The old man led them past the main building to a wrought-iron gate, the only opening in a long wall of pink masonry. Inside was an intricate garden—a bank of scarlet, a bed of yellow and white blooms, hedges clipped into geometrical shapes—surrounding a pink bungalow. A shingled roof sloped to a wall made of glass. A waterfall splashed. Fountains and statues poked up from the shrubbery.

Victor tried easing the gate, but its weight took over and shut it with a *clang!* "Do you . . . is this where you live?"

"We're staying here," the old man replied. "They call it the Admiral Raphael Semmes Cottage. Although I wonder what the poor man would think if he woke up in this place. Now, you lads step in here. Lavatory's second door on the right, plenty of soap and water."

Butch trailed Victor into the big white-tiled bathroom. "Everybody act like we was Typhoid Mary or something."

Victor touched the cut on his eye, and watched himself flinch. "I don't know about you, but he's right about me. Look at me. I look sorry." There were two sinks. Victor set to scrubbing himself in the one on the left. Before long the worst evidence of his beating was gone.

When he turned, Butch was wiping the dirt from his face on a monogrammed towel, without the interference of water. He showed all his teeth—an imitation of a smile—and said, "I don't wash for nobody."

"Fine with me."

Butch dropped the towel on the floor and led the way back to the garden. Victor touched one of the red-throated flowers to see if it was real.

Edgar Gilliam walked around the house. "Ah, much better," he said.

From behind him came a startling sound: a steady thumping, interrupted by faint little cries, as from someone being beaten.

Gilliam smiled. "The woman I love! Come on. Oh—lad, forgive me, but I've reached the age where I can't remember my own name, let alone yours. Give it to me again."

"It's Victor. Victor Sylvester."

"V for victory, eh? That's a very old name. You should come through all right in the end with a name like that. And this one is Butch? Right." The old man peered around the corner. "My dear, are you flagrant? I have some people for you."

The moaning had nearly died out. The old man waved them around the corner. The back garden was designed around a turquoise pool in the shape of a seahorse. Beyond, in a circle of sunlight, a large lumpish woman was pounding someone on a steel cart with wheels, a hospital cart.

"Would you look at that," murmured Butch.

Whoever it was had gone limp. Two arms dangled from under the towels. A band of pale flesh lay exposed, and it was there that the large woman directed her blows.

The poodle zipped from side to side, setting up a hateful racket. On the table, a shiny chrome radio played a daytime drama.

From the towels came a groan of pain, or pleasure, or both.

"Come on, lads, nothing to fear but fear itself," Gilliam said. "Hilda won't attack you without an exorbitant payment."

Hilda noticed them then, quit pounding, and looked up, blowing a bead of sweat from her lip.

"Why'd you stop?" came a muffled demand. "You haven't been at it—"

"The mister is back."

The dog skittered into the bungalow.

The towels stirred. Victor found himself looking into a re-markable face, a dramatic, almost catlike arrangement of sculpted cheekbones and deep eyes, taut flawless skin. He had seen a picture of that face. Those eyes, the fiercest green eyes, gazed at him as if they could drill holes through his head. "Well?" she said. "Edgar. The meaning of this!"

"Beg your pardon, my dear, this is Victor, and his friend there is Butch. I've engaged them to serve as our guides to the exotic bayou country. I knew you'd want to meet them. Fellows, this is Madame."

"Hey," said Victor. At once it seemed the dumbest thing anyone had ever said, and she registered the same reaction.

"Not funny, Edgar." When she brought an arm around to prop up her chin, Victor was shocked to see wattles, the sagging upper arms of a much older woman.

"It's not intended as humor, my dear. They're natives of the vicinity and I've taken them on for the week."

"What day is this, Edgar?"

"Monday, I think."

"Your day to go completely insane?"

Edgar chuckled.

Madame's eyes never wavered in their examination of Victor. It was as if no one else were in the garden. Victor looked to the old man for help, but her gaze had him fixed.

"I presume you speak English," she said.

"Yes, ma'am."

"How old are you?"

"Sixteen," said Victor.

Butch gaped at Madame as he might a dangerous fish.

"You're in some kind of trouble with the authorities. That much I can tell." She propped her chin on a fist.

"No. No ma'am."

"Yes you are. I'm a sound judge of character. You're hiding something. Some trouble. And that one's been in jail more than once." She looked over her shoulder. "Hilda. Vermouth."

Hilda trundled away.

Edgar sat in a carved cedar chair. "Madame's learned to read faces as well as some people read the newspaper."

"What do you mean?"

"Madame was once a spy."

"A *spy*," Victor marveled.

Madame smiled a tight little smile, as if she'd heard the story once too often. She examined her razory fingernails, then flicked her eyes up at Victor. "Edgar exaggerates. I did a few small performances for our government in the Great War. A spy is someone who lies for money. I am an actress. I did it for love. You're too young to know what I mean."

"Are you in the movies?" said Victor. "I thought maybe I'd seen you before."

"Don't waste my time, little boy. I don't give autographs. And you didn't get that mess of a face playing a dumb innocent. Now tell me what you did."

"Okay. Okay. I got into a fight."

"Edgar, take this lying child away." The servant appeared with a tray and one tiny blue goblet. Madame drained it. "Another. This is so distressing."

"My dear, I've interviewed Victor at some length, and he tells me his friend here is trustworthy. A contract has been made."

"Edgar . . ." She rested her chin on her arm, and looked up, beseeching.

"Constance," he said, "you may intend to lie around this deadly place having your muscles undone, but I don't. These boys and I will be off exploring."

She blinked. "Well, I suppose this one is rather attractive, in a *National Geographic* sort of way," she said, waving her finger at Victor. "But really! This one! What is its name?"

"Butch," said Butch. "Don't wear it out."

"Don't you think he's just a bit much, Edgar?"

"My dear, the decision's been taken."

"Well, when you find out what secret they're keeping from you, I reserve the immediate right to lord it over you."

Edgar laughed. "I wouldn't deny you your greatest joy in life," he said. "The torturer returneth. Come on, lads."

The tray seemed too delicate to balance in Hilda's big hands, yet she brought the goblet within Madame's grasp without spilling a drop.

"I think we should work on the small of the back," said Madame. The long fingers tipped the glass, set it down, pulled the towels over her head.

Hilda set to kneading.

"Wow," said Butch, as Edgar steered them out by the elbows. "She's your wife?"

"There are times I don't quite believe it myself." Edgar led them to the gate. His eyes were the same crinkly blue as his suit. "Come," he said, starting off.

"She's a movie star, isn't she," said Victor, following. "I've seen her somewhere before."

"Madame doesn't believe in the movies. Calls them the nightmares of the vulgar. She was an actress of the legitimate stage, in her youth."

"I bet she was one good-looking woman," said Butch. It was the closest to a compliment Victor had heard from him yet.

"That she was. And she still is, to me."

"She got a name?"

"It's Ida, but if you tell her I told you, I'll dismiss you on the spot. She's known professionally as Madame Constance Belair. She'll rather you call her Madame. You may of course call me Edgar, since we're to be partners." He waved his cane at a blackbird that sat in his path. "Boys, I've been married to that woman for twelve years, and I've never known her to be wrong in her estimations. If you have something to tell me, perhaps you'd better do it now."

"I—I'm not in any trouble, I swear," said Victor.

"Me neither," said Butch. "We were just wantin to help you out."

"There is something, though." Victor selected each word. "Something I saw."

Edgar leaned on his walking stick. "And what was that?"

Victor took a deep breath and told about the dead man, the noose, the sound in the bay, the collision, the black submarine. Edgar's mouth opened wider and wider, until at last he closed it and yanked off his dark glasses. "What flag did she fly?"

"No flag. I heard them talking inside it. It was German, I think. I've heard Hitler on the radio. It sounded like that."

"Like Hitler." Edgar shook his head, turned to Butch. "And you saw this too?"

"Hell no. Far as I know old Sandy made it all up. See, I just come along to see about this boat of mine he—"

Edgar fixed Victor with his clear stare. "Are you telling the truth?"

"Yes sir."

"A submarine."

"Yes sir."

"In this bay."

"That's right. I guess it's kind of hard to believe."

"Not at all." Edgar started off down the slope. "Any fool with a shortwave receiver can hear them out there at night, talking to each other. Hurry on, lads. I want you to show me some things."

Victor had to run to keep up. "You've heard 'em?"

"Bloody godless pirates. As long as they're on the seas, no one's safe."

"Do you think they're gonna invade?"

"Invade? Here? Why on earth would they do that?"

"Well . . ."

The old man paused, in his haste. "My boy, they've got their hands full with the Royal Air Force. I'm afraid Alabama is the last place on Hitler's mind. What he has of one. No, I think you happened upon one of ours. A Navy skipper who had taken leave of his chart. It wouldn't be the first time."

"But don't our submarines carry a flag?"

"I'm not sure. I would think so. We'll find out." Edgar quickened his stride.

"They sunk eighty-somethin ships just last month," Butch put in.

With a wave to the boy in the marina shed, Edgar struck off down the avenue of boats. The afternoon heat boiled up from their shiny white decks. "Come, lads," he called, "I have a chart!"

Victor had been so sure no one would believe him. In the cage he thought he was all alone, at the end of the world, detested by his own father, swearing he would never need anyone, ever again. But maybe he did have a friend or two in the world, after all, after Willie, the one who always loved him best, who would love him forever no matter what he did. Here were two strangers acting as if they believed him, acting almost like friends.

He trailed them to the last slip, the great polished-oak motor yacht with the flying bridge. "Now look here, Butch. This is a yatchet."

Butch dropped his voice to a whisper. "Keep him talkin, Sandy. If we can't find somethin to steal from *this* man, I'm gonna give up and go back to school."

17

I T W A S H O T as ten summers. The sky was pale blue, full of towering clouds. A gathering of bay shrimpers stood in the sterns of their ratty boats and watched the *Constance* go by. High above deck on the flying bridge, shielded from the sun by a snappy red awning, Victor waved to the shrimpers as if to confirm that he was a millionaire.

Edgar Gilliam told them to make themselves comfortable.

He had a theory, he said, and they'd have to go out a ways to test it. Then he went below.

Butch stretched in a canvas chair on the foredeck, drinking beer from the brown bottles Sarah brought him, one after the other. "They done sent me to heaven," he crowed.

To Victor, who spent the afternoon up on the flying bridge trying to figure it out, the *Constance*'s path seemed aimless wandering. They steamed down the shore, veering in along the strand of big summer homes and then out, down the miles of uninhabited woods.

All the pain in Victor's face came to life as he looked across the stretch of water to Willie's island. Could a person give shape to a big piece of land, to the sculpture of trees, sand, marsh grass, glinting tin? Some of the air had gone out of the island. The beaches slumped into the bay. The trees wore Spanish moss as a sign of their age, vertical brushstrokes of gray. Were they starting to wither?

What would his father do when he found the dangerous animal out of its cage? Set out to catch it, to finish the punishment? More likely *Good riddance, one less mouth to feed, always trouble, that boy*. He could act as if Victor never existed, as if he were a figment of his family's imagination. He could do that. He could.

The shore fell away for the Bon Secour River. The pilot turned west along the miles of unsettled white dunes, the peninsula leading to Fort Morgan.

Victor's heart bounded at the view. From this height the immense five-pointed brick star was visible from miles down the beach, behind its grassy earthworks on the finger of pure white sand. It looked like real war with its searchlight towers, vehicles, radio aerials. The red brick flanks offered no handholds. Cannons poked from narrow slits in the walls. Antiaircraft guns, giant ungainly things, bristled at the edge of the water. A jeep raced along the perimeter road. Men in uniform hurried down oyster-shell paths.

The *Constance* moved into the bay's open mouth.

The warm moist wind stirred around Victor. He held on with both hands as the shifting currents set the little platform to rocking. They passed Dauphin Island, headed south into the Gulf.

The sun stayed in one place, burning a white hole in the sky. Seagulls wheeled down to perch on the railing near Victor's head. He moved his eyes over the dazzling pattern of waves. His eyes went out of focus. He found himself staring into a brilliant blur.

He dozed. He passed hours in this blur.

By the time he came back to himself, the sun had gone level and gold in the west. Butch was snoring away in his chair. There was nowhere in sight.

Victor picked his way down the ladder. "Butch. Hey you. Wake up."

Butch snarled and covered his eyes.

"Get up," said Victor. "You're burned to a crisp."

Butch stirred. "Leave me alone."

"Listen. We're out in the middle of the Gulf."

At last Butch sat up, blinking. He rubbed his ear and looked over the side. "What you mean?"

"I mean we went out of the bay a long time ago and we been headed south ever since. Straight out. Look around you."

Big open-sea swells had the deck slowly rolling. Butch found his balance against the rail. "Reckon they mean to thow us to the sharks?"

"I think it's a good chance we didn't come out looking for birds," said Victor.

Behind them, Charles opened a door. "Mr. Gilliam wishes to see you both."

They followed down carpeted stairs. Belowdecks, the floors were laid with thick rugs, the walls hung with murky oil paintings, the lamps strung with crystals that split the lamplight into colors. It might have been a fancy apartment in a city except for the way the crystals tilted and clinked when the boat felt a swell.

Charles motioned them into an ornate dining room with red velvet walls, a long table and chairs of dark massive oak. Models of sailing ships sat on little shelves around the walls, lit by individual brass lamps. The table was set with china and candles, polished silver, flowers in a Chinese vase.

Edgar Gilliam came through a door at the room's other end, talking. "Well good evening, I trust we all spent a pleasant afternoon. A siesta does me wonders, especially when I'm exploring. Were you gentlemen well taken care of?"

"You bet," said Butch. "I tell you, gramps, this is one slick setup."

"Thank you, Butch. And please, I insist. It's Edgar. Lads, there's been a slight change in plan. I'll explain everything after our supper."

"We're a long ways from land," Victor said.

"That we are, sir, eighty miles." The old man drew out the carved chair at the head of the table. "Sit, sit! Never talk business on an empty stomach, Victor. I learned that lesson from a very large and successful businessman."

Edgar raised a porcelain bell. Before he finished ringing it Sarah swung through the door with three steaming bowls on a tray. The boat rolled. She tilted the tray and brought it around in a well-rehearsed balancing act.

"Victor, take your seat. She can't serve you standing."

Victor obeyed. It was the oddest soup he had ever seen, but it smelled good. It was pearly pink, with some black mushy things swirled around and some other chewy white things. The heat of it stung the raw place in his mouth. It tasted like bits of fish in a nice tangy broth.

Butch was staring at his. "What is it?"

Edgar smiled. "Soup."

"It's good," said Victor.

Butch took a sniff. "I don't eat somethin I don't know what it is."

"Magnificent!" Edgar patted her thin brown arm. "Sarah, you've outdone yourself!"

She bowed her head, hurried out.

Butch prodded one of the white things. "It ain't octopus, is it?"

"Oh, no," Edgar said. "It's some sort of oyster and prawn concoction, I think. Sarah hails from the French Caribe. She does the most surprising things with seafood."

Butch sat back in his chair. "That ain't no oyster," he said. "What else we havin?"

"Be quiet, Butch."

"Don't tell me to be—"

"Boys, boys," said Edgar. "There's some sort of roast on the way. Butch can take his chances with that."

Butch folded his arms. "So we goin to Cuba, or what?"

Edgar dabbed his mustache with his napkin. "Not tonight. We're in the Gulf due south of Fort Morgan. We've dropped our sea anchor."

"We're stopped?" Victor put down his spoon.

"Ah—hmmm . . ."

Sarah arrived to replace the bowls with plates of steaming pork roast, melted apples, and some kind of pink chunky salad that Victor knew instantly he would never eat, no matter how hungry he was.

Edgar waited until she was gone. "One doesn't talk in front of servants."

"You sure are being nice to us, Mr. Gilliam."

". . . Edgar."

"I mean, Edgar. But I thought you were interested in looking for birds. There aren't any birds this far out." Victor watched Butch eating roast pork and apples as if it were the last food on earth. He raced through the pink salad without stopping to see what it was.

Edgar poured more wine for himself. "Anyone?"

"No way. That stuff's sour," said Butch.

"Ah, well. To answer your question, Victor, I really have no interest at all in birds, unless they're properly roasted and served on a bed of rice."

"I figured," said Victor. "We went through a whole herd of pelicans up in the bay and you hardly even looked."

Edgar wielded fork and knife. "Still, it wasn't an accident that we met. I need your help. Not exactly the kind I mentioned before."

"You want to find the submarine," said Victor. "So do we. I think we can do it. But we should be up in the bay. I've got this idea there's something up there they want."

Edgar nodded, tasting a forkful of apples.

Victor traded a look with Butch, who lifted his elbows from the table and began serving out seconds for himself.

"Mr. Gilliam, there's something you're not telling us," Victor said.

"Quite a lot, actually." Edgar wore a mild, harmless smile. "What you didn't realize is that the other night you threw quite a sizable wrench into an already complicated plan."

"I guess you'll let me know what you're talking about when you're ready," Victor said.

"The U-boat." The wine left red droplets on the tips of Edgar's mustache. His eyes glittered with news. "You spotted it. You . . . collided with it. Surely you realize that wasn't supposed to happen."

Butch dropped his fork.

"That was U-641," Edgar said, "a type Seven-C submarine of the German navy."

Victor suddenly saw himself eighty miles out in the Gulf on this boat with a man he did not even know. *Honey boy, what a fix* . . . "How do you know that?"

"The commander is Captain Franz Henkel of the southwest Atlantic hunter force," said Edgar.

"What are you, a Nazi?" hissed Butch, throwing down his napkin.

"Just the opposite," Edgar said. "I'm an unreconstructed American. A pillar of the Grand Old Party. I'm also a very rich man. I love America. As long as that demented Austrian holds Europe, I won't sleep through a night. Besides, my father's mother was a Jew. I believe that disqualifies me as a Nazi."

Victor's mind whirled with junctions, wires and questions, connections. "But you acted like—you didn't believe me! You said it had to have been from the Navy, like that was the first you'd heard of it!" He folded his napkin and placed it beside his plate.

Edgar's gaze was still friendly, but the grandfatherly smile had been replaced by something sharper, an edge. "The man you met yesterday. Glass. He's not who you think. He's an agent of the government."

"Which one?"

"Don't be ridiculous. Ours. The Federal Bureau of Investigation."

"Like on 'Gangbusters,' " Butch put in, looking proud of himself.

"Exactly so. Now, Victor, if you'd mind looking at me in some other way than as a traitor, I'll try to explain." Edgar lit a cigar, puffed a blue cloud.

Victor struggled to keep his voice steady. "Why'd you bring us all the way out here? You planning to get rid of us?"

"Oh, tosh. You have a nimble imagination, my boy. Not at all. Just to keep you out of harm's way. You'll admit you've demonstrated an amazing talent for turning up at the wrong time. Anyway. I think you'll enjoy what's going to happen tonight."

Clenching the cigar between his teeth, Edgar slipped from the room and returned with a large green globe of the earth. He set it on one end of the table, started it spinning with his hand. "It's a big world, Victor. See how fast it goes around?" He stopped the whirling with his finger. "This is us. A speck on the globe. This is Germany. Here. That boat left the port at Brest, here in France, seven weeks ago. Do you see how far they had to come?"

"Sure," said Victor, "but why are they here?"

"They want to give up. Surrender. They've made an offer, and we've accepted. A shipshape Seven-C, the best boat they've got, in exchange for good treatment when they land."

"They're Nazis, and they want to give up?" Victor did not believe it.

"Some of them are Nazis. The crew. They have passengers. Friends of Madame. These people have been working for our side in secret, but things are too warm for them now. They've made friends in the *Kriegsmarine*, the navy. Officers who are convinced Hitler must lose the war. They'd rather fall prisoner to one of the Allies than continue to serve him. Do you understand? They've laid hold of a boat, infiltrated its crew, and they're all set to turn the whole bundle over to us."

"Your wife," said Butch, coming up from his slack-jawed silence. "She's friends with these Krauts?"

Edgar spread his palms over the northern hemisphere. "Madame has friends everywhere," he said. "She knows people on all sides. That's why she's been . . . useful to our government on occasion. She stays in touch with these people. She's an actress, so she can move in any circle she likes. On occasion they've passed information through her."

"I knew there was something fishy about her," said Butch. "She wouldn't look me in the eye."

Victor watched Edgar's fingers encircling the world. He wondered why the truth couldn't have been revealed a little closer to land. "Are you telling me she set it up with the U-boat captain to come here?"

"It was more in the way of a message received from their side," the old man said. "She contacted the FBI. We met Glass. They wanted a place that was off any track, beaten or otherwise. Madame and I had summered here, so we passed the suggestion. No offense, but nothing much happens along this particular coast. And there's no one around to see it if it does. Or so we thought. We hadn't counted on you."

Victor got up from his chair. "They sailed that thing all the way from here"—he pointed to France—"down this way, and around Florida, and all the way up the Gulf, just to give it up?"

"That's right." Edgar ran his thumb over mountainous bumps.

"That's nuts!"

"But this isn't the only location, Victor, and that's not the only boat. There are three. They all left Germany with the mission of dropping spies along the coast of North America. Two of them will do just that. They'll land sometime this week, one in Florida—right over here, see?—and the other somewhere in New England, it's not clear. They're loyal. We've alerted the authorities. There'll be greeting parties waiting for them. U-641 was assigned to come into the Gulf. The officers have arranged all this without the knowledge of the crew. But they've been forty-eight days out at sea. I imagine they'll be wanting a breath of fresh air. I shudder to think."

"Why don't they just give up? Why'd they have to sneak around and sink my boat and run and hide?"

"Lad, you rushed in where angels fear to tread," Edgar said with a pained little smile. "The night before last was the night. You must understand, it is very important for these officers that they be captured. Not give themselves up. For the safety of people they left behind, it must seem they fell into enemy hands. Do you follow me?"

"I think so."

"I don't," said Butch.

Edgar clapped hands. "Charles! The map!"

Obviously Charles knew just which map to bring. Edgar spread it on the table and put down his finger. "The plan called for 641 to enter Mobile Bay here—through Grants Pass, out of sight of the fort. High tide and a full moon, so the tide would drop rapidly. He would surface and throw up a protective screen—that fog you saw—while Roy Glass ferried the passengers to us at the Hotel. After my wife had identified her friends, Glass would signal the captain, telling him to proceed with the plan."

"A signal with the lighthouse," said Victor. "That's why he was out there."

"Then Henkel planned to beach himself by accident on a sandbar, whereupon Glass would call in the Coast Guard patrol boats from the fort, they'd handle the capture, and the transaction would be complete." Edgar turned up his hands. "A neat plan. But you happened onto the scene just about the time the captain put out his smoke. You know what came next."

"He ran into me."

"Well, however it happened, the captain was nervous enough as it was, and when you two . . . met, he gave up and retreated."

"I sure as hell didn't sink *his* boat," said Victor.

"But you put a scare into him." Edgar folded the map. "Sent him out of the bay and halfway across the Gulf of Mexico. He was convinced the plan had been compromised, that you were the Coast Guard or something. He had his guns trained on you. I'd say you're quite a lucky young man. After Glass found you floating and was able to talk to you—to find out what you'd seen—he enlisted me to take you out of the way while we tried to set it up again." Edgar stubbed out the cigar.

Victor waved at the smoke. "Why couldn't you just tell me?"

"You might be the talkative type. We didn't think so, but you never can be sure. What if you'd gone straight to the Coast Guard with what you'd seen? Their ignorance is crucial. They might have ruined everything. There are fifty lives hanging in the balance. We rather thought it wouldn't hurt you to spend a night at sea."

Victor pushed away from the table. "So, that whole business when your wife was looking us over. That was an act too?"

"She's an actress." Edgar reached for the bell. "I'm just a businessman myself. I'm not accustomed to all this excitement. But I've never been one to turn away when a good cause presents itself." Sarah appeared. "Quite a fabulous meal, my dear. We're through now. I'll take coffee in my study. Gentlemen? Coffee?"

"Not for me," said Victor. Questions still wormed out of him. "What about that man I found?"

Edgar waited until the door swung closed behind Sarah. "Please, Victor, I urge you. Loose lips, you know. And we happen to be on a ship." He stood from his chair. "I don't know who that might have been. Glass sent someone to see about that. We think it must be one of your local affairs."

"I'm not so sure." Victor stood from his chair. They had all lied to him. For some reason they wanted to draw him in. Edgar took the role of the befuddled old bird-watcher, Glass played the coast marshal, and Madame rounded out the illusion with her performance as the grande dame. Victor felt like the only member of the audience too stupid to notice the stage, the actors, the rehearsed tenor of their lines.

"Victor, I need your help," the old man was saying. "We're a part of the plan. We've anchored at a specific spot on the chart." He touched it with his thumb. "Very soon Henkel will see us with all our lights up. We'll exchange signals. He'll know to proceed, that the damage has been contained. He wants a look at you through his scope before he returns to the bay."

Butch stretched up from the chair. "Hell, Sandy, you must have put the fear of God into him."

"Guess I did." Victor followed the old man into a study littered with nautical charts.

"It's an elegant plan, don't you think?" Edgar said. "My quiet bit for the war effort. FDR will be proud."

"You mean that U-boat is out there right now," Victor said, "looking for us?"

"That's correct."

"What's gonna happen to the Krauts?" said Butch.

"Prison camp. Believe me, they'll prefer it. I'm told the prisoners of war eat better than many Americans. Shameful, I think. My wife and I will assist her friends in getting through—but there, that's enough. You know everything now."

"What's the FBI need with you? Can't they do this themselves?"

"We're what's known as a cover, Victor. A civilian craft

doesn't have trouble with the Coast Guard. Besides, someone has to foot the bill for the operation. In case something goes wrong, they'd rather certain . . . politicians didn't know."

"You don't think the Germans'll send somebody to get their submarine back?"

"Let them try. It will be in the hands of the United States Navy in the morning."

Charles appeared at the door. "Sir. A word with you."

Edgar rose for a whispered conference. "Come on, lads," he said. "This may be something."

They went into a tiny closet of a room, rife with radio gear: boxes, tubes glowing, headsets, green radium dials. Edgar sat in a swivel chair, placed a phonelike contraption against his ear, and began spinning the large dial as smoothly as any safe-cracker.

"You could run you a radio station here," said Butch.

"Shhh." Edgar flipped three toggle switches. The round speaker crackled, then a buzz, a smell of overheated wiring, a fading hum . . .

"*Hoppel poppel.*"

Those words, most clearly. A guttural electric voice. Static crashed. Edgar twiddled the dial.

"*Hoppel poppel.*"

"Is that German?"

"Yes."

The signal whistled and spat.

"What's he saying?"

Edgar smiled. "Scrambled eggs. It's the opening code." He reached for the microphone, pressed the trigger with his thumb. "*Hoppel poppel haben wir nicht. Aus,*" he said.

"*Haben Sie gebratene Eier? Aus,*" the box squawked.

"*Ja, ja. Möchten Sie Schinckenspeck? Aus.*"

"*Ja, bitte. Aus.*"

Edgar turned to see the amazement he had inspired. "I've just told him we're fresh out of scrambled, so he ordered them fried. I offered a side of bacon. That's the opening code. Now he has some checking to do."

Victor shivered. "Can he see us?"

"Not yet. Quiet now. Listen." Edgar turned up the static fuzz. Behind it Victor heard rapid yakety-yak in that strange, bitten tongue.

"There's more of 'em!" Butch stared at the speaker as if it might leap from the wall and attack him.

"At least two . . . one calls himself *Messer*. That's 'Knife.' The other is 'Tiger.' A long way off . . . they're looking for someone."

"For us? We gotta get out of here!"

Edgar strained to hear. "For someone called *Berg*. 'Mountain.' Knife is saying that he and Mountain were supposed to make a . . . hmmm, *Verabredung*, an appointment, a rendezvous. And this fellow Mountain didn't show. I wonder if that's not our friend Henkel."

Butch said, "I thought they was fighting in England and all. Never knew there's so many down here."

"These two chaps talking here are somewhere way east, probably off Florida. The Big Bend. That's where 641 was supposed to drop his cargo."

"*Das ist Berg.*" The voice was so close it might have come from a man on the other side of the wall with his mouth to the speaker. "*Ich habe mich verirrt. Aus.*"

"*Verloren! Gott in Himmel!*" The faraway German exploded, a staticky splutter.

". . . *es ist ein Sturm, ein Orkan* . . ."

"What's he saying?"

A shadow came to Edgar's face. "He's just told his leader he's lost. Says a storm blew him off course, a big storm. *Orkan.*

A hurricane. Flimsy excuse, seems to me. Of course they're wondering why they haven't seen anything of it."

"Did they hear you?"

"I don't think so. Here's—he's sending them his coordinates . . ." Edgar snatched a chart from the middle of a stack which tumbled and unrolled around him. "Ahh, good show. He's giving them a position off St. George's Island. That's two hundred miles from here." He glanced up. "That means he's still with us. For a moment there I thought he'd bailed out."

The chatter went on for more minutes. Edgar translated a phrase now and then. The conversation closed with an exchange of *Heil Hitler!*

Butch paled.

"Oh, yes, they're quite open," said Edgar. "It's part of their program. They hope to frighten the merchant captains by talking a lot on the radio. Make them think there are more U-boats than there are."

"It sounds like there's plenty," Victor said, amazed.

Edgar reached for the microphone. "*Jubiläum, Jubiläum,*" he said. "*Die See ist sehr ruhig. Aus.*"

"*Können Sie mich nach der Jubiläum? Aus.*"

"It sounds like 'jubilee,' " Victor said.

"Very good." Edgar punched the trigger. "*Ja. Es findet eine Party statt. Vorbei und aus.*" He turned down the dial. "Our friend wants a lift to the party. Come. Shall we say hello?" He sprang from his chair and past them, up the steps two at a time.

Victor stumbled over Butch's heels going up. They came out on deck. Every light was ablaze, the night velvet dark. Edgar walked to the stern, waving his arms over his head. "This is history, lads," he called. "Come have a look."

They went to the rail, but it was like trying to see into the night from a lighted-up house. The waves were swelling and

falling. At last Victor began to make out sparks in the water,
a spatter of diamond lights spreading every time a breaker went
over. It was phosphorous. You could see it only on dark nights
like this.

"There!" Butch leaped up. "I see it!"

Where he pointed was nothing.

"About five hundred yards due east, lad." Edgar kept waving.
"Looks like a shadow."

"It all looks like shadows," said Victor.

Butch turned abruptly. "Jesus Christ, I ain't stayin out *here!*"
Fear grabbed him like a hand. He pried himself loose and ran
down the deck and vanished down the stairs.

Edgar reached into his jacket and came out with a long,
ungainly pistol, which he aimed at the sky. He fired. A red
streamer rocket shot up, bursting red, scattering. "Keep looking, lad."

"I still don't see it," said Victor, and then he did.

So it was not a dream.

He had known it but not quite believed it.

It was a void long as a tanker. A darker part of the darkness.
It was the enemy now. The other night, in the water, he was
too dazed to be sure.

Now he was sure.

As he stared, its outline sharpened: the stubby barrel-shaped
tower with a sort of pulpit at the front, a platform surrounded
by railings, then the cluster of spikes and antennae, the sloping
stern like a great fish with its tail tucked under. That was where
he hit.

A red tracer zipped up from the pulpit, dissolving. An
answer.

Victor felt a strange kind of courage, verging on anger. He
had whipped this thing. He alone had sent it under and fleeing.
It was the enemy but Victor was strong now. If it wanted to

surrender he would help. Surely it could see him in the glare. *Come and get me.*

Edgar lowered his hands. "That's not according to plan."

Victor could not look away from the blackness of it. It hovered there, riding the glow of the waves.

Edgar cupped his hands. "Either my eyes are deceiving me, or the captain is submerging. He's supposed to exchange signal lights and proceed on the surface to the bay. He's not to dive until we're just off the fort. His batteries or something."

A sudden breeze set Victor's teeth chattering. "It looks like it's just f-floating there to me," he said.

"Lad, you stay here and keep him in sight." Edgar moved back from the rail. "I'll run down and find out what's what. I don't like this."

He disappeared.

Victor was alone with the shadow. This was the monster he had come out to chase, and now it was looking at him. He could see less of it than before. It flattened, stretched out, kicked up white foam at its stern. Only a short length of darkness showed.

The wake churned, a white tail as long as the ship, moving at a distant angle across the stern of the *Constance.* The barrel of the conning tower grew shorter and shorter, then disappeared in the froth, tearing a line of hissing bubbles.

Victor followed the line with his eyes. There was darkness and phosphorous starlight to the horizon, and on that horizon, hovering just above it, a single light.

A lighthouse. No. Land? They'd been steaming away from it all day. A twinkling light, only one, and as soon as Victor saw it, it went out.

The trail of bubbles pointed to where it had been.

Victor heard in his head the cold electric voice from the wall. There were men under this water, out past that very wave.

The whole eastern side of the sky lit up bright as lightning—a flash, neon blue, turning yellow and silver-hot white, and a giant volcano of purple red yellow blue fire erupted from the water, billowed skyward from a giant ship all ablaze. The concussion slammed over the waves and struck Victor in the face. A second explosion. The thunder forced air from his lungs.

A big ship, a cradle of burning, a floating platform of fire launching enormous red spheres. Skyrockets whistled and screamed, trailing fizzy reflections in the water.

Charles groped to the rail. "Great God."

"It—something blew up!"

Edgar burst out on deck, a wild look in his eyes. Butch came right behind him.

It happened so fast. Red lightning flashed and exploded, reflecting on low-hanging clouds. The fire spread across the horizon. The waves were on fire. Fireballs blew to the sky.

Butch wore a rapt expression. "Would you look at her burn."

"A tanker." Edgar sounded strangled. "A gasoline tanker. Look there. Survivors."

Victor turned on him. "I bet this wasn't part of your plan."

"Some sort of trap. We—we walked in. Charles! Get those lights out! Now!"

Charles ran for the wheelhouse. The lights died, and that made the fire even more spectacular. The disaster was a mile away, but Victor felt heat on his face and he saw the reflection sparkling in Butch's eyes.

Inferno spilled from the wound in the side of the tanker. Tiny black specks hurtled down through the glare. People in the fire.

A great column of smoke rose, lit from below.

18

THE TANKER broke in two. The front half sank. The superstructure leaned crazily and sat burning on the water.

The darkened *Constance* drew closer, running through rivers of flame. Wreckage rained on the waves. Fragments fell hissing in puddles on deck. Curls of ash floated down, and a volatile smell: fuel on fire.

Butch watched the conflagration with his mouth open. Edgar muttered instructions to Charles and vanished below. Charles shouted to Victor for help.

Victor pulled stacks of flotation rings from a cabinet, carried them to the port rail, and dumped them at Butch's feet. "Get a move on. There's gonna be men in the water."

Butch turned, his eyes full of awe. "Nobody left alive outta that."

"Looks like Edgar made a deal with the wrong Nazis," Victor said.

"I know what you mean," Butch said. "That thing give me a real funny feelin when I got a look at it."

"Yeah, I noticed. You run like they were shooting at *you*."

"Man, a Kraut is a Kraut, what I say." A rumble came from the remaining half of the ship, still a quarter-mile off. "Anytime somebody gets all chummy with one on the radio, I got to stop and think."

Charles struggled under a big pile of netting. "Come help me here!"

Victor took one end; they hooked the eyelets in cleats along the port rail. "I bet you never figured this was gonna happen," Victor said. "If it wasn't for us, those Germans wouldn't have never laid eyes on that ship." When they let go, the net unrolled down the *Constance*'s side.

Charles drew up to full height. "Mr. Gilliam knows what he's doing. Now bring those on here."

Across the water, the rumble grew into a groan. The stern tilted slowly—a last scatter of explosions—then the forecastle tipped up at a drastic angle, rolled, and plunged under the water.

The wave raced across, crashed over the *Constance* like a storm swell striking a dinghy. Victor was thrown to the deck. He looked up to see water surging around Butch, snatching him, washing him to the edge. Victor scrambled through the torrent, grabbed his arms. Together they slammed into a metal post.

The great wave receded and left them there.

Butch was shouting: "We're hit! We're hit! They got us! Turn loose! We're sunk!"

"No! Be quiet!" Victor untangled himself. "That was a wave. From where it went down."

Then he heard shouts beyond the rail.

He got to his feet. The water was littered with junk, some pieces still burning, some with men hanging on. "Over here!" they were shouting, and "Hey, buddy, here!" and whistling, waving their arms.

"I see a bunch of 'em," Butch called.

"What if they're hurt?" Victor said, waving his arms as Edgar had done. "Can they see us? Go turn on some lights!"

Charles cupped his hands over his mouth: "*Are you hurt?*"

"Over here, man! Come on!"

In the dark it was hard to tell men from the wreckage. Victor sailed life rings toward likely targets. The first two fell short.

"Great throw!"

"Over here!"

Then Victor got the hang of it, hurling the things so they floated out long and pretty. He could tell which ones fell close by the answering shouts.

A racket from over the rail—feet scrabbling against the hull. A man grunted, fell back to the water. Victor leaned over the side. Dark faces strained up at him.

"Got a rope?"

"Hey kid! Give us a hand!"

Butch tossed the coil of rope, but he had forgotten to tie it to anything so it hit the water and sank.

More men thrashed out of the dark. Three of them sprang to the net, clinging like spiders, inching up. The eyelets gave way and they tumbled back into the sea. The net fell over them.

"To the stern!" Victor cried. "Go around to the stern! There's a ladder!"

A desperate shout—"I can't see! Jimmy, help! I can't see!"

Butch tied another rope to a cleat, tossed it over. Two men fought over it. "Hey, one at a time!"

Victor raced to the rail where a hand had a grip.

"Get back. There's more behind me." A powerful man, dripping wet, hauled himself up the last rungs and onto the deck. Two more came after him. Their clothing was riddled with burns. One was bleeding from his head.

Butch hauled a man in by his shoulders, then leaned down and reached for the next one. Butch was strong. It took him a while to come to, that was all.

A balding man struggled up the ladder, crying out each step. "Where are you, Jimmy?"

"Right behind you. Go on."

Victor seized him with both hands. His clothes had been burned away. He was not balding. Little tufts of burned hair stood away from his head. He held his eyes. "I can't see."

Then his friend was there. "It's okay. It's Jimmy. Lay down. It's just temporary. You're okay."

They were big burly men, but as soon as they came over the rail they collapsed to the deck heaving, coughing, wiping their eyes. "I think that's it, Sandy," Butch hollered.

The man who was first over the rail approached Victor, the light from the ship still burning in his eyes. "Who's your skipper here?"

"Mr. Gilliam. Edgar Gilliam. He's down below. I'll go get him."

He slipped down into the carpeted quiet. A light burned in Gilliam's study.

The old man did not hear him come in. He bent over the microphone, his eyes closed, his face closed, listening to the earpiece. He mashed the trigger. "But you must know this is highly upsetting! Out!" He listened a while. "I don't care anything for contingencies. This wasn't a contingency. There's not a—"

Victor heard the tinny reply in the earpiece.

Edgar faced away, his quaking hand holding his spectacles over a chart. "How can you be sure it wasn't? He knew all the . . . everything was just as you said. We had a confirmed visual sighting. *Confirmed*, now. Out."

Victor peered over Edgar's shoulder. He had his hand on a large, tattered chart showing Mobile Bay in the top left quarter, the expanse of the Gulf crisscrossed by blue lines. A hand-drawn red stroke led from the mouth of the bay to an X in the middle of nowhere.

This must be that place.

"Well then obviously our plan is compromised. I'm going to have Uncle Sam and his whole family out here any minute. Over and out!" Edgar flung the earpiece against the wall.

Victor cleared his throat.

"My stars!" Edgar gasped, dropping his glasses. "You gave me a shock. How long have you been there?"

"Not long."

"What is the situation? Have we found anyone?"

"Nine so far," said Victor. "Still looking. They want to talk to you."

"Are they hurt?"

"One guy's all burned. Real bad. They got him lying down. Most of the rest look okay. I don't know how they got out of that thing."

Edgar looked on the floor around his feet. "Lad, do you see my spectacles?"

Victor knelt to retrieve them. "Here. Who were you talking to?"

"Glass. He says it wasn't 641. Couldn't have been. It must have been someone who knew all our codes, who knew just where to be. He hasn't been able to raise Henkel at all." Edgar smoothed the wrinkles from the Gulf. "Something odd here, you know? He talked as if he almost expected it. As if nothing has happened. But it has."

"Yeah," Victor said, "there's one ship sunk and a bunch of guys dead."

"I don't see how we can continue. If that captain was an impostor—how did he know where to intercept us? Was he going to try and bluff his way through?" Edgar paced the tiny room. "Or was he intending to put his torpedoes through *us* when that ship happened by? The double cross! Perhaps through some coincidence the . . . the torpedoes . . . no, that doesn't make a bit of sense, does it?"

To Victor, the only logical theory was a simple one: the old man was a fool. You could not trust a U-boat, a Nazi, no matter how he might sound on the radio. You couldn't play games with the enemy. The minute the German captain spotted that tanker, he turned back into a Nazi. He had no choice but to attack.

"If they'd meant to get us they'd have done it," said Victor. "I think maybe somebody just pulled a big trick on you."

"I suppose I'd best go talk with these men." Edgar sighed. "Lad, it goes without saying that I haven't much experience at this game."

"We've got to tell somebody about this," Victor said, following him up the stairs. Edgar moved like an old man again, no spring in his step. When he opened the door to find the deck lit up bright as day, he turned on Victor. "I ordered those lights out! What are they doing on?"

A shout arose from the survivors clustered around the wheelhouse. The pilot approached from their midst, hands behind his back. "Pardon, sir, I turn them on," he said. "These— these men are still wanting to look for the other ones. I tell them I am taking orders only from you, but now they are driving the boat."

"A mutiny, is it? Not on my boat!" Edgar pushed past him. Two steps brought him face to face with the ringleader. "I am the owner of the *Constance*, and I demand to know by what right you've taken command of a civilian vessel!"

"Sorry to hurt your man's feelings," said the wide-faced, powerful sailor, with an expression that was not the least sorry. "We're still missin five of our crew. They got to see us to find us. My name's Jackson."

Edgar shook his hand. "What is your rank?"

"I'm four-F, servin stateside, sir, merchant marine, like every man here. I was Captain Ellis's mate. He's one of the missin."

More men sidled out beside Jackson, looking bruised and greasy, sopping, smudged, but still plenty tough.

"Leave the lights on, Perkins." The pilot scurried away. Edgar turned back to Jackson. "What was your ship?"

"*Eugenia Rae*. Tanker. We left Tampa for Mobile, night before last. Full load of gas. But I guess you saw that when she blew."

"A merchant ship then. Did you see what caused the accident?"

"Pardon my French, but it don't take a goddamn genius to see it wasn't no accident."

Edgar pressed on in his starchiest voice: "You're saying you were hit by enemy fire?"

"Well sir, unless you was packin torpedoes on your fancy little cruiser here, I'd say that's a good guess."

"Everyone's fortunate we came along, then," said Edgar.

"Everyone but five," Jackson said.

A shout rose at the rail: "There's one! There's one!"

They pointed where he was pointing, but when the thing bobbed into view, it was only a severed length of pipe.

"Pirates." Edgar shook his head. "No one is safe."

The men muttered agreement.

"I put in a call to the Coast Guard," said Edgar. Only Victor knew it was a lie. Only he saw the old man's hands shaking as he embellished it. "I called the post at Fort Morgan. They're sending two patrol boats. I'm to cut my lights and head directly for Mobile, get your men to a hospital."

"There's nobody else out there, Jackson," a man said. "We got to get Earl to a doctor. He's bad."

"If it was me, I wouldn't want to be give up on all that easy," said Jackson. "Who's down with Earl?"

"Jimmy."

"I'll go see."

The men moved to the foredeck, buzzing among themselves. Butch was still bent over the side.

He straightened. "Hey Sandy! Come here! Hurry!"

Victor started over. "Got another one?"

"Hell yeah," Butch called, and then his feet went out from under him.

Two hands slapped the rail. One groped up, desperate for a hold.

Victor ran to him, leaned over, hooked his arm under an arm, and lifted with all his strength.

Butch caught the other arm.

"Pull!"

The man landed on both feet.

He slung water from his hair.

He was Joseph.

He was.

19

I—I MUST be dreaming—
Good God
It is you
Little brother
It's you
What the hell are you doing
Are you okay?
How did you—what are you doing out here
I don't believe it

"*Vic!*" Joseph threw out his arms. They came together. The hug got tighter and tighter until Victor was sure his bones would be crushed. He felt the pure strength of his brother, trembling wet.

"Did you—did you see what—what hit us?"

"A U-boat. A torpedo from a U-boat. What are you doing out—"

"Goddamn! Feel my heart! I'm about to have a heart attack! Are—are they all okay?"

"One guy says he's blind, but what are you—"

"Whose boat is this?" Joseph said. "What are *you* doing here?" He exploded in laughter, pounded Victor's back, embraced him again.

"How did you—did they let you out of the Army? I thought you were in England! What are you doing here?"

"Damn!" Joseph leaned on his knees like a sprinter just done with a mile. "All the places I might have got sunk, all the people who might have come picked me up, it's my own little brother! Goddamn! What a stroke!" He whooped and smacked Victor so hard he had to take two steps. "They didn't get me, Vic, they couldn't kill this here boy! They tried, they shot it right out from under me! How you like that? *How do you like that?*"

Some men were on their feet now, lighting cigarettes. Jackson came over. Joseph clapped his shoulder too. "They didn't get us, hey Jackson? They got the tub but they didn't get us!"

"Yeah, they sure as hell got 'em a tub," said Jackson. "Looks like you the last one we'll find. There's four still out there. We're damn lucky." He wandered off to the pilothouse.

The shock had Victor jangling like a set of keys. It didn't feel right. Why was Joseph on a gasoline tanker in the Gulf of Mexico? It wasn't right the way he came up from the water . . .

He was dark from the sun. He looked younger by ten years than the other men.

Hadn't Jackson said they were all 4-F merchant marines? That couldn't be right . . . Joseph was 1-A if ever there was one. He'd come back crowing from his physical. The Army doctors told him they'd never heard a better heartbeat on a white boy. Why was he out of uniform, working on a tanker with this gang of deckhands?

He was made out of muscles now, his flesh fine and hardened, as if he'd been shaped by a knife. His face was the same, sunny Joe; when he grinned, a big space showed between his teeth. His hair was cropped short so it stuck out in all directions. His freckles had merged into one red.

He came over to hook his arm around Victor's neck; he was clammy and smelled of the sea. He surveyed the luxury of the *Constance*, looked around at the shiny fittings, the parquet deck. "Vic, you landed in some mighty tall cotton, didn't you, boy," he said. "What the hell . . . ?"

"It's a long story," said Victor. "I guess you got one too."

Sudden darkness overwhelmed the boat. One by one the men gave up looking. They stretched out or sat by the rail, exhausted or stunned into silence.

The engine sounded a surge of new speed.

Victor stood where he was, feeling the damp from his brother's embrace. What happened to the war? What is wrong with this picture?

Dear Willie, Joseph is back. Like you said. They sent him back. He's OK. Me too. Saw a ship sunk by a Nazi U-boat. Joseph came out of the water. No joke. Wish you were here. Love, Victor.

It seemed impossible. It was a miracle. Joseph had come home just in time to help Victor fight his own war.

PS Where did you go?

20

VICTOR FELT the nudge of Joseph's foot. They lay on their bellies, hanging over the prow in the rushing wind. Where the *Constance* met the waves, it split open the phosphorous glow, like a razor slicing darkness to reveal the stars.

"But Joseph, why were you on a tanker? Wouldn't the Army bring you home on a troop ship?"

"Those are full of wounded and stuff." Joseph stretched his arms. "The tankers pay real good now, thanks to all the torpedoes. Hell, Vic, I swear. I thought tonight that was it, I was dead. They couldn't pay me to jump off the side of that sucker again. Look at me. My hands won't quit shaking. I was just sitting there, drinking a goddamn cup of coffee, and there was a thunk and the whole damn thing blew all to hell. It was like sleepwalking, brother, getting off that thing. They teach you how to escape from a sinking ship, but this wasn't like that. I don't know, I don't know . . ." He put his head on his arms.

Victor turned on his side, propped his elbow. "Are you out of the Army for good?"

"It's just a medical furlough. Broke my knee in a jump. It was my bright idea to come home."

"When do you have to go back?"

"Don't worry. They'll let me know." Joseph looked back at the men sprawled asleep on the deck. "You don't have to make a big deal about me being in the Army in front of these guys.

They're all four-Fs. They'd feel real bad if they found out I was a GI."

"They don't know?"

"When they hired me on, I told 'em I was American, wanted to get home. They didn't ask. They needed a hand. It gave me a little spare moola for when I got here. Or it would have." He sat up, a frown on his face. "I had three weeks' pay in cash in my locker. I had big plans for that money. I was gonna take you to New Orleans, show you what a little city life does for an old country boy. But hell, I'm lucky to get out with my hide."

Joseph sat quiet a moment, then he said, "Remember that song Willie used to sing? 'Were you there, were you there when that great ship went down' . . ." He bashed an imaginary guitar on the deck. "Guess what else was in my locker. Goddamn it."

"They must sure cuss a lot in the Army."

"Hell, yeah." Joseph grinned. "It's the only goddamn way you can get anybody to listen to you." He strummed the air with his hand. ". . . 'when that greeeaat ship went down?' How's it go? 'Husbands, childrens, wives—all the—little bitty children dieeed.' " He still had his big rolling voice. "Well. I'll have to ask Willie."

Victor swallowed. "Joseph. I got something to tell you."

"Something else? You already told one whiz-bang of a fish story, Vic."

"It's Willie."

Joseph turned with cold, even eyes. "What's the matter."

Victor could not speak.

"She's dead," Joseph said.

He nodded.

"How long?"

"Sunday . . ."

Joseph slammed his fist on the deck. "Well that ain't hardly fair, is it, her to die just when I—when I was on my way home to see her?"

"No, it ain't," said Victor. "There ain't a single fair thing about it."

Joseph stretched out flat, his face in the spray. "How did Daniel . . . how is he?"

"How do you think he is?" Anger foamed white inside Victor. "He's out of his mind! The minute she died, he tore into me like I killed her myself. Like—like he gave a damn about her!"

"Course he does, Vic. She's his mama."

"All he ever did was nag at her drinking and get me to look after her."

"But she's his mother."

"I know, I know," Victor said, and to his horror he found he was the one crying, not Joseph. "But *I* didn't kill her! All I did was leave her alone for two seconds, and she picked that exact *minute* to die!"

"That's Willie, all right."

"But he—he locked me in the cage, Joseph. Old Pop's dog pen. In the boathouse." It shamed Victor to weep before his brother like a child, but he could not help it. All the words came out pouring, the meanness, the rage on their daddy's face dragging him over the yard. He told about Willie on her bed, how she was the only thing that kept Daniel from coming across and strangling him. The kicking, the beating. The jail. "I think he broke my ribs. Look here." He pulled up his shirt. "It's all blue."

"He used to beat me like that, Vic. Back when I was the only one big enough for him to hit. I remember one time . . ." Joseph's voice trailed over the side.

"Well, I don't know about you," Victor said, hiccuping now,

"but I can't—go home. I can't ever go home. He put me in that—in that cage and he left me. Like I was a dog. He didn't care if—if I lived or died."

"You'll go home," said his brother. "You'll go home and he'll tell you he's sorry. I promise."

"Ha ha." Victor wiped at his tears. "That's a joke."

"He will. Big Joe's here, boy. He ought not to treat you like that. He was upset."

It was so easy for Joseph. Everything. Wave a hand. Say a word or two. Make it all right.

"Look, Vic. A porpoise. It's been a long time since I saw one." Joseph leaned through the rail. "Willie used to say it was the best good luck."

"I don't care. I hate her for—for dying like that."

"And I hate you had to be there for all that, little brother. You loved her the best. I know that. She loved you better. Used to say you got all her good sense."

He rolled on his back. "She didn't do it to you, Vic. Didn't do it to anybody. You remember that time we all got on that old pontoon boat, all the cousins and uncles and aunts, and went down there for Thanksgiving dinner? Nah, you were too little." Joseph appeared not to notice Victor's tears, or else he was telling this story to give him time to stop them. "All the way down the river, everybody's bragging on Willie, we're all tasting that fine oyster dressing of hers and the cranberry sauce, and we get there and she's gotten into the whiskey for the lane cake and passed out. Hadn't even lit the stove. She always had lousy timing. All she ever wanted was to stay out there where she belonged, folks to leave her alone."

Victor took a deep breath, held it, let it out slow. "This coast marshal guy came out one day," he said, swallowing. The hiccups were gone. "Or I guess he was the FBI, like I told you, I'm not sure if—anyway, he tried and tried to get her to cover her windows. She wouldn't do it. The next thing you know there's a body floating up and a U-boat in the bay and Willie's dead. There just ought to be some connection."

"I don't get it," Joseph said. "What did Daniel have to say when you told him this stuff?"

"He never gave me a chance. He wouldn't believe me."

"You never know . . ."

Victor sat stiff and apart. "You weren't here. You were off over there somewhere, oh, you're the big hero. They got a picture of you right up next to Jesus."

"I didn't want to go, Vic. I got drafted, remember? If I had my way I'd have stayed with you and Willie, catchin specks and hangin out."

"That's not what you said. You said you couldn't wait to go. And all your letters, you said—"

"It's not like you write in a letter, Victor. It's something else." Joseph scooted out on the bowsprit.

Victor spoke in a rush: "I was gonna join up. I wanted to be just like you. I was on my way, had it all figured out. I was almost there. Then everything happened."

"Listen to me. They'll come after you soon enough. It ain't fun. It ain't games like we used to play. It ain't like snatch the flag. You saw that tonight. Besides, hell, you ain't old enough."

"Yes I am."

"No you're not."

"You think I'm still the same as when you left." The heat rose in Victor's face. "I'm not. A whole lot has happened since then. I'm sixteen. I'm not just a kid."

Joseph yawned. "They say you spend the rest of your life wishing you were sixteen again."

"Not me. I'd rather be dead."

Joseph stretched on his side, peering down into the water. "He's still there, Vic. He ain't gonna give up till you look."

Victor leaned way out into darkness, the spray. There were two porpoises, one on each side of the prow—arching flashes of animal light, plunging out of the waves and back in, racing the boat at a swift perfect pace. "Look, Joseph. There's one on this side too. One for you, one for me."

"No, uh-uh." Joseph's yawn was a song. "It can't be us. We're still here. One is old Pop and one is Willie, see? They finally got back together." He pulled up his knees.

For a while Victor watched the porpoises run, then he curled into a ball, facing away from Joseph. They went to sleep barely touching the backs of their feet, the way they used to do.

21

HOURS AFTER dawn the *Constance* steamed past a mountain of coal, the tallest thing on the horizon. Cranes and barges and spider machines nibbled at it from all sides. From there to Mobile endless docks bustled, one great ship nudging the next and the next. How could one place feed so many ships?—tankers, cruisers, tugs, tenders, cargo ships, the white banana boat, a flattop carrier, gray Navy destroyers, everywhere sailors and stevedores.

At the edge of the water lay a vast yard of incomplete ships, gigantic animals that had crawled up on shore to die—skeletons, parts of skeletons, carcasses without hides. Men scampered like insects along the framework of their bones, welders applying lights at great altitudes, wielding tiny glittering suns. A truck raced by, tossing up a cloud of pink dust.

Then the shipyard gave way to a serene line of wharves and warehouses, a few larger brick buildings, broken-down waterfront mansions. The pilot steered *Constance* to a wharf where a little crowd of boys waited beside a white ambulance marked with a red cross.

The survivors gathered their blankets around them and tottered over the gangplank, followed by two men bearing a stretcher.

The crowd stayed quiet, pointing and whispering among themselves, until one boy worked up his nerve: "Hey mister, was it Germans? We heard it was Germans."

"How many'd they get?" chimed a voice from the back.

"Did you see 'em?"

Charles cast off the lines, and the *Constance* moved back from their questions, back down the river and across the bay.

J O S E P H . Stay here and go with us." Victor had promised himself he wouldn't say it again, but too late: it was said. All the way up the lawn from the yacht basin, Joseph glanced over his shoulder and into the bushes as if someone might sneak up on him.

He did not walk with a limp.

They stood in long shadows just outside the pink wall surrounding the bungalow. Edgar had gone in to call for the car.

"I already told you," said Joseph, "I want to go home, and get Mother to fry me up a mess of okra and maybe some chicken, and some butterbeans. I'll eat till I'm full. Then maybe I'll call up old Mary Stringer and take her up to the Cut and Shoot and drink beer . . . reckon she's still around?"

"Joe. I don't know what this old man's up to. I'm not sure he knows himself. But they're coming back! We've gotta stick close. This is for real. They sunk you. What more proof do you want?"

"You've got to be careful," said Joseph. "You might be getting into something you can't handle."

"You can't just take off, Joseph. I need your help."

"Vic, listen a minute. I don't know what all this means, but as far as I'm concerned it's got to wait. I've come four thousand miles and I want to go home. This man's gonna give me a lift. If you want to stay, stay. I'll come back if you need me. But I just got out of the middle of it. I didn't come here to get right back in. I want to go *home*."

The sunlight revealed little lines around his eyes. Something had changed him. Something. He talked like the old Joseph, looked like him, moved with the same carefree grace. But this wasn't the leader of expeditions, first in line to be injured at whatever daring or dangerous scheme they dreamed up: leaping headfirst into muddy water, asking their daddy for money, going off to fight Hitler. Once Joseph had been full of big talk about what he would do to the scrawny loudmouth bastard when he got his hands on him. Now all he wanted was to curl up at home and eat a good supper.

"Let him go, Sandy." Butch blew his nose in his hand. "He'd only just get in the way."

"Vic, this the kind of trash you run around with these days?"

"Watch it, brother man," Butch warned.

"Hell," said Joseph, "I know it gets lonesome out there on that island, but I didn't know how bad it got."

Victor flared. "Butch let me out of that cage. Nobody else did. I owe him for that."

Butch said, "You're damn right you do."

But Joseph was ignoring them both for the blond girl with the tennis racket, the long brown girl in white pleated skirt and white blouse who came striding down the lawn. "Hel-lo," he said under his breath.

"Woo woo," said Butch. "Looka hyuh."

"Shhh." Victor batted him. "I've seen her before."

"Well *I* haven't," said his brother.

Victor knew the slender tapered legs, the loose-limbed way she walked, swinging her arm. He had memorized her as she ran down the dock that evening.

"Hello, boys." She held her tennis racket in front of her face like a fan. "Have you seen Grandfather?"

All three opened their mouths to answer, but no sound came out.

She wore a mysterious smile at the corners of her mouth. "He's about this high, and he's got a big white mustache."

"Baby, whatever you lost, I'm here to help you find it," Joseph said.

She gave a little unamused laugh. "Charming."

"Prince Charming, to you. And your name is . . . ?" He ran his hand through his hair.

Victor spoke up. "You looking for Edgar?"

Her eyes sought him out. She was cool, unapproachable, flawless. He had not seen her face that night, and only a profile that morning out on the balcony, but he recognized those bottomless green eyes, those imposing cheekbones. Her eyes were green smoke. For a moment Victor had the sensation that no one had ever looked at him before.

"Yes, his name's Edgar," she said.

"You're his—he's your grandfather?" Those unshakable eyes came from Madame!

She approached the iron bars. "I know you from somewhere. I've seen you before."

"I guess." Victor could not help blushing.

She covered her face with the racket. "Oh, I know now. You're the Peeping Tom."

"I don't—I don't know what you mean," Victor tried.

"At the yacht basin. I knew you were watching." A wayward smile played on her lips. "We both did."

"I just—soon as I saw you I went on, I mean, I quit looking."

"Uh huh." She laughed, a silvery note. "Little boys have to watch to see how it's done. Is Grandfather inside?"

"Yeah." Victor was aware that Butch and Joseph were staring at him, but he was too red to look back.

"See you." She drifted away, tossing behind her a long trailing glance, like a gift.

Victor examined the ground. His ears hissed. He might have been deep under water. Butch pounded his shoulder. "I think she likes you, boy!"

"They don't make 'em like that anymore," Joseph said. "What did you do to her, Vic?"

"I saw her. Kissing this guy."

"Mm, *mm*."

Victor kicked a tuft of grass. He pulled on a curl that was tickling the back of his ear. "The old man never said anything about her."

"I know why," said his brother.

A long black automobile came crunching down the oyster-shell lane. Someone had taken a normal-sized shiny black car and stretched it out longways.

Butch gave an appreciative whistle. "This old man has one of everything."

The driver got out. "Is one of you Sylvester?"

"See you later, Joseph. Have a good time at home. Give 'em all a big howdy for me." Victor surprised himself. He hated himself when he sounded that way. Of course he loved his brother. But he couldn't help feeling deserted. Again.

Joseph turned. "I'm going. You got to look out for yourself."

"I can do that," said Victor. "I been doing that."

"I'll talk to Daddy. It'll be all right . . . gonna shake?"

Victor hung back.

Joseph grabbed his hand, pulled him in, hugged him, slapped his shoulder. "Hell, you know I'm coming back, now I got a look at *her*. You call up the store if you need me. Mr. Jesse still there?"

"Sure."

"He'll come get me."

"Sir . . ."

Joseph stepped into the car and stretched back on the wide seat. The driver shut him in. He rolled down the window, grinning. "Can you see the look on Daniel's face when I drive up in this?"

The car moved away on a cushion of silence.

"Gentlemen." Charles stood at the gate. "Mr. Gilliam requests your presence."

"You sure know a lot of fancy talk, Charlie." Butch strutted into the garden. "Sandy, you reckon they eat books?"

"Literacy has no bearing on good breeding, sir," said Charles.

"You can say that again."

They were halfway down the pink wall when the girl reappeared. She seemed surprised to see them again. "Charles, who are these boys?"

"I believe, Miss Diana, that this one is Victor, and the other is referred to as Butch."

"I bet you're Victor," she said to Victor.

She could not have been that much older than Victor, but no girl his age ever looked so arranged, so pampered. Golden curls spilled over one shoulder, constrained by a lavender ribbon. So this was what money could do for a girl. Make her perfect as a fancy orchid in a greenhouse, too dazzling to look at for long. In place of the tennis racket she carried a hanger, a dress covered over with tissue paper. "Charles, would you call the car down."

"I'm sorry, miss. It's just been sent away."

"But this is Grandmother's *dress*. For tonight."

Victor popped his jaw, trying to open his ears.

"I'll have the hotel send a taxi, miss. Wait here." Charles went back through the gate.

Diana let her gaze wander to Victor, as a piece of the scenery. "Do you have some business with Grandfather?"

He straightened and tried to look older. "Yeah, I guess we do."

"You're not working on the boat, are you?"

"We already been out on it," Butch told her, "you shoulda seen it, what happened—we was out in the middle of—"

"Shut up, Butch." Victor cut his eyes. "Don't listen to him. He got sunburned and it went to his head."

"And it looks like you got something worse," she said. "What happened to you?"

Victor blushed behind the bruises. He'd almost forgotten them.

Butch spoke up. "His daddy—"

"Shut *up*."

A yellow Eastern Shore taxi pulled to the gate.

The girl teased Victor with her eyes. "Are you coming to the dance tonight?"

"You mean me?" He blinked. "I don't—I didn't think so."

"I don't really want to go either, but we have to. It's in Grandmother's honor. If you change your mind, maybe you could ask me to dance." She tilted her chin, walking by. At the gate she said, "I might say no, but you always could ask."

She handed the dress to the driver, stepped in.

"I ain't believin that," Butch said. "She got a thing for you, Sandy!"

"Sh-hhh! She can hear you!"

The driver slammed his door and drove off.

"She sure is pretty," said Victor. "You think she—no." Those were sweet words hanging in the air. He looked at the spot where the taxi had been. Keep yourself on the tracks, think of what you have seen, what you have to find out, what you hit. Still—

"I think she got bad eyes," said Butch. "What would she want with such a ugly old boy?"

"That's what I want to know," Victor said.

Edgar appeared from the side garden, dusting his hands. "Is Diana still here?"

"No." Victor waved at the gate. "She's—she left. You never said anything about her."

"Angel of beauty, is she not? She's my wife's granddaughter, but she's dearer to me than any blood relative. Poor girl. Her parents died before she ever knew them. Diana came to us as a child."

"Is she in on all this?"

"What? Our plan? No, of course not. The boys keep her so busy she hasn't had time to notice. You know young girls. They haven't much interest in worldly affairs." Edgar shook off the thought. "Well. Any rate. Come with me. There is news."

They followed him through the ferns, past the seahorse pool. One section of the glass wall slid away to reveal Madame in a turban of shiny blue silk, interwoven with sparkly gold threads, clasped with a diamond pin.

Her face was even more dramatic than Victor remembered: a rush of red in the cheek, sharp eyebrows swooping over those

eyes, a ruby shine on the lips. Her gown, a floor-length robe
in the same deep blue silk, shimmered when she placed one
impatient hand on her hip. "Time waits for no man, Edgar,"
she said, "and neither do I."

"We were coming, my dear. Of course you remember young
Victor, here, and his associate Butch."

"Edgar, you do have a positive talent for finding the *crème de
la crème*." She swiveled, her hand still in place, and stalked into
the cottage.

Stepping over the threshold, Victor found himself in an enormous room, bright with crystal and brass lamps, tall candles
in silver holders, a chandelier. He'd never seen so many lights
on in the afternoon. It was the living room, he supposed, with
hallways that led off at two angles. Prominent among the pieces
on the vast white carpet were a white leather sofa and chair, a
bright silky-scarlet chaise longue, a mahogany bar inlaid with
a beveled mirror, mahogany stools carved to match. Victor heard
a radio, the smooth croon of Crosby. What was that song?
"Night and Day."

The little puffball dog leaped and yapped at Madame's hand.
"Bless his heart, snookums." She snapped her fingers, which
sent the poodle into a frenzy, lunging for her hand. "Is he mad?
Yes he was. Yes he wasums. Come here." She led it down the
hall to a bedroom and slammed the door in its face.

"Good riddance," said Edgar.

It took a moment to see past the splendor of the room to
Roy Glass at the far end, his back to them, talking on a white
telephone. A vast canvas filled the wall behind him—Farragut's
battle, the same whistling shells as the picture in the hotel
room, but twice as large. The original.

Edgar opened a cabinet crowded with cut-crystal bottles.
"Your usual, dear?"

"We ran out of vermouth last night while you were out

playing Captain Bligh," she said. "This is a remarkably unciv- ilized place to have three stars in the Michelin. I sent to the bar, and what they sent back I wouldn't serve to a dying man. I would not be surprised if Hilda has to go all the way to New Orleans to find something I can abide."

"A shame." Edgar poured a golden liquid into a tiny stemmed glass.

"So of course I haven't had my massage," she went on. "Imag- ine the knots from my head to my toe. And then all the con- fusion. Naturally we waited up until God knows what hour."

"Unavoidable, my dear. Here. Will a sherry suffice?"

She drank it in one gulp. "I hate it. You know how I hate it." He filled it again, and she drank. "Brr. It's awful. Again."

"Yes, yes, but everything's all right now. Your husband has come home to see about you." Pouring a scotch for himself, Edgar shot a wink at the boys. "Drink for you gentlemen? What's your poison?"

Butch said, "Huh?"

"What would you like?"

"Oh. Whiskey."

"Same for me," said Victor. If he was going to stand on this thick carpet and act like a rich grown-up, he might as well have a drink. He tossed it back, as Madame had done. It went off at the back of his throat, a velvet detonation. His head filled with smoke.

Madame switched off the radio. "Edgar, how much do these boys know of our plan?"

"Everything. I was obliged to tell them. Couldn't very well spirit them off into the Gulf without a word of explanation, could I?"

"You might have." Madame glanced at Roy Glass, still mur- muring into the phone. "Roy's afraid we may have lost our chance."

Glass replaced the receiver and walked down the room toward them. "Good news."

"What's that?" said Edgar.

Glass acknowledged Victor and Butch with a nod. He was dressed like a flashy advertisement in a magazine—rumpled linen pants and white shirt, red polka-dot necktie. His hat lay beside him on the lacquered table. "My men have spoken with the Maritime Commission," he said. "Yours was the only witness report on the accident. There was nothing to see by the time the Coast Guard arrived."

"And the crew?" said Edgar.

"They have finished giving statements," said Glass. "They have agreed in all respects."

"That's good," said Edgar. "Very good."

"Fine to see you boys again," Glass said. "Victor, I was sorry to hear about your grandmother. And I'm sorry I could not tell you the whole truth before, but Edgar has explained it to you. This must be your brother."

"No," Victor said. "This is Butch. A friend of mine."

Butch stood near the door, wary, as if he might need to make a run for it. "You the guy from Gangbusters?"

"You might say that. Where is the brother?"

"He went home," Victor said.

"Where is home?"

"Not far from here. Magnolia Springs."

Glass turned. "Do you think that was wise, Edgar? Until we have all the loose ends tied up?"

Butch edged into a chair.

"The lad seemed mostly grateful to have been pulled from the sea in such short order," Edgar said. "We left the rest of his crew at Mobile, but he wanted a ride to his home. I obliged him. He understands the delicacy of our position. He's assured me he'll be discreet."

Madame set her glass before him on the low white table. "And how much does *he* know?"

"My dear, I do wish that you would trust your old infirm husband. The lad is a soldier on furlough. He'll not interfere." He poured out more sherry.

Glass started to sit, changed his mind. "Boys, you are going to have to try hard to understand what I tell you. Our friends on U-641 broke radio silence early this morning. That was indeed the boat you saw and signaled, and they did indeed attack and sink the *Eugenia Rae*. We regret the loss of life, but we intend to carry on with the plan. It's that simple."

If this all was a scheme to get some Germans out of Germany and capture an enemy submarine, Victor thought, it was the most roundabout way to do it that anyone could have invented. "He came all this way to surrender, but instead he sunk that ship?"

Madame curled fingers around her glass. "Listen to what Roy is saying."

"Did you overhear our friend's conversation with his comrades?" Glass gestured out to the bay. "Just before Edgar began the code sequence. He was under suspicion. He had disappeared from his pack. His chief instructed the others to confirm his last reported position."

Edgar moved around the bar, his gaze shifting from the boys to Glass, and back. "You remember that, don't you, boys."

"I ain't sure," said Butch.

Glass sat, hands on his knees, facing them. "Our friend believed he was in danger. He thinks the other captain may have overheard Edgar's code sequence. His chief put out an order for the others to begin a rendezvous. One of them—288—his name is Klaussen—sent word he was nine miles from Henkel's position, and would move directly toward him. Of course our friend had no choice but to withdraw from the operation."

"But he didn't withdraw!" Victor insisted. "He sunk that ship!"

"With a comrade approaching, and the sudden appearance of the merchantman, our friend acted as he is sworn to act. He fired on the ship. The other sub arrived in time to serve witness, and send word to their chief. That let our friend off the hook."

Something did not fit. Victor put down his drink. "You mean he sunk that ship just to make the others think he wasn't turning traitor?"

Roy Glass said, "That's right."

"But he is turning traitor? Later on tonight?"

"In a manner of speaking," said Glass.

"That doesn't make much sense to me," said Victor.

"Me neither," said Butch. "Fact is, ask me, you oughta start over from the beginning."

Glass smacked the table with his hand. The glasses jumped. "You must understand how important it is that these men be captured. They must not surrender."

"But people got killed on that ship," Victor said. "That counts for something."

Madame coiled on her barstool, jangling bracelets, lustrous and lithe as a snake. "Edgar, I think this one has the fragile beginnings of an actual mind," she said. "Child. This is war. People get killed. It's unavoidable."

"Those men knew the risk when they signed on that tanker," said Edgar. "I'm told they're paid well."

A grandmother who looks like a movie star. A grandfather who makes excuses for a torpedo. The world is full of strange wonders. Up to now Victor's idea of old people was Willie—wrinkled, shrinking with age, cooking fish on the stove, shooing flies from the kitchen—or old Pop, not even a memory, just a cage for bad dogs. It was odd to imagine how Victor might have turned out as a Gilliam, if instead of his own God-fearing spare-the-rod father and mother he'd been born to people like this, in a luxurious place like this cottage. Would he be perfect and blond, like Diana, or the same homely boy in fancier clothes?

"None of this is our fault," said Roy Glass. "We had no way of knowing the merchantman would come along. None of this would have happened if our plans had gone off the first time." He smiled without humor. "You were an unforeseen event."

"They're coming back?" Victor said.

Roy Glass stood a long time without speaking. "I am not sure how much of this should be discussed in front of you."

Victor kept his voice even. "That thing ran into me."

"Don't you have a home you should be going off to?" said Madame. "Don't children still do that these days?"

"No," Victor said, "they don't."

She lifted an eyebrow at his insolence. "This is a game for grown-ups."

"I'm not playing." Victor squared his shoulders.

Madame settled the glass on the edge of the bar. "Nobody's playing. I've got an idea about you, though. You've been listening to the radio too much. You have a head full of ideas."

Victor met her gaze. "If that thing comes back in, I'm going to be out there. I know all about your plan, inside and out. I saw what happened. If it wasn't for me and Butch, half those men would have drowned."

"Tell her, Sandy."

Edgar shrugged. "He's right, my friends. These lads are in it. Can't help that now."

"This is a dangerous time," Glass said. "We cannot have any further interference."

"The responsibility's mine." Edgar slipped his arms around his wife. "You just do what you can to make sure we don't have last night all over again. If our friend can't make up his mind, we may have to make it up for him."

"Well, Roy? I believe my husband has a point." Madame stood up, stretched her arms. "I would rather cut off my fingernails than go to this awful dance tonight, but the poor simpletons have to throw something every time someone with the slightest reputation comes through." She laughed. For a moment she looked as young as Diana. "Then again, I suppose they could do worse than me."

"It is all arranged, Madame," said Glass. "Everyone will go. It is part of the cover. Very important that you not deviate from the schedule. If anything happens, you will have been at the dance all evening, then retired to your rooms. We'll handle everything." His spectacles magnified his milky blue eyes. "Our friend will pass into the bay at two-thirty, and our rendezvous is at five."

"Good! That gives us plenty of time to dance," said Madame.

Edgar smiled. "Is that what you'd like, my dear? Take in the youth in their party regalia?"

"We can't take these . . . boys, can we?" she purred. "*Look* at them."

Edgar clapped his hands. "Of course we can. I'll have Charles do something. I think it's a wonderful idea."

"Edgar, I do love your style." She kissed the air by his cheek.

The old man beamed. "And I thought you married an old fool for his money," he said.

"I did." Madame patted his hand. "You can tell what a man's worth by how much he's got. You're the richest man I ever met. Now make a drink for your poor old sweetheart. She's going to have a nap."

"My Constance," Edgar said, swaying her side to side. "What would I do without you?"

"Or I, without you," Madame said. Only Victor could see the cold, studied look in her eyes when she said it.

Roy Glass opened the door. "Bring the boys to me when you are done with them."

Charles appeared in his place. "Sir?"

"Charles, we're all going dancing. Take these lads off and make them presentable. The shop in the hotel. Have them open it up. Then take them to Mr. Glass."

Charles looked as if he'd been asked to clean up after a dog.

Madame stifled a pretty yawn with her hand. "Well, go on, you can do that, can't you? And then take the night off, all of you."

"Of course, Madame. Thank you." Charles bowed to the boys. "Gentlemen. Come with me."

22

T H E S O U N D of a band floated over the lawn, through the live oaks, the open French doors. They played just a snatch of a tune—a rinky-tinkling piano, a conversational roll on the sax, the small crowd of brass piping up. Then the drummer went *bit! bop! bit! bop!* and the whole thing fell apart. They murmured among themselves, noodling, tuning, horns finding the same note from other horns.

Victor stood on the balcony, admiring the night and the music and the suave new self he saw when he looked down. It seemed the band was tuning up because Victor had never looked so fine. The shiny new wing tips were shining, the white trousers pressed to a knife-edge. The white collar prickled his neck. A striped necktie and blue blazer, a real Navy blazer with gold buttons.

It was something what money could do. Take a gangly old boy from the river, wash him good, put him in these duds, put him up on a hotel balcony, and you got a whole other boy. Victor felt hungry and mean and good-looking, or at least not ugly as before.

After all, there was a certain look in the eye of that girl . . . Diana.

He wondered what his daddy would say. It would be some kind of revenge just to see the look on his face. He was a poor man, proud of it. He would take one long look at Victor's getup and spit on the ground. He used to point out the hotel from the deck of his boat and say boys, get a look at some people who don't know the worth of a dollar.

Willie would say, You're a right lookin fancy. Where on earth do you think you're from? Turn around, let me get a eye full of you. Heard a preacher once who said clothes was the invention of the devil, there weren't none in Eden till the snake come along . . .

What would Joseph say? What was he doing right now?— sitting down to a mess of vegetables, probably, ordering the children around, basking in the glow of being a hero, and home. Just his face in the house would shine away some of the gloom Willie must have left, passing through.

Victor banged his fist on the bathroom door. "Come out of there. The band's starting."

No sound from the other side.

This was the room where Victor had awakened after the collision: the flowered stretch of carpet, the canopy bed with its draping of mosquito net. He was beginning to think of it as his own. Glass had handed him a key, then headed up the stairs at the end of the hall.

Victor banged again. "Hey. Come on."

"Go to hell," came the shout.

"What are you doing in there?"

"Kiss my ass."

"If you don't come on I'm gonna leave you." Victor squinted at the mirror as if to see himself for the first time. Fine clothes, all right, but still his scrawny bruise-battered face, one tooth bent over the other, jets of hair sticking out. He spit in his palm and tried to tame the angles.

The door crept open and there was Butch. If Victor thought he looked half as ridiculous as that, he would go hide in a closet. The hotel shop carried only the one style for men, and on Butch the clothes looked oddly misshapen. The trousers bunched at his shoes; the buttons on his shirtfront threatened to pop; the jacket rode up on his neck. He had tied the tie with a square knot, and gotten a comb through his hair, but that just made it bush out all frizzly on the top of his head.

"If you say one damn word," he said, and that was all.

"I didn't say nothing." Victor pulled on his chin to keep from busting out laughing.

"I look like a goddamn idiot," said Butch.

"No you don't."

"Well if *you* do," Butch said, "so do I. I ain't goin down there."

"Aw, why not?"

"Forget it."

"I bet you there's some good-looking girls there," Victor said. "You never know."

Butch flung his jacket to the floor. "You can have 'em. I thought we was goin out hunting that thing."

"They want to keep an eye on us till then, don't you see?

What they don't know, we'll be keeping an eye on *them*. I'm not just going to kill time. I got an idea. Glass is gonna take us to this dance, right? Once everything is going on, I can run up and take a look."

Butch plopped in the chair. A shirt button sprang free. "A look where?"

"He's got a room up the stairs, right down yonder."

"What are you lookin for?"

"I don't know exactly." Victor retrieved the button and handed it back. "But I bet I'd find it. I need you to keep him busy while I look. Are you with me?"

Two sharp raps, and the door opened in.

Roy Glass, in a dark silky dinner jacket. "Are you ready to go?"

"I ain't goin," said Butch.

Glass smiled. "After Mr. Gilliam was so kind as to . . . furnish you with these clothes? Take a look at you! You both look like human beings."

"Go to hell." Butch slumped back in the chair, and made a choking sound, pulling at the collar.

"He's chicken," said Victor. "He thinks everybody's gonna laugh at him."

"I just don't like puttin on some monkey suit so I can go stand around and look at a bunch of dancin assholes," said Butch.

"See what I mean?" Victor handed up the jacket.

"I need to know something from both of you," said Roy Glass. "Will you play by our rules tonight? We do not want any surprises."

"We're not the ones," Victor said. "Go talk to your Nazis out there."

"Everything is all set. You must realize how important it is that we not make a misstep. You have come into something you do not completely understand. It can be . . . dangerous." His steady smile tinted every word with a threat. "I ask only that you follow my instructions."

Victor said, "Let's go to the dance."

Butch flopped the jacket over his shoulder. "I ain't dancin," he said. "I'll go down there but I ain't dancin."

"Do we understand each other?" Glass opened the door.

Victor walked past him. "I understand you, if that's what you want to know. Come on, Butch."

"I was better off in my own clothes," Butch muttered, limping down the hall.

Victor waited while Glass locked the door. "You coming?"

"I hope you have heard what I said."

"Sure." Victor walked on. He was proud of himself. He'd stuck up to Glass, made no promises, given nothing away. He was walking a tightrope somewhere high over the truth. For some reason they wanted him to see what would happen tonight. That man in the swamp might have found out something. And he was as dead as any man could be. Victor would need all his balance.

A shower had slickened the grass, left the eaves dripping, the air full of mist. Clouds hid the stars. The bay was nothing but dark, and a rhythmical lap on the shore.

The ballroom joined the wings of the Hotel. The band was into a real number now, the trumpet cutting the air with its notes. Before blackout curtains, you could see the dancers from offshore on nights like this, shimmering like exotic fish through the curving glass wall. Now the only signs of life were the music and a tuxedoed fat man standing in a dim alcove.

When he opened the door, the band swelled in the night. A voice rode across—a woman scatting along on a clarinet line:

"Oh we're goin'
 I don't know where we're goin' but we're goin'
 Yes, we're goin'
 The only thing I know izzzz—we're goin'
 Feel the rhythm runnin' to you
 You know tonight's the night"

Victor caught a glimpse of men in uniform, girls flashing by in crinoline. Lights glittered and swam.

"These young men are with me, Wiggins," said Glass.

"Thank you, sir." The fat man swept the door open.

The room seemed to have no ceiling—it was high, a deep violet blue, with tiny yellow electrical stars twinkling in familiar constellations. This perfect sky rose in a dome over the dance floor, where couples twirled and stepped.

"God," said Butch, going in.

"It's really something," Victor agreed.

A red spotlight struck a great mirrored ball, spreading spackles of light. The band pumped the tune on the stage, which was shaped like a seashell.

Roy Glass had stopped for a word with the doorman.

The air sparkled with chatter. At the far end of the room was a long bar, a mirror stacked with bottles, a crowd weaving in and around.

The players' knees were hidden by inverted wooden seashells emblazoned TF on front. Two drummers pounded a jungly beat on brass kettles. A Negro's hands blurred over the xylophone. Victor put his hands in his pockets and soaked up the noise. He forgot Glass and the Gilliams and Diana and everything else in that big wash of music, the pure sound that went straight from the horns to his ears.

The bandleader, a wiry man with a long baton and a wispy

mustache, marked the time in the air with his wand, smiling blandly at his singer.

She strained on high heels to reach the globe-of-the-world microphone. Her face was tilted up at the spotlight, a dramatic wave of ink-black hair down over one cheek. Her voice was big, husky, smooth as that permanent wave, an effortless vibrato from this chubby little dot of a woman in a glittery dress. She snapped her fingers and sang.

> "There's a small hotel
> By a wishing well
> I wish we were there
> Together"

Victor stepped aside for a crowd coming in. The girls squealed as they entered the magical light; they whispered and giggled and stood at the edge of the dance floor. Five fellows a little older than Victor slunk toward the bar.

Glass came in behind them.

"Great band," said Victor.

"I have some arrangements to make." Glass touched Victor's elbow. "I need you to stay here."

"Glad to." He smiled. "This is terrific."

"Where is Butch?" said Glass.

Victor waved at the crowd. "Over there. Getting accustomed." Butch huddled against a wall, wide-eyed at the profound abundance of girls.

"Keep an eye on him till the Gilliams arrive, will you?" Glass's friendly clasp had steel in it. "Have a good time. Have a dance. I'll be back." He went around the bar and disappeared through a swinging door.

Another surge of people pushed Victor into the room.

Slowly the dancers were spreading in twos and fours among the blue-draped tables. This song was slinky. A trombone purred. The dancers swayed, touching. The lights went reddish and low.

Victor drifted through the perfumed crowd to the stage. The singer perched on a little white stool at the edge, smoking a cigarette while the players kept the rhythm in their knees. The lead trumpet swung high and brought the song down with a nice ironic descending scale. Victor started clapping before anyone.

The bandleader bent to the mike. "Good evening ladies and gentlemen thank you so much," he said in a slippery voice. "Thank you thank you. My name is Tommy Fossey and these are the Bandits of the Beat!" On cue, all the band members gave out a little howl, which was supposed to sound outrageous. "What a beautiful beautiful evening and so many ladies just as beautiful . . ."

The singer put out her cigarette with her toe, stood, smoothed her skirt. When she smiled, little dimples opened in her cheeks.

Tommy Fossey raised his hand. "But if you think the girls you have here are sweethearts, I turn your attention to the young lady we've brought all the way from her hometown of Sanderson, Texas, our raven beauty, the queen of the Bandits, the voice of choice, welcome Miss Dinah Anderson!"

Of course! That was it! From the radio!

Butch came up with a glass of beer in each hand.

"That's—that's Dinah Anderson!" Victor exclaimed. "She's a big star! I've heard her on the radio. I never imagined she'd look like that, though."

"What you mean?" said Butch.

"She sounded kind of . . . blond."

Butch nudged his elbow with a glass. "Here, take this. She does got a sweet little behind."

The bandleader was making a speech about our rugged GIs

fighting for freedom and how we would come to victory in the end.

Someone waved from across the dance floor.

Edgar and Madame were taking their seats at a large round table just to one side of the stage. Madame wore a long wine-red jeweled gown with a turban to match. Edgar looked regal in his tuxedo. People turned to admire them.

"Come on, Butch." Victor led the way through the throng.

"Ho ho, lads," Edgar boomed. "Don't we all look the part! Charles didn't do so badly by you after all."

Victor took the chair Edgar held for him. "Thanks for the clothes. This is great."

Butch sat, too. "Never seen so many painted-up girls in one place."

"Didn't I tell you?" said Victor.

Madame kept her head high, her eyes to the stage, a slight distracted smile to acknowledge the whispers about her. She tapped her fingernails on an ivory cigarette holder.

Tommy Fossey kicked off a stomp version of "Beer Barrel Polka."

A waiter appeared. "Oh good evening, Madame!" He bowed to kiss her hand. "Evening, sir. We're so lucky to have you with us!"

"Oh, no," said Madame, "it's we who are honored."

The waiter looked flustered and impressed. "I must go find Mr. Reginald," he said.

"Bring us a drink on your way, won't you, friend?" Edgar said. "Rye for me. Neat. Madame will have what she always has, won't you. Boys? Should I be corrupting you with such regularity?"

"I'll take a beer," said Butch. He appeared to be enjoying the view of Miss Dinah Anderson's curvy legs.

"I'm fine," Victor said. "Where's Diana? Isn't she coming?"

That brought Madame's attention around. She smiled and put her thumbnail behind a front tooth. "Look at you in your fancy new clothes. You're very nearly respectable, aren't you?"

Victor squirmed. "I don't know about that."

"Edgar, look at them. Don't they look respectable?"

"They do indeed." The old man's eyes lifted past them. "Now here comes our beautiful flower."

She *was* beautiful making her way through the crowd: that deep tan against the white satin dress. "Isn't it grand?" she said, scanning the room with a tentative smile. "A Tuesday night, and it's festive as *anything*. You'd never know there's a war. Hello, Grandmother. It's all for you!" She leaned down for a kiss on the cheek.

"Hello, dear. You're lovely. Where's Bill?"

Diana's smile vanished. She sank to a chair. "He's been called back," she said. "They sent his squadron to New Jersey! What could he possibly do in New Jersey? I think it's just awful." She stuck out her lip in a pout.

"You mean he's already gone?" Madame put a cigarette into her holder. The waiter appeared with a light, and the drinks.

"This afternoon. He left me a note. Can you believe that?"

"My dear child," said Edgar, "Uncle Sam is fighting a war. He doesn't have time to wait for young love."

Diana put her chin in her hand. "Well I think it's perfectly horrid! He hasn't been here a week."

"Darling, they don't care a thing about that," said Madame. "They're men. Always running off to play soldier or something. Don't be sad. He'll be back."

"I'm not sad, Grandmother. If he wants to go off and leave me alone in this horrible place, that's fine." She glared at the band as if she wished they would hush.

"You're not handsome it's true
But when I look at you
I just—oh, Johnny, oh, Johnny, oh!"

Edgar watched the dancers with a cryptic smile.

Diana had taken the chair directly opposite Butch and Victor, but she noticed them only now. "What are you looking at?"

"Not you," said Butch. "I like a gal with a little more meat on the bone, like her there." He waved at the singer, who was favoring him with little winks from the stage.

Victor admired the sparks in Diana's eyes. *A girl with a fuse*, he told himself, *a short fuse*.

Then her annoyance turned into amusement. "You look like bad boys who've been sent to church. Look at their clothes! Grandmother!"

"I know," said Madame. *"Très misérables*, don't you think?"

Butch drained his glass and lifted his finger as Edgar had done. The waiter appeared at his elbow. "Another for the young gentleman? Ladies, something?"

Diana said, "Yes. Bring me something strong. A vodka."

"We don't want to get out of our head, Diana," said Madame.

"Bring me a vodka, with tonic water," said the girl, "a tall glass."

"Diana . . ."

"Go on, bring it," Diana told the waiter. "Grandmother, I could kick and scream and throw a tantrum, but I'd rather do the adult thing and just have a drink."

The music stopped. A drumroll, a little trumpet fanfare, and the spotlight settled beside the bandleader on a thin, nervous young man, shiny as his waxed mustaches. "Ladies and gentlemen," he quavered, "an important announcement, if you please. As you all know, this isn't the usual Tuesday night at the Hotel, and that's due to one lady, one lady alone. She's here with us tonight. She's our guest of honor."

Victor watched the subtle tension in Madame's face, the lift of her shoulders. She placed one hand on the other and stared off into the middle distance as if he must be talking about War Bonds, or someone else.

"What an honor. What a great honor it is for the management of the Hotel, whenever she graces us with her presence." He read from a slip of paper in his hand. "Star of Broadway and London and the great stages of the world, she is a living legend of the theater. She has performed her unforgettable Lady Macbeth for the crowned heads of Europe, and received accolades from the likes of Sarah Bernhardt and the great Caruso. Now she's known for her patriotism and her contributions to USO charities and the Ladies' Auxiliary of the Red Cross. Ladies and gentlemen, please join me in a round of applause for our distinguished guest, Madame Constance Belair." He started the clapping, the paper between his fingers.

Spotlights came to dazzle their table, a polite ovation. Madame arose with a smile, blew a kiss. "Thank you, thank you," she said. "Thank all of you." She sat just at the right instant, Victor noticed, before the lights wandered away.

"Wasn't that lovely," said Edgar.

"Lovely," she said through her smile.

The young man fluttered up to the table. "Good evening, Madame, I'm Reginald Peavey, you remember, on the telephone, oh my good gracious, we're just *so* excited to have you here with us this evening, such an honor, I saw you perform once at the Saenger Theatre in New Orleans, it was—well, what can I say?—it was marvelous, and when I heard you were at the Semmes Cottage, I said to myself, you've just got to do something!"

"Thank you darling," purred Madame, clasping his fingers,

"of course I remember. Who could forget? This is precious, this whole thing, the orchestra, your little speech—just *too* precious."

Butch leaned over to Victor's ear: "When do we puke?"

Reginald Peavey hovered a while, making a fuss. When he left, Madame turned to Edgar. "Remind me to go anywhere else in the world next summer."

"Ah, be gracious, my dear," Edgar said, sipping rye. "You're a star. They have to make a commotion over you." He put a match to his stubby cigar. "Besides. Like the man said. I think it does everyone good to pay homage to a truly patriotic woman. I drink to you. Here's to my beautiful and patriotic wife." He raised his glass. "Come on, everyone. It's a toast."

"Thank you, Edgar," Madame said. Her eyes narrowed.

"Here's to the USO and the Red Cross and Betsy Ross and Martha Washington," said Edgar, his glass still aloft. "And my wife, Madame Constance Belair."

"All right, Edgar, that's fine." Her smile was tight. "Maybe we've had enough to drink for one evening?"

"Maybe we haven't had nearly enough." Edgar's eyes glittered as they had when he told Victor about the Germans, the U-boat, the plan. "I particularly liked the way he kept returning to the word honor," he said. "Isn't there something you've been forgetting, my dear?"

Reaching into her evening bag, Madame examined her face in a compact mirror. "Looks fine to me, Edgar." She stood. "Why don't we dance?"

The old man watched her, unblinking.

"Well? Are you going to let me stand here like a fool?"

"*Grand*father," said Diana.

Edgar pushed up from his chair. "No, of course not, my dear. Delighted." He took her hand and led her to the floor. The song was "The Tennessee Waltz," slowed way down.

Victor straightened his tie and coughed. Diana paid no attention. He coughed louder.

She turned. "Something caught in your throat?"

"No, I'm fine," he said. "I just. Well. I mean—I wondered if you wanted to dance or not."

Diana pursed her lips. "Why should I?"

"Well," Victor said. "This afternoon you said . . ." He looked to Butch for help, but Butch was intent on Dinah Anderson. "I don't know. I can't dance. I thought you might show me."

"Don't you think you're a little young for me?"

"No," said Victor. "How old are you?"

"Almost twenty." Diana toyed with her glass. "Oh, why not? Nobody wants to have fun anymore. At least someone cares what I want to do." She got up. "Let's go."

The music screeched to a halt, and all conversation. Every spotlight swiveled to Victor.

Trailing her to the floor, Victor caught Madame's glance of approval, mixed with a warning.

In a million years of dreams, he never expected to dance with this beautiful girl in a ballroom to the swell of a big band, but here he was. "Put this hand here," she told him, "and hold this one. That's it. Now just watch my feet."

The pattern was easy, the beat not too fast, and before the first song was over Victor had unlocked his knees and was actually gliding her across the floor. If only he had a picture! "You're not so bad," she said. "Ever do this before?"

"Oh, nuh-uh." Victor sidestepped her toes.

"You're supposed to come in a little closer."

With a thrill his hand came to the warmth of her back. This was the closest Victor had ever been to any girl, and he marveled at the softness, the touch of satin, the sweat on his hands, her aroma of powder and faint perfume. He had crept to the edge of this moment, and here he was skating across. He wished his whole body had a memory, so he could live this tingle over and over for the rest of his life.

"I think you look kind of sweet all dressed up," she said, her voice just a breath in his ear. "No, watch it. One, and a two."

"Like this?"

"Mmmm . . . I know you're working with Grandfather on —whatever it is. He said he trusts you. Doesn't he seem strange tonight? Out of sorts. I thought he was awful to Grandmother just then."

"I guess he's got a lot on his mind," said Victor, trying to find the rhythm with his feet.

"Oh I know. This project of theirs. They've been up all hours. He was fine until he took that trunk call, and he's been a grump ever since. He shouldn't spoil her big night. As soon as this song's over, I'm going to say something."

"You know what's going on? This—project? You know what it is?"

The question didn't seem to bother her. "A little," she said. "They're always involved in some intrigue or other. They love it. It keeps them young. Look. Aren't they handsome?"

Victor had to agree. The Gilliams might have been a dance team from the movies, moving with confident elegance, every step spontaneous but somehow predestined. And yet there was a studied distance between them, like old partners going through a routine.

Victor felt a tap on his shoulder: a muscular man in full Army uniform, who said "May I?" and danced Diana away without waiting for an answer.

Victor blinked. His feet felt spongy and light. It had been a trance, her touch, the fragrant lights and music, and now it was broken. What was coming over him?

Now was the time. Diana in the hands of the Army, Edgar

and Madame caught up in their performance, Glass off attending to unknown details. Even Butch was transfixed, by Miss Dinah Anderson. Victor did not hesitate. He walked past the bartender, behind the bar, through the door.

The kitchen: a billow of steam: two Negroes looked up from their cast-iron pots: Victor nodded and kept going. He went through a dark dining room where three elderly couples hunched over their plates. They thought he was a waiter and tried to get his attention. The maître d' did not look up as he went by, down a long hall and into the night.

Mist was drifting on the lawn. Victor stole across. There was a light at the top of the stairs.

The door squealed. Cringing, he placed his foot on each step, to make the least noise, and paused at the landings to listen.

When he reached the third-floor landing he took up a clay pot of marigolds, leaned out the window, and pitched it at a stretch of sidewalk. It shattered, a crash.

A door opened above. Sudden footsteps.

Victor ducked into an alcove, pressing flat to the door. He prayed he was skinny enough. The footsteps went past him, on down the stairs. The door squealed and banged shut.

Go on. Quick. He'll be back.

A light shone around the door at the top of the last flight. In his hurry, Glass had not even closed it. Victor took three steps at a time. The door swung in to a large room, the attic slope of the ceiling, a bare wooden floor, battered desk, iron bed, telephone, washstand, a big stack of *Life* magazines.

The wide drawer in the desk was locked, the other drawers empty. An assortment of dark clothes hung on a pole in the corner. Inside the humming electric icebox Victor found a quart of milk and a wilted tomato.

No other sign that anyone lived here.

The only possibility was the narrow arched doorway covered by a brown curtain.

Victor drew it aside.

What he saw made him cold.

A hooded lamp cast a faint light over an array of radio equipment much more elaborate than the transmitter on the *Constance*. A long oaken table held seven black boxes, hissing, with wheels and dials and knobs and cords running among them like a convention of snakes. Tubes glowed soft orange. Two telephones sat on a large round speaker beside a hand microphone and a telegrapher's key. An ashtray was mounded with butts.

In plain sight was a machine that had to have been designed for some important evil. It resembled a typewriter, with a wooden lid on a hinge and three sets of alphabet keys, steel pushbuttons that stood away from the panel.

A slat folded down in front, stamped with ENIGMA on one side and *Klappe schliessen* on the other. A metal plaque in the lid told a lot more, all in German, beginning with the words
ZUR BEACHTUNG!!!

Something to do with a code. Had to be. Victor knew all about codes from *The Boy's Guide to Secret Detecting*, the single most popular volume in the Bon Secour High School library, but the rows of numbers and letter pairs charted in the lid were way beyond that.

Why would an FBI agent have a German code machine?

Victor turned to a side table stacked tall with cardboard folders of black and white photographs, dozens and dozens. He thumbed through: ships, factories, fences, walls, a street in a city, a blurred face. The port of Mobile. A wounded soldier in a hospital bed. The silver belly of an airplane, the stern of the banana boat, live oaks at Bellingrath Gardens.

Maybe the FBI had captured the machine, and Glass was using it to lure the Nazis.

But why all these pictures?

And why, in the last folder, were there six different views of Roy Glass, apparently snapped when he was unaware of the camera? Here climbing from an automobile, there walking out of a barber shop, standing by a woman on a sidewalk . . .

Something wrong. Victor looked closer. The man in the photographs had the same wire spectacles, the careful blond hair, but he wasn't Roy Glass. He was thinner, with a square jaw. Someone who looked a whole awful lot like Roy Glass but was not.

Victor knew who he was. He'd seen him only once, from a distance—headed down the yard, dejected, Willie pointing him off her porch—but this was the first coast marshal. The very first man who came to get Willie to cover her windows.

The resemblance was startling, as if Glass had studied these pictures for the purpose of transforming himself into this man.

Victor flashed from the pictures to the face of Roy Glass to the dead man, mottled blue, gold wire spectacles.

Glass was not the coast marshal. He'd said that much. But he had taken the coast marshal's place, even down to his looks.

Maybe he was not an FBI agent, either.

Mild static, and far away, the electric stammer of Morse code. Victor grazed a key with his finger.

He needed this proof.

He shut the lid, snapped the snaps, snatched up two folders of photographs, backed through the curtain. Glass was bound to be back up those stairs. What was in the locked drawer? Must be something important, as careless as he'd been with everything else—diamonds, maybe cash or gold bars. Victor worked a metal ruler into the crack. The cheap lock gave way with one yank.

He found a camera about half as long as a man's hand, a black leather binder, and a deck of Aviator playing cards. He gathered everything and slammed the drawer. Time to flee. Remember the last time you waited too long . . .

This was proof. Now all he had to find out was just what it proved, and maybe somebody more important than Butch would believe him.

Lugging the machine by its handle, tucking everything else under his arm, Victor slipped from the room. He left the door as he'd found it, ajar. He moved fast down the stairs. Where could he hide these things? A tree was his first idea, a nest of branches at the top of a gigantic live oak, but some wind might knock it all to the ground. He crept onto the lawn. The machine was heavier than it looked. Under that wheelbarrow. No. In a pipe or a culvert. On a boat—but it might sail away.

A good safe place out of the weather. Strange forces were everywhere, not just out under the waves.

He noticed a bullet-shaped bus parked around to the rear of the ballroom, beside an unlit doorway. A ribbon down the side of the bus said BANDITS OF THE BEAT. Silver trumpets leaked out around the stage door. Victor opened it. A big swell of instruments washed down the narrow stairway, a Glenn Miller arrangement flowing like fast water. More steps led down to the right, an apparent dead end. Victor went down. Tucked under the stairwell, a little half-door opened to a crawl space under the stage.

He got on hands and knees and dragged the machine through a maze of pipes and crossbeams, directly under Tommy Fossey and his orchestra. The big sound masked his noise. Sawdust sifted down when the drummer's foot thumped the boards overhead. Through the wooden lattice at the front of the stage Victor saw dancers from their knees down, ankles twirling and stepping.

He squeezed the machine behind a narrow row of posts, where no one would ever find it.

Squares of light fell through the grid. He opened the leather binder. The first three pages were torn from a radio log: dates, times, numbers, FREQ and HZ and KHZ and code names like WALTER and DAVID and FATHER. Scribbled half-lines described the conversations: "Says to confirm 7842 if not aware" and "Reduce aims in flow, re: MALCOLM" and "Load? Other factors? No on procedure." The last message read "OK CATALOGUE."

Next came an assortment of Mobile & Ohio railroad time-tables, "Port Activities" columns clipped from the *Register*, Help Wanted notices with red circles around shipyard jobs.

Then a map, drawn in black ink on a sheet of flimsy typewriter paper. The scale was wrong, but the shape of the bay was distinct. A dotted line entered through Grants Pass and ran straight to a fancy doodled X in the deep water west of a series of squiggles. Those must represent Willie's island, Weeks Bay, the river. Another X in a box on the bend in the river—right at the mouth of Noltie Creek. A third X on the point, where the Hotel would be, and a triangle for the Middle Bay light. Dotted lines connected everything. This must be the plan for tonight's rendezvous.

The orchestra whammed to a finish, provoking a storm of applause from the floor.

Victor flipped through more pages in a crabbed hand, *Stunde* and *überwachen*, *Benzin* and *Werft* and *infiltrieren*, and it might as well have been in Chinese. At the back of the folder he found one page in English—a typewritten draft of a cable.

COMMUNICATION/EYES ONLY/ABWEHR

MOTHER and FATHER have divergent aims necessitating a separation by the controller. MOTHER is most reliable. FATHER has been excluded and is considered unreliable. Word received cf. ARABELLA of inquiries in her AO re:

credentials, unsuccessful deflection of same inq. Origin unknown but possible FATHER. Will proceed with separation. School is in. All quiet proceeding. Successful insertion five of crew L. Three not yet in place. Transfers of info. to come. Sugg delay all further detachments pending outcome. Must discuss problems transp. with ONE. Elimination of local interference will continue in pace with HQ reported desire to continue CATALOGUE.

RAYMOND

It didn't make much sense without knowing who was who, but it had a flavor of dark and complicated evil.

RAYMOND must be Glass.

MOTHER and FATHER might be Madame and Edgar, in which case Edgar was "unreliable."

If Victor and Butch were the "local interference," they might be in worse trouble than that. Depending on how things went with CATALOGUE.

The deadliest-sounding part was the simplest: "School is in. All quiet proceeding." That sounded like a scheme with a history and a serious future.

Victor returned the papers to the binder, and tucked it in a narrow slot beside the machine. The bandleader's amplified voice vibrated the stage: "Thank you thank you . . . round and round and round she goes, and where she'll land, nobody knows!"

Half the cards in the Aviator box were not cards at all, but pieces of thick card-sized cellophane. Victor pulled one out. Rows of black dots made a pattern on its face; minuscule numbers ran along one edge.

Roy Glass was a spy. Victor knew it beyond any doubt, and in the rush of knowing he remembered Glass in the lighthouse, flashing signals and blowing the horn to the fog. His smooth astonishment the next morning, when Victor described what he hit. His subtle performance this very evening. His masterful lies in the Gilliams' bungalow.

The signs had been written in English and only Victor had seen them all. Who else knew the truth? Edgar? Madame? Diana, who whispered in Victor's ear she knew more than she was telling? Were they all in on the game?

He had to find out. Play dumb, play along, and find out.

He crawled back through the forest of pipes, his head grazing the stage, and squeezed out through the opening. Of course he'd blackened the knees of his pants. He was tempted to run up for a look at the band from backstage, but if he could blend back into the dance before he was missed, he would have completed his mission and observed the first law of Secret Detecting: Never get caught.

He slipped in the way he'd gone out, through the kitchen and past the bar. The music was hotter and faster now, double time "Tuxedo Junction." Dinah Anderson was nowhere in sight. Boys jitterbugged and the girls let them. Victor threaded through the crowd. Lots of girls, bigger smiles. He examined the front of the stage, to make sure no one could see past the latticework.

Diana sat alone at the Gilliams' table, a drink in her hand.

"What happened," said Victor, "did everybody already call it a night?"

"Oh, it's been a night, all right," said Diana. "What happened to you? You've been crawling around on the floor. Very nice. Well, you missed the big show." Her eyes were bright, whether from tears or vodka Victor couldn't tell.

"Tell me what happened," he said.

She brushed hair from her eyes. "It was terrible. Grandfather got very nasty, just all of a sudden. I didn't notice until they were into it. I was dancing. I had no idea he was drunk. By the time I got here, Mr. Glass was just trying to get him to leave. Grandfather was pointing at her, telling everybody she wasn't Constance Belair, she was Ida, Ida Simpson from Jasper, Alabama, no matter who she pretended to be. Oh, awful, he was yelling and she was just staring at him. Like she meant to kill him." Diana shuddered. "They made me stay here. It was like—he went crazy! He kept saying I know who you are, I know who you are . . ."

Victor had seen the pictures. He had read the radio log. "Where did they go?"

"The bungalow." Diana gathered her hair in one hand and began retying the ribbon. "That's why I stayed. Mr. Glass wants you down there."

"Let's go," Victor said.

"Go ahead. I'm supposed to go to the boat and wait." She wiped the wet circle from the table with her hand.

"Have you seen my friend Butch?"

"The last I noticed he and the singer were getting to know each other."

"That sounds like Butch," Victor said. "Listen, I had a good time dancing and all."

"Don't get your hopes up," she said. This must be the same clean, cold smile she gave all the boys. "I'm not too reliable."

That word again: how much did she know?

"There's some things I ought to tell you," said Victor.

"Work on your dancing." Diana stood up from the table. "Then we can talk."

23

THE FROGS and night bugs hollered for all they were worth, until the darkness beneath the great arms of the live oaks came alive with gonking and buzzing. Whenever the door swung open, the wail of the orchestra stirred the creatures to greater demonstrations of noise, as if they resented the imitation of their music and were driven to drown it out.

The great lawn was dark, foggy, empty except for a couple kissing near the ballroom entrance, and Victor sneaking along the bushes toward the bungalow.

He did not want to be in the open. Something was happening now. The frogs would not lie.

Nothing moving outside the pink wall. The gate screeched on the bricks. Subtle lights under palmetto fronds illumined the curving walkway.

Listen to the bugs, is what Willie would say. They are trying to tell you if only you'd listen.

Victor walked around to the garden. The pool glowed jade green. He wished he could always live in danger; it brightened the colors and made his heart beat fast. He would remember forever each step he took on this path. Would he see the monster tonight? This life seemed more real than his own: this skulking and lying, pretending and scheming, stealing, hiding, detecting. He was out to discover something for himself. This was the most important thing he'd ever done.

Remember. Only you saw it all. Only you know where the proof is hidden.

The glass door glided open.

"Look who's here." Madame had removed her turban, revealing coal-black hair pulled tight against her skull by a silver buckle at the back. "Come in, boy. We've been waiting for you."

Victor stepped in. Edgar was not in the room. Roy Glass sat on the scarlet chaise longue, his jacket tossed over the cushion. "Where did you go?"

"Sorry," said Victor. "I got to . . . talking to somebody and we went outside for a while."

"Ah, romance." Glass smiled. "And young Butch?"

"I think he's talking to somebody too."

Madame resumed her place on the white leather chair, and lifted her glass to her lips. "I don't think you need to worry about him, Roy. He wasn't paying much attention."

"Where's Edgar?" Victor was aware how brightly his question rang.

"He's not feeling well," said Madame. "He's not himself. He's sleeping right now."

"Is everything still set for tonight?"

"As always, a slight change in plan," said Roy Glass. "I do not think it will put us behind." He reached into his jacket and came out with a blue-black revolver, which he grasped by the barrel and handed to Victor. "Go ahead. It's not loaded. You may need to know how to use it tonight."

Victor sighted down the barrel. The metal was cold in his hand. "You sure it's not loaded?"

"Very sure. Point it down and pull the trigger."

Victor could not help closing his eyes when he pulled.

Click.

"Now. Aim it at something on the wall, support your wrist with the other hand, use the sight, brace yourself, and practice firing."

Victor aimed at the painting of Farragut's battle. Six clicks, six silent explosions.

"When it's live ammunition, you will feel a kick and you must work very hard to keep your footing," said Glass. "I hope you won't have to find out. Aim for the middle of the man. Let the bullet do the rest."

"Okay," said Victor. "Why do I need to know all this?"

"We have had a defection," Glass said. "Someone has decided to end his participation in our plan. Hand it here. See this lever, this is the safety." Why was Glass wearing gloves?

Leather gloves, like hunters wear in the winter?

All spies wear gloves. It's their way. They don't want to leave fingerprints. Another alarm bell went off inside Victor. After all he had learned, maybe he should have had a second or third thought before strolling back into the midst of these people. He took a tentative seat on the leather sofa, where he saw a clear path to the door. "Who defected?" he said.

"My husband, it seems," said Madame, without a trace of irony. "I don't know who put these ridiculous ideas in his head, but he's become convinced that Roy and I are lying to him."

"Lying about what?"

Glass thumbed bullets into the revolver.

"Our plan. Everything." Madame lit a cigarette without bothering to use the holder. "He keeps insisting I'm not who I pretend to be. I think the poor man has lost his mind, if anyone wants to know what I think."

"He is concerned," said Roy Glass. "He has every right to be concerned. This is a dangerous business, and he knew it from the start."

"Oh come on, Roy, I can't stand this any longer." Madame smoothed her shiny red gown. "Let's do it."

Glass snapped the gun shut and placed it on an end table, within Victor's reach. "I'll go wake him." He went down the long hall to the bedrooms.

Being alone with Madame in a room was like having a spotlight turned in your face. You couldn't see who was directing the glare. She flicked her ashes at Victor. "Has Diana gone to bed?"

"That's what she said."

Her smile was a frown. "She's a beautiful girl, isn't she."

"Yes she is," said Victor.

"You stay away from her."

"Yes ma'am." Victor inspected his fingernails. "I thought it was great, that speech they gave about you. I wish I could have seen you in one of your plays."

"Ha," said Madame. "You may get your chance."

Glass led Edgar Gilliam down the hall by his arm—or a much older man who looked like Edgar, shuffling into the room, his eyes swollen, white hair standing up on his head, white feet sticking out of blue pajamas.

"Hello, Edgar," Madame said in a firm voice. "Did you have a good nap?"

"What time is it?" Edgar held up his arm to shield his eyes from the light. He looked like one of those bone-thin refugees in the newsreels. "I . . . I don't know—what happened. What did you do? What . . . are you . . . "

Glass steered him to the sofa. The old man rubbed his eyes with his fists, opened wide, squeezed them shut.

"Edgar has been making inquiries in Washington," said Glass, walking a wide circle as if the old man were wounded and might attack him. "He wondered whether I was who I said I was, and he decided to check."

Edgar closed his eyes and inclined against the cushion, dozing.

"He talked to the wrong person at the Bureau," Glass said. "No one had heard of me. He thinks he has alerted the authorities. He decided we are working for the other side."

"But you are," Victor said. "I found out. I know all about you."

Glass looked up with faint amusement. "Oh? What is it you know?"

Victor took a deep breath. "CATALOGUE."

He watched the word flicker over their faces, an involuntary wince.

The smile died on Glass's lips. "You know too much," he said.

Madame came over to shake her husband's arm. "Edgar," she said, "sit up, Edgar, and try to wake up. Roy, I think you gave him too much."

Suddenly Edgar coughed, put his face in his hands, shook himself up out of sleep. The effort was painful to watch. "I don't know—what you've done to me." He held one hand against his eye. "I'm on to you now."

"Here we go again," said Madame. "We should have let him sleep."

"I've made calls, I've made calls," Edgar said. "You won't get away with this. It's going to be stopped."

"You haven't called anyone," Madame said, stretching up, going to the icebox. "You've been in that room, sound asleep, since you made such a fool of yourself. And of me. I hope you're satisfied."

Edgar's attention drifted around to Victor, hovering there on the edge of his seat. "Lad, I'm glad someone's here to see this. Do you understand what has happened? My dear wife and this man, this—this man have schemed against me! I've been played for a fool!"

"I'm not sure," Victor said, standing, "maybe I ought to be going."

Roy Glass moved between him and the door. "We need you," he said. "We're not finished with you."

"Lad, run and get the police," Edgar said, "make a call to the Coast Guard!"

"Victor is reasonable," said Roy Glass. "Aren't you? You just want to help. Isn't that what you said?"

Victor eased down to his seat. The revolver was inches from his hand. "It seems like you can handle all this without me," he said.

"But you're wrong," Madame said, swooping past. "You're just what we need. Your timing is perfect."

"Tell me one thing," said Victor. "The coast marshal. The first one. What did you do to him?"

"Ah, the unfortunate Roy Glass," said Glass, pulling the fingers of his glove. "Yes, I believe you met twice, did you not? One time when he wasn't himself."

"That was him in the swamp."

"Needless to say, he was never supposed to make such a public appearance," said Glass. "It won't happen again. A shame you did not heed our warning. Everything is a mess."

Ceiling fans turned lazily on the ceiling. Madame leaned against a fluted column along the gallery at the side of the room. "Edgar," she said, "I wish you had talked to us before you *did* anything. We could have explained it all for you."

"Quite sure of that, my dear." Edgar sat rock-still, his hands between his knees. "You have a script for every occasion."

"As it is," Madame said, "you've left us very little choice. We've come this far with Roy. We can't possibly go back now. What do you want us to do, just abandon the plan?"

Edgar's hands trembled. "The plan is corrupt," he said. "If

you're my wife, come with me. We'll leave this place. We'll have nothing further to do with this man."

Madame pulled on long white gloves. "We've been playing with fire a long time, Edgar. You can't just—stop playing."

The old man waved at Glass like a piece of the furniture. "You said he was FBI. You lied to me. I would never have done it if I'd known—if you'd said—"

"Of course you knew," Madame said. "You knew all along! You know who my friends are! How did you think Roy was able to set it all up?"

"The result is the same," Glass said, reaching to lock the door. "What difference does it make who pays my wage? People take sides in this business, Edgar, but does that mean they cannot talk to each other, work with each other? It's too bad. Who knows, I may be working for your side before it's all over."

Edgar sank to the sofa, shaking his head. "But this is wartime, this is treason and espionage during wartime," he said.

"We land a few men, then we leave the country," said Glass. "What is the harm?"

"It's not going to happen," said Edgar. "It's over. Too many people know. They heard me in the ballroom, I made sure of that. This lad and his young friend know everything. If anything happens to me, there'll be witnesses."

"We have a plan for that, Edgar," said Glass. "You know me. We may put it off a night, but we always have another plan."

Madame said, "Roy. This is useless. I'll do it. Give it to me."

Roy Glass lifted the gun by its barrel.

Victor was not afraid. He would die running. If it came to him now in the back, he could take it and die. The truth was his. He could die knowing that. The evil was real, and it was not in him. He backed around Glass with a hard bitter burn in his eyes. "You can kill me," he said, "but I have something you want."

"Don't hurt the boy," Edgar said.

"We don't intend to," said his wife. "We want to make sure neither one of you gets in our way again."

Her hand closed on the gun. She strode half the length of the room to stand in front of her husband. "Roy, tell me again. Feet apart, one hand bracing the wrist, aim and—"

Victor dove for the floor. The world slowed down *bang* why did she shoot him *bang* get down out of the way he's dead oh my God *bang*.

Edgar's pajamas erupted, dark blood spreading and pumping over the white leather cushion, a stunned look on his face, like a child. He cried out but it came out a wheezing of air.

Madame stood with the gun outstretched, her hand still supporting her wrist.

Victor had never seen anyone die. It happened so fast. That was not Edgar, that wounded animal thrashing, collapsing on its side, a mess on the perfect white sofa, a hand grasping, that sound, that hollow rattle, a tremor, and then his head lay on the coffee table beside a vase of white roses. His eyes stared, amazed.

Victor looked into the hole of the gun.

"Hello, yes. Hello? This is Roy Glass, can I speak with— oh yes, of course, Miss Haines, how are you—listen, it's urgent. Can I speak to—sure, I'll hold on. Yes. Hello? Wiggins? Glass. Listen. I've got a boy here, holding him with his own gun. Seems he broke in here at—yes, the Hotel—he broke into one of the guest cottages here, and it looks as if he's killed a man. A guest, a Mr. Gilliam. Yes. You better get down here. Sure, I know. That's the way it—what? Oh. The Semmes Cottage, third one on the right. Better hurry. His wife. She's hysterical."

24

THEY GOT ME. It's done. I'm in jail. Real jail. The Fairhope jail. Help.

Wish I'd listened to you when you told me stay home, boy, don't go out looking for trouble, because you surely will find it. Well here I am Willie I found it so what can I do?

They got me out of their way. Edgar Gilliam too. In one quick little killing that was over Willie quicker than you could imagine, in the time it takes you to count one, two, three. Now I see how it happened. I was so worried about that monster coming up from under the waves that I never saw the monsters around me. All along they meant to get rid of Edgar then fix it so it looked like I killed him. It fit with the rest of their plan.

She shot him then poured herself a drink. She and Roy Glass congratulated each other. They toasted each other and kept the gun on me and hardly looked at Edgar lying there dead. They didn't say much until the cop got there. All at once she was worked up hysterical pointing at me, yelling murderer! murderer! Right off a stage.

The cop said yes ma'am and yes sir, he picked up the gun with a rag to make sure my fingerprints stayed on it, he took a look at the old man's body, put his handcuffs on me and took me away. An ambulance came flashing its red light about the time he was throwing me in his police car.

I tried to tell him. I did. Mister, you got it wrong, you don't understand, this is a setup, she killed him, I swear! I saw! He looked at me like I was a disease he might get. Slammed the door in my face. All the way up the road I was begging. I told him about the U-boat and what they were up to. The more I told him the less he believed.

You believe me don't you?

He said Glass has been the coast marshal ever since there was one. Five years. You and I know it's a lie. We saw that other Roy Glass and I wish you were here now to tell them for me. There were two. The first one is the dead man I found.

Help.

I know it's a sin to pray to somebody besides God but I'd rather pray to you if it's okay. I don't figure God has much use for me the way he's been working things. Never meant you to die alone Willie. You know it. And the only one that's got it in for me worse than God is your son my daddy. If I knew you forgive me it wouldn't matter what either one of them said. I'm in terrible trouble I know. I would ask you to put in a word with them or the law if I thought it would help, but I think it's too late.

I know. Stupid. Stupid to play along with these people. Dumb as the old man trusting Nazis on his radio. I don't know Willie when I looked around and saw you dead, it bollixed me good. You made sure the sun came up and like that. Without you it all fell apart. Things went wrong. That cage. A monster came out of the bay. This wild boy, you knew him. Butch. Where was he when I needed him. Then the dead man. The ship blew up. Joseph came back. Now he's gone. I'm in here by myself. After you I haven't got any family at all. All those up in that house are just strangers to me. What is happening *this minute* is the start of my own life.

I went out looking for it, yes I did.

But I am not as stupid as I used to be. I won't be in this jail forever. I hid the proof where they never will find it.

Awful to see that old man. Blood is darker than I ever knew. It ran all down the white of that couch. And his eyes were open. He knew what hit him. I thought about you. Yours were closed. I bet down on the dock it was peaceful. I bet you didn't mind it so much. Who were you waving to, Willie? To me?

They locked me in here and left me alone and I cried for you. You and the old man, now isn't that queer? I thought I was past crying but I'm not I guess. Doing too much of it here lately. I can't help when it comes over me, just a flood of sadness washing me down the gully you cut in the earth when you died.

Hope it's all right where they buried you. Maybe I'll get to see it some time. Wish I could go back to the island. It hurts the way you promised it would.

There are spies here.

Help. I hope you can hear this.

25

MILES ACROSS the flat fields, within sight of the spring at the head of the Magnolia River, the Sylvester house huddled in a grove of sycamore trees. The first light of dawn revealed that it once had been white. A tin-roofed porch faced the street. A blue star hung in the front window. A white sand path ran from the back door to the landing at the slender green river. The shrimp boat was gone.

In her room at the back of the house, Victor's mother stretched her arms. The sheets were old, soft as skin, the sweetness of night cream embedded in the cotton, the musty smell of all those years married. You couldn't wash that smell out.

But her husband's side of the bed was cool. That was how Ellen liked it. She could take all the time in the world waking up. She knew plenty of fishermen's wives who pined for their men out at sea, but she never did. She liked her husband to go off and leave her alone, make money, bring it back to her every so often.

She loved the smell of Daniel when he'd been gone a while, after he'd come in and taken a bath and squeezed lemons in his chest hair and rubbed Old Spice all over himself. She loved him then, for a day or so.

Then it was back to his old way, the surly belligerent way, the shouting, the tears from the kids. The smell of shrimp coming out in his sweat. Ellen would start wishing she were a Catholic so she could have some beads to count the days until he was gone again.

His leaving brought peace to the house. The children minded her.

She rolled on her side to cough. The cigarettes were bad but she had to have them. Everybody's got something that's just going to kill him one day but he's got to keep having it.

Like the children, Joseph then Victor then Roxanne then Margaret Ann then Doolittle then the one who didn't live, and then Peanut. With the birth of each one, she felt a piece breaking off the far end of her life. But she just kept having them.

Suddenly she remembered why she felt happy this morning. Joseph. Her oldest. Her baby. Alive and not killed in the war. His coming brought joy to the house. The children adored him.

She would make a big breakfast. It might take the whole month's egg ration to feed him, but she would do it.

Bluejays made a racket outside. Ellen raised up and sat on the edge of her bed, rubbing her toes. She lit her first cigarette. The cool smoke went off in her mouth like a bell.

E L L E N kept serving his plate, and Joseph kept eating: pancakes, cheese eggs, link sausage, tomatoes, big steaming pools of grits, biscuits, more biscuits. The other children sat in a ring at the table, bedazzled, watching him eat.

"I need pancakes lots worse than you, Roxy," said Joseph, stabbing his fork on his sister's plate. "Getting a little thick in the hips, ain't you? Time you turn fifteen you'll be big as a house."

"Oh shut up," said Roxanne, but she grinned because she knew it wasn't true. "You're not a bit more mature than you used to be."

Margaret Ann kept patting her curls and telling about things her friends had gotten for their birthday, to remind everyone that her eleventh was coming up next week.

Doolittle could barely stay in his chair, laughing and clapping hands at everything Joseph said. "Hey Joseph," he cried, "how many Krauts do you get to shoot?"

"Krauts? Well let's see," said Joseph, drizzling syrup. "About a hundred and fifty a week, I reckon."

"Jiminy!"

"Joseph, don't tell the child that," said their mother at the stove.

"A hunnerd and fifty!"

"Course then there'll come a full moon, see, and you can double that. Cause they can't see at night. See, Krauts don't believe in eating carrots. Once the sun goes down they just kind of stumble around. If you put up a wire you can trip a dozen at once."

All the children laughed. Only the baby seemed oblivious to the newcomer, preferring the green mushy stuff in his plate.

"There's a whole bunch of Krauts over at Elberta," said Margaret Ann.

"No carrots," said Doolittle. "Wow."

"Julia Harttung's from Elberta," Margaret Ann went on. "She said sometimes they take down the American flag when nobody's looking and put up the German flag."

"They don't do it," said Ellen. "Where you children get your stories I don't know."

That stung Margaret Ann. "Julia *said*. Her daddy's a German. She said they did it at the post office and they had some fights with these other men."

"I want you to stop talking to Julia Harttung," said her mother.

"She got a genuine rhinestone bracelet for her birthday this year," said Margaret Ann.

Roxanne carried plates to the sink. "Joe. Where's your guitar?"

"I lost it."

"What do you mean? That was . . . that was your favorite thing."

"I was on a ship that got sunk, Roxy." Joseph might have been talking about someone he didn't know. "I had to leave the guitar."

Their mother put down the dish she was washing. "When?"

"Night before last."

Suddenly Doolittle looked ready to cry. "You lost your guitar?"

Ellen circled the table. "Oh my God, son, why didn't you say? What happened? Where were you? Were—are you hurt? How did it happen?"

"It's okay. Really." Joseph swallowed the last bite of pancake. "I was on my way home anyway. We were right off the fort. I'm okay, Doo. Don't get upset. I didn't get hurt."

Doolittle fled the room.

"Oh, he's been so upset since—since Victor went off, with Willie in here and all," said their mother, untying her apron. "I'll see after him."

"Jesus," said Joseph when she was gone. "What's the matter with everybody? Is it the way I look? They keep running away."

"It's just a lot of things," Roxanne said. "Mama goes a little crazier every day. And Daddy's bad when he's home. He's worse than he was on us. He brought Willie in here and laid her out on this table, right here, Joe. He left her all day. You can't expect to come home and everything's like you left." She glanced over her shoulder as if their father might be standing there.

"I know. I know," Joseph said. "But we'll all be okay."

A knock on the door. They jumped. "Anybody home?"

Joseph carried the baby to the door. It was old Mr. Jesse, from the general merchandise. He had thick glasses and a long curved beak, like a parrot. "Looking for young Sylvester," he panted. "Call on the telephone."

"Hey, Mr. Jesse, that's me. Who's it from?"

"Don't know, I just brought the word." The old man started down the steps. "Hurry on now, I don't like to tie up my line."

Joseph handed the baby to Roxanne, and followed him. Roxanne watched his effortless stride up the street.

She was drying the last plate when her mother squeezed out a rag to wipe the stove and said, "Aren't we lucky having our Joseph back home."

"Where's Victor?" Doolittle's sullen face, in the door.

"Let's count our blessings, Doo. We got Joseph, and Victor's all right, Joseph says, and the Lord looking out after Daddy."

Then Joseph was on the porch, in the house. His hurried step spoke of disaster. Ellen held her soapy hands up to fend off the news.

"Mother, come in here a second." He walked to the back.

She went, steeling her mind.

Joseph sat on her bed. "Vic's in trouble."

Victor?

"What trouble?"

"I don't know. It's all mixed up. He's in the jail at Fairhope."

"The *jail!*" The door curtain billowed into the room. "Joseph, what in the world?"

"I don't know. Those people he was hanging around with—there's somebody dead. They had him talking all kinds of foolishness. I'll go see about him. I might need money. How much have you got?"

"About forty dollars."

"I've got twenty. That won't be enough."

"Joseph. What do they say he did?" She faced him down with her eyes. "Tell me, son."

"Somebody got shot, Mother. They're trying to put it on Vic. He's not sure what the charge is. I don't think they've charged him yet."

"Oh my dear God." Ellen felt for her throat. "Victor."

"He didn't do it. It's all mixed up."

"Your daddy will kill him. This will be the end." She reached into her purse and held out four bills.

"You got any more tucked away?"

"No . . ."

"If somebody else calls here, don't go answer it." Joseph squeezed her hand. "Just stay here. Don't tell the kids. Not even Roxy. I'll tell 'em something."

"I'm going with you." Ellen turned blindly to her closet: what do you wear to a jail?

"You stay here. I bet I can talk to the man," Joseph said. "I'll be back with Vic before you know it. Give your old boy a little credit. Where's the keys to the truck?" He bound her with a hug and whirled from the room.

She heard his boisterous announcement to the children, a call from an old *girl*friend, Joe going on a *date*, hoots of derision. She stared at her eyes in the mirror.

The old pickup started with a grind and a cough.

She forced her hand to pick up the brush. Starting at the front, she moved it through the tangle, stronger strokes now, her hair smoothing out, falling back at her neck. It was long and light brown, hanging thick at her shoulders. She refused to pin it up or curl it or cut it short like other women her age.

A F T E R N O O N shadows crept across the floor. The baby was down in his crib and nearly asleep when the knock came.

Go away!

But it sounded again.

Go away!

Ellen went to the window.

A man she did not know, on her porch.

He looked like the man she imagined would come to tell her Joseph was dead. A dark hat. A gray suit, a gray face in this heat. A briefcase in his hand. Knocking on her door.

She held onto the collar of her dress and walked to the screen. He was such a young man to be bringing news. Not unkind, in the face. Not kind, either—the face of a statue. Beyond him, an automobile glittered dark blue in the sun.

"Is this the Sylvester residence?" His voice was supple, like fur.

"Yes it is."

"You're Mrs. Sylvester?"

She nodded.

"Is your husband home?"

"No. He's off on a trip. Can I help you?"

"You have a son, Joseph Sylvester?"

"Yes I do." Her hands were ice. "May I ask who you are?"

"Yes ma'am." He held out his wallet, a badge. "Special Agent Enos Roberts, from the Mobile office Federal Bureau of Investigation. Is Joseph here?"

"No he's not." Ellen felt a hand closing on her throat. Her own hand.

"May I come in?"

"I have children," said Ellen. "I mean, I have other children. Why don't we talk on the porch." She stepped through the door.

26

VICTOR HUNG up the telephone and rested his head on the wall. "He's coming to get me. He told me to find out how much the bail is."

Officer Wiggins gazed into his ledger. "Bail's set by a judge," he said. "The judge is in Mobile. This a felony charge. You got to be moved."

"How long do I have to stay here?"

"That's up to the judge." The officer led Victor by the arm toward the rear of the jail. He looked like somebody's uncle— a big man with delicate ears, a fleshy neck, stomach hanging over his belt. He was soft and probably slow. He was the same man who'd guarded the door at the dance.

At the back of his jail were four cells exactly alike, lightless cinder-block cubicles with hard cots, cold floors, iron bars. Victor was the only prisoner. "Look," he pleaded, "you got to help me. I never killed anybody. Look at me. She took the gun from Roy Glass and shot the old man herself. This is a frame-up."

Wiggins regarded him at arm's length. "Frame-up," he said. "Would you listen at that."

"I'm serious," Victor said. "I told you, I can prove it to you. He's a spy. If you'll take me down there I'll show you."

Wiggins opened the cell on the right. "Go on in."

"Mister, you got to listen to me!"

The big ponderous head nodded up and then down. "*I* ain't got to do nothing, but *you* got to get back in your cell."

Wiggins slammed the door, shot the bolt. He carried a tin percolator to a hot plate beside the sink.

"I got proof," Victor said.

The officer spooned the last of the coffee into the basket, and rattled the bag. "Call me when this thing starts to steam." He started up the hall. "I got some paperwork."

"Why won't you believe me?" cried Victor. "You think I made all this *up*?"

The telephone rang. Wiggins stopped. "Son, I have heard a lot of folks say how they didn't do whatever it was they done," he said, "but yours is the wildest one yet." He nodded away up the hall.

Victor slammed his fists against the bars. He kicked the bars with his feet. He slammed his whole body into the bars. This was jail. The real thing. Not an animal cage in a boathouse, but a cage built to hold a strong man.

It made him want to break out and commit some real crime. Find the ones who sent him here. Let them see how it feels behind bars.

He sank to the floor.

He wondered if Wiggins was in on it too. Maybe it was impossible that the whole world was scheming to help deliver spies to the shores of Mobile Bay, but then why did the signs all point that way? Roy Glass—oh yes, a smart man. Persuasive. He'd fooled Edgar Gilliam, all right; probably hadn't been too tough to convince this baggy policeman he was some kind of Secret Agent Undercover U.S.A.

Victor sat on the floor by the cot, reliving the mute, childlike shock on the old man's face when he died. Why didn't they kill Victor while they were at it? Probably they couldn't resist the neatness of the stroke: old Mister Moneybags and his guilty conscience out of their way, the nosy young troublemaker behind bars, charged with his murder.

A curl of steam from the pot. "Your coffee's boiling!"

Wiggins returned.

"Look, call the Coast Guard," Victor begged. "Ask about a tanker that was torpedoed night before last. In the Gulf. The *Eugenia Rae*. I was out there. I saw the U-boat that sunk it. I heard the old man *talking* to it."

Pouring coffee into a stained white mug, Wiggins leaned on the sink and said nothing.

"Well, let me call 'em, then. Come on, mister. You got nothing to lose."

"You had your telephone call. You get another one tomorrow."

"That's too late! Don't you understand?" Victor heard the shrill in his voice. "We've got to stop them. I'm not playing! Those are real Nazis out there!"

"You simmer down." Wiggins eyed him, curious. "I'd think you'd had about enough trouble, your age, mixed up with a murder, without coming up with some wolf story. What is it, you want to be in the newspapers? Let me give you a piece of advice. The minute you start spilling all this to the judge, he's gonna put you away for life. Just on the principle of it."

"Not when I prove it," said Victor.

"I work nights for Mr. Glass, at the Hotel," said the policeman. "If he was up to any kind of—funny business, don't you think I'd seen it?"

Victor gripped the bars. He sensed a chink: keep the pressure on. "He's real smooth. Every lie is better than the last one. Even Edgar didn't know everything they were up to, till right at the end, and she was his wife! The minute he found out, he threatened to blow the whistle on them. So she killed him!"

Wiggins shook his head. "It don't wash." He moved up the hall.

Another bell, the front door. Victor mashed his face between the last bars to see who it was—

Joseph, sauntering down the corridor behind the policeman. "I swear, Vic," he boomed, "get a little drunk and you land in jail."

"Joseph, I'm sure glad that's you."

"You're damn right it's me. I hope you're happy you made me miss dinner." He grinned at Wiggins. "I'm just home on leave from overseas and I can't get enough of my mama's cooking."

The officer did not acknowledge this surge of amiability. He lifted the key ring from its nail on the wall.

Victor's heart jumped. "I'm getting out?"

"No, I'm getting in." Joseph lost his grin. "For ten minutes. The officer tells me they won't let you go till a judge has a look at you."

Wiggins pulled on the heavy door. Joseph stepped in and flung an arm around Victor's shoulder. He smelled like fresh air. "Don't worry. We'll figure out something."

The door clanged shut.

"Man, they trapped me," said Victor. "I walked right into it. I knew that Roy Glass was up to something, but I never figured on Madame. I found out a whole bunch about them."

Victor told. Joseph listened. "They don't want me around. They killed him and made sure it was my fingerprints on the gun."

Joseph whistled. "Damn. I told you. Those people are dangerous."

"Every time somebody turns up dead I get blamed," Victor said.

Wiggins came to the bars. "Son, you said your name was Joseph Sylvester?"

Joseph squinted out at him. "That's right."

"That your truck outside?"

"My dad's. What's the problem?"

"Looks like neither one of you boys going much of anywhere," said the officer. "I got a call. Seems there's a federal guy on the lookout for you."

Joseph went white. "For me?"

"Yep. Called from somewhere down in the county and put out a want for that truck. He ain't gonna believe you just come walking in my front door." Wiggins chuckled. "This is his lucky day."

"Listen, buddy, there's been a mistake—"

"That's what your brother said, too." Wiggins poured hot coffee. "If we just kept the ones who thought they belonged here, we'd go out of business. I'll come back and sign you in soon as I call that man back." He flipped out the light and lumbered away.

Every time Victor thought he had seen the worst they could do, a new tentacle reached out and wrapped around someone. "Joe. That's got to be Glass. He was worried because Edgar let you go home. Soon as he got me taken care of, he went out after you."

"Yeah, it could be," said Joseph, sinking to one end of the cot. The blood had drained from his face.

"Is Mama all right? Did you tell her?"

"I couldn't help it. I thought I'd need money. Man, it's dark in here."

"What did she say?"

Joseph looked at his knees. "She didn't say anything. She's worried for you."

"We got to get out and do something." Victor paced the cell. "If Glass has been down to our house . . . I knew it. God, am I stupid. I told him right where we lived, everything."

Joseph shook his head. "It doesn't matter," he said. "I think this one came looking for me."

"Well, he already knows where *I* am."

"Victor."

"What?" Victor stopped pacing, and turned. A mask had fallen away from Joseph's face. He had worn it well—cheer and bravado almost from the moment he came over the rail of the *Constance*—but it slipped in that instant, and he did not try to put it back in place. A hard, resigned sadness in his eyes, fierce shame. He looked everywhere but at Victor.

"This isn't your man," he said. "This is somebody else. I've been waiting for him." Joseph tucked his foot under him on the cot. He was nerveless, somehow vacant, a husk.

"Joe . . . ?"

"That torpedo was aimed straight at me," he said. "I knew it. I was sitting there with my coffee and it blew and I said well, they've got you. You can't get away from them. Not even here."

"I don't understand." Victor eased down to the other cot. He had wondered what difference the Army had made in his brother, what glamorous stories of war he'd brought home. Never dreamed they'd be locked in jail, or that Joseph would have this sick look on his face, the lost voice of a stranger, when he set in to tell.

"It's war," Joseph said. "It's a war. You don't even have to be fighting. They'll get you anyway. Look at you, Vic. They got you good and clean. And me too. Hook line and sinker."

"But Joseph, you got out of that ship. You're okay. These people are spies. You and me are just part of their plan."

Joseph's eyes glimmered. "Just hold onto your plans for a minute, brother. That man is the real thing. He's looking for me. I'm a criminal now, Victor. I'm a deserter. I left the Army and left England and got on a boat and came home. There. I said it. There it is. Are you satisfied now?"

Victor blinked.

"I told you to let me go home in peace, but you had to get yourself thrown in jail." Joseph slammed his fist on the wall. "And me with you."

Victor turned all the way around on the cot. "You mean you—you just left?"

"That's right. You got it. I deserted. Say it, Vic. Hell, you can't even say it. You think you're in trouble, but you didn't *do* anything. You'll get out. I'm guilty as hell." The sadness disappeared in the flash of his eyes. "All I did was take off. But there's a war on, you know, and that's what they call a capital offense, Victor, how's that for laughs? You know what that means, don't you? That means they shoot you. I'm going to get shot. And then it means you and the rest of them, you won't be able to go to Moore's Store, even, because everybody will know. It'll be in the papers. They love it. There's nothing worse than a deserter. They'll turn me into a bad example."

Victor's horror overflowed. "Joseph, how could you do that? You just took off? What were you thinking about?"

"I thought you'd try and understand," said Joseph. "I'll tell you what's funny, I was looking at this book about great criminals of the past, you know, England. And this fellow said one thing they all had in common, they didn't know they were criminals until they'd already done their first crime. Nobody sets out to do something wrong. They do it by accident once and find out how easy it is. Sometimes it's the first thing they've ever done right." Joseph pounded his fist on his knee. "That's how it was for me, Vic. I did it. I left. I'm glad I did. It was easy. It felt good. I knew what they'd do to me if I got caught. That just made me run harder."

So this was the answer—the distance he kept from the other survivors of the *Eugenia Rae*; the nervous glances over his shoulder; something he said about the war, how it wasn't like in a letter. . . . "But your letters, Joe! You never said you wanted to come home."

"The letters were lies, Victor. Lies. I wasn't even over there when I wrote most of them. I been working tankers for six months in the Gulf. Wilbur forwarded all your letters to me. I wrote letters back and sent 'em to him. He ran 'em through the censor and mailed 'em."

"Wilbur?"

"Dumb old cousin Wilbur. Believe it or not. He's got this great job in London. Headquarters. Records Division. He can get anything. He helped me."

All those fragrant V-mail pages folded, refolded, all the hours Victor spent filling in the censor's marks with his imagination . . . all lies!

"I told him I had to come home and see Willie, sick as she was," Joseph went on, as if, now he'd started, he wanted to get rid of it all in a rush. "I wanted a discharge but the best he could do was a three-week pass, and then the fool went and used my real name. Didn't notify my unit. They put out an AWOL. By the time he figured out I wasn't coming back, he was up to his neck in it. He played along. He faked up some papers to calm down my sergeant."

Too much to grasp all at once. Sure, Victor had seen pictures of deserters in the *Register*, right there alongside Axis Mary and

Tokyo Rose. How could Joseph be one of those white-faced, terrified boys? What could have happened to him?

"Wilbur must have sprung a leak," he was saying. "All the FBI offices have my picture. They got close in Brownsville three weeks ago. I been expecting them ever since. I just—I just thought I'd get to stay home a little longer—"

And now Victor saw tears streaming down his brother's face. His expression was frozen like stone, but the tears were streaming and the wall was beginning to crack. "Talk, Vic, say something," he said, sucking in breath.

Victor wished they were little boys again, so he could sit down and put his arms around Joseph, but they weren't little boys and he could not do that. So he said, "I don't know what to say. I can't get my mind around it. I thought you were so brave. I wanted to be just like you."

"I'm sorry." Joseph wiped his eyes with his sleeve. "I'm sorry. I can't be your hero. I'm not a hero."

"Oh, stop feeling sorry for yourself!" Victor cried. "You're so full of talk about how good it felt and how glad you are, but it's killing you. I never seen you like this. Why'd you do it? Why'd you leave? Were you chicken? Is that it?"

"Keep it down back there," came the shout.

Not long now until night. Shadows stretched from the front of the jail all the way down the hall, just touching the bars.

"There was something I couldn't take," Joseph said.

"I don't care what it is. I don't care. Just tell me." Never mind that they were not boys anymore, that Joseph was older . . . Victor sat on the cot beside his brother, he put an arm around his brother's shoulder. Some of his own loneliness went away then, some of the pain he had prayed to Willie about.

Joseph shrugged out from under his arm and pulled his other foot under him. "It started out good," he said. "I was the best. The most pushups. The fastest four-forty. They told you when to get up in the morning, what to wear, when to pee, when to pick your nose, and then at the end of the day they kicked your butt and sent you to bed. Just like home." His smile was bleak, but he went on as if he had practiced this story to himself a hundred times.

"I made some good buddies. I guess that was the best part. The only good part. This one fellow Darden, from South Carolina. Double-A screwup all the way. Great guy."

"You talked some about him." Victor leaned against the wall, his feet off the end of the cot. "Didn't he drive a jeep through the officers' club?"

"A motorcycle," said Joseph. "Valentine Dance for the officers' wives. Darden went through wearing some whore's red silk slip on his head. He got three weeks in stir. He was crazy. Him and me just looked out for each other right from the start. Fellow members of the smartass brigade. The drill sergeant hated us but he loved us. He said we were the worst pair of screwups since Leopold and Loeb. He must have loved us or hated us one, cause at the end of it he made sure we both got the same orders, same squadron, both of us Airborne. Howellton Army Base. England."

"Airborne is parachutes?" said Victor.

"Right."

"They always cut that out of your letters."

"They start you jumping off a box about this high"—Joseph held out his hand—"and then move you up two steps, and up, and before you know it you're flinging yourself off a tower. All you got is this big rubber band around your middle to keep you from busting your brains on the ground."

"But you did it . . ."

"There ain't that much to it. You and me used to jump off that tree at the spring, just as high, and we didn't have a rubber band. Darden was ticklish about it. He didn't come along near as fast as me. But he got to where he could do fine as long as he shut his eyes when he jumped. Don't ask me. It seems like it'd be scarier. Finally they took us up in a plane, and taught us static line. You got this belt around you that hooks on a rail. When you jump, the line jerks your chute open, so you don't have to count or do any of that. You keep your eye on these light bulbs by the door. One red and one green. The red one comes on at takeoff and stays on, so everybody looks red. Red and scared.

"But brother, the minute that green one comes on they slide that door open and run you out of it, go go go, fast as the jump master can holler. And you better carry your ass out that door, cause there's somebody right behind you and five more behind him. If you so much as stop to take a second look, that jump master will scream in your ear and sling you out the door. It's pretty goddamn hard on the nerves, let me tell you. Once you get up in that plane, it's the real item."

Victor hardly dared breathe. "It sounds bad."

"The day before Thanksgiving. Our seventh jump. Lucky seven. If you hit within a quarter-mile of the target, you'd go active duty. If you missed, you'd go back and start over. They took us way up there, circled around to give us a good look at the target. Darden was standing ahead of me. I could smell his Juicy Fruit . . ." Joseph's eyes clouded over. "He was all red from the light and he had this big grin on his face. That light went to green and the door opened and it was windy as hell, the jump master yelling go! and he went and I went. The line unrolled from my pack, just like it was sposed to, then it jerks you up hard but when I looked down the line was gone. Nothing there. Just the end of it, flapping in the breeze."

"Jesus," said Victor.

"That's right. That's what I said. Jesus H. Christ. I died, Vic. I died right then. Forty times that first second. I could see myself dying a hundred thousand times before I ever hit the ground. It wasn't like flying at all. It was falling. Like a rock. I fell just a second before I hit something. A parachute. Got tangled up in the ropes and then I grabbed hold of some legs and it was Darden." Joseph drew up his knees and hugged them. "My buddy. I hung on. That was it. I hung on. And here's what I can't figure out. For the love of God, Vic, I can't figure it out. His chute was open. I didn't hurt it a bit coming through. But he, he started kicking me. Hard. Right here. Hard as he could. He thought we would both die if I hung on. He had to save himself and he tried to kill me to do it. He tried his best. I fought him. He beat on my head with his fist. I kept yelling his name and my name, telling him we'd be okay, quit kicking. But he never did. All the way to the ground."

"How the hell did you ever hold on?" Victor said.

"Believe me. I wasn't about to let go." Joseph's voice was the stranger's again: empty, afflicted.

"Yeah. I guess not."

"He broke these three ribs with his boot. We landed all messed up, top of each other. He got up and took off running. I'd had the wind knocked out. I just laid there and thought, you're alive . . . and I thought, your best friend tried to kill you. This is the war, this is what you have got yourself into. This is what you are here for. To get killed."

"But you didn't get killed," said Victor.

"That's the hell of it, Vic. I got real good and close, but I didn't get it. Doesn't that say something to you?"

"Like what? Like you're lucky?"

"Yeah, that's what I thought there at first, how goddamn lucky I was. Hell, Darden was only looking out for himself. That's what they teach you. It's in the handbook. The life of a soldier is his most important weapon. Without that weapon, a soldier cannot fight.

"But then I was laying on this stretcher while this medic poked me all over, and I got to thinking about Darden's face. When he tried to kick me off him. That big shiny grin he had, just before we jumped. See I thought, maybe he didn't want you to go active, maybe he hates you because you're ahead of him. Maybe he put a little nick in your line."

"You mean—you think he tried to kill you? Before you went up?" This was not like any war story Victor had ever read. He had read *The Army Boys on German Soil*, but all the Army Boys were on the same side. "Why didn't you tell somebody? He was your friend and he tried to kill you twice?"

"You don't know who's your friend." Joseph turned his face to the wall. "I think maybe it did something to me. When my chute wasn't there and I died. That's about how alone you can be, Vic. Knowing out of everybody in the whole goddamned world, it's your turn to die. I don't know. Maybe it was that line's turn to break. I thought maybe Darden, or somebody else in the squad. Or somebody in the parachute plant. Or somebody in the bushes. But all of a sudden I felt *picked out*.

"I went back to my squadron. They'd all heard some kind of a story about it. When I came in they looked at me. Patted my back and said was I okay. That was the last any of them wanted to know. Darden never spoke to me. I started looking at everything . . . different. I got real careful. I didn't know who the enemy was. My sergeant, the Germans, the guys. Darden. Too many to count. I didn't want to jump. I didn't want to pick up a gun. I wasn't any good anymore."

"What did you do?" Victor said.

"The list went up. Darden got active duty. I got sent back to jump off the box. And that's when I made up my mind, brother. I'd been picked out and come within that close of it. That was a signal. Take off. Get out of here while you can. Right then I didn't care how. I just knew I had to come home."

Joseph sat breathing in, breathing out, his chin on his knee. "Here I am. They got me. And that's why they're gonna shoot me," he said. "Because I came home."

Victor had spent his whole life wanting to be Joseph, and suddenly Joseph was no one to be. "We can't let them take you," he said. "We can get out of here."

"They'll just find me again."

"We can get *out* of here!" Victor grabbed his brother's shoulders and shook him, hard. "You can't give up. There's enemies here too. You can't walk away and not fight!"

"Watch me, Victor." Joseph settled back on the cot. "You just watch."

27

T H E Y   H E A R D the bell out front, Wiggins harrumphing at someone. They traded a look. "It sounds like her," Joseph said.

"Oh God. It is."

Officer Wiggins led their mother down the corridor.

The light bulb swung as she passed. Victor had the ridiculous idea that she would be locked in with them too.

"Is this where they are?" She sounded mad.

"Here, Mama," said Victor.

"I can't see them. Haven't you got a light back here?"

"There's a war on," said Wiggins, but he flipped the switch.

The collar on her blue dress stood up all around. Her hair was blown to a frazzle. "I can't believe you would keep human beings in the dark like that. Joseph? Are you boys all right? Has this man hurt you?"

"We're all right," Joseph said. "I'm sorry you had to come all this way."

"Mama, how in the world did you get here?"

"In the whaler. I like to have drowned. I hope you both are proud."

They sat on their side of the bars, looking down.

"Well?" She tapped her toe. "What am I supposed to do?"

Officer Wiggins retreated.

"What do you think your father will say when he hears about this? He'll be home any time." Her voice now a shiver, now brimming with anger. "What will he say?"

"It won't make any difference," said Joseph.

"A man came to my house, Joseph Sylvester. He stood on my very porch. He said . . . he said you were—a deserter." She came to the bars. "Tell me what he means."

"He's right. I am. I left my unit in December. I've been working on tankers." Joseph grabbed the bars, his eyes shining. "Mother. I knew it would hurt you. That's why I lied."

"Oh, I don't want to know," she said. "All the way here I just knew you would say it wasn't true."

"But Mama—"

"Victor, hush. I'll hear from you in a minute."

"He doesn't have to speak for me," said Joseph. "I'm not afraid of the truth. I left because if I'd stayed, they'd have killed me. I knew it. Just as sure as you're standing there. I'm sorry about the war but there isn't anything about it that is worth getting killed over."

A little tremor seized her. She leaned on the bars to control it. "I was scared for you, too," she said. "I had the most awful dreams. I kept praying and praying they would send you home."

"They didn't. I came home myself."

"You came home to your mama. . . . They ought not be able to make a law against that. They won't take you back, will they?"

"They'll put me in prison," said Joseph. "It's a crime, what I did."

Victor noticed he spared the further details. "Joe, what if you said you got hurt," he said, "you got hurt and you didn't know what you were doing?"

"Victor, for God's sake, the idea," their mother snapped. "How many wrongs do you have to pile up to make a right? Don't you see that's how you wind up in jail, telling lies and getting into trouble?"

"It's not like you think."

"Oh? What is it like? Why don't you take a turn?"

Victor saw her mind was set, but he stumbled ahead anyway. "I met these people. I found out some things they didn't want me to know."

"What people? What things? What did he say about this man getting shot?"

Victor felt the blood in his face. "There were two, Mama. One I found down in the swamp. The other was an old man I knew. I saw them kill him. They put the blame on me."

"What are you talking about? Son, what on earth have you gotten yourself into?" She tried to touch his hand through the bars, but he pulled away.

"A lot happened, Mother," he said. "I couldn't stay down at Willie's. I couldn't come home. Daddy wanted to kill me. I saw something. I can't explain it all yet. But I had to find out what it was."

Ellen folded her collar down. She started to speak, but emotion overcame her, and she turned away.

"Mother, you ought to go home," said Joseph.

"Can't I just pay that man some money and you come on with me?"

"We tried." Joseph handed the bills and keys through the bars. "Here. Take the truck. When Daddy gets home, tell him to call to see if we're still in here. If we are, he better call that lawyer in Daphne."

"I can't tell him," she said. They could not see her face. "I won't. We'll work this all out and he won't have to know."

Victor moved closer. "Mama, it'll be all right."

She dug into her battered old purse for her Zippo and a cigarette. She inhaled a chestful of smoke, let it sharply out. "You don't know what it does to me to see the two of you. I always had such a hope for you boys. I won't be able to hold my head up."

"Yes you will," said Victor. "We'll get out, and we'll prove it to you."

"Did that man give you something to eat?"

"Not yet."

"It would be just like Fairhope to try and starve you to death."

Victor couldn't help it; he smiled, and that made her as angry as when she came in. "Don't you smile at me, boy. I don't want to see you smiling while I'm standing here."

"Mama, I'm not your little boy anymore."

"No, you're not. Look at you. You're sure not the boy I raised." She backed away, to the door. "I'm going home. I'll be back."

Her heels clicked up the hall. She stopped for a word with Officer Wiggins, and then she was gone. A layer of blue smoke floated on the air.

The silence held until Joseph broke it. "Boy. She was burned."

"Yeah," said Victor.

"Victor?"

"Yeah?"

"You're right," said Joseph. "We got to get out of here."

"Now you're talking. What's he doing up there?"

Joseph strained to the corner of the cell. "There's somebody else with him. Another cop. A younger guy."

"Is it night out there yet?"

"Just about."

"I don't know," Victor said. "It seems like everything I ever tried to do went wrong."

"Oh, don't listen to her," said his brother. "She's just burned and you need to get your mind off it."

Victor said, "I just wish I hadn't seen that look on her face."

"Yeah I know."

And they sat, remembering it.

28

THE PIER at Fairhope was a plank promenade running straight out from the foot of Bay Street for two hundred yards over shallow water—waiting, at all hours, for anyone who cared to pick out a path across the uneven boards, being mindful of fishhooks and invisible gaps which could cause you to fall or spill your bait. On hot nights like this, there was always somebody. People fled their kitchens and rooms to come sit in the dark over the bay, where a breeze might get at them and where, if they dangled a chicken drumstick at the end of a string, they might catch a blue crab for the gumbo.

On this night there were plenty of sweltering people, couples

out kissing, a sprinkling of serious fishermen, a whole crowd
hurling cast nets off the end, children rampant underfoot. The
moon was past full. The weight of the air seemed to flatten the
water.

A feeble glimmer reflected on low clouds over the city of
Mobile. To the south, a curve of darkness showed the sweep of
the shore to the Hotel, interrupted by the piers and pier houses
of the rich summer homes.

From one of the smaller piers arose a faint cry: *Jubilee!*

A man casting his net heard the cry in mid-throw and let
go too soon. The net hung on a nail. He swore, looking out
to the south.

Jubilee!

The Negroes at the end of the pier stopped talking first.

Some men told the children to stand still and hush.

One by one, down the pier, people turned, not quite sure
what they'd heard or where it came from or whether they'd
heard anything.

Jubileeeeee!

A wondering buzz advanced toward the shore. Everyone knew
what the word meant, even children so young they had only
heard stories. It meant all the fish you could gather from the
shallow water, where they had come to lie still for your hand
or your net. It meant a gift straight from God, and everyone
had been waiting for it. Soon they all were peering down from
the pier, muttering:

Did you hear that?

Sure as hell did

I don't see any fish

What was that?

Jubileeeee!

Well damn!

I hadn't caught nothing all night

Did he say jubilee?

Come on Mavis, get yo things together

Hadn't had one since thirty-six

Yeah, but it's just that kind of a night—

Tackle boxes slammed shut. Good bait was reeled up from the water. Couples left off kissing and looked around at the commotion.

One man broke into a run, yelling, "Jubilee! Jubilee!"

Where?

Down yonder

Has anybody seen

South of town! By the Hotel!

Jubilee!

Two automobiles started at once and screeched away from the pier. Some of the serious fishermen carried lanterns down to the water and went wading in, probing the shallows with dip nets. One came up with two middling flounder on his first try, and let out a shout that carried new hope to the end of the pier.

People hurried along the sand. More cars revved to life. Drivers flipped on headlights and raced off, forgetting the rules of the blackout in their haste to roll down windows, honk horns, and shout "Jubilee!"

Word spread up the hill, from porch to porch among the houses on the bluff. Telephones rang. Supper came to a halt. Garage doors flew open. Pickup trucks coughed, started.

Soon the little streets were jammed with vehicles, people running and laughing and calling to neighbors: a whole town leaving its supper to head down for the water.

The one who first raised the cry passed among them, unnoticed, walking uphill against the flow.

At the head of Bay Street he climbed up on a white marble obelisk set in a little park, a monument to something; it was too dark to read. From this bluff he had the best view of the crowd spreading south from the pier, the pinpoints of lanterns among them, excited shouting, cars appearing from nowhere all at once.

A long, mournful siren arose in the middle of town.

At the front of the jail, Officer Wiggins turned up an ear. "What was that?"

"Fire horn," said the younger policeman.

Wiggins went to the door. "Probly Corcoran messing with the wires again, but maybe one of us better run see." He folded his arms. "Sure a lot of traffic for a Wednesday."

"I'll go," the other man said. "You keep an eye on our vistors. I'll be back in a minute."

The horn sounded again.

The young man slid into the patrol car and drove away. Wiggins stayed in the door, watching the confusion of automobiles.

"He's outside," Joseph whispered in the dark. "Look on that nail."

"We can't reach 'em . . ."

Wiggins came hustling down the hall, breathing hard. He went to a green metal cabinet and began rooting around in back. A long-handled net came out, then a shorter one, then a lantern and three work gloves.

Victor linked his fingers through the bars. "What's going on?"

The officer's face flushed as he stooped to gather the nets in his arms. "Young fellow says it's jubilee! First one since I don't know when. Everybody's down there already!"

Victor opened his mouth to answer, but he felt Joseph's touch on his knee, a caution.

"Maybe you can get us some fresh fish for supper," said Joseph.

"We'll see. Barnes'll be right back." Wiggins snapped out the light and carried his things to the front, out into the street.

"What a stroke," Joseph said. "Look around. Do you see a broom or something?"

"Shh. He's coming back in."

Headlights played through the front window, drifted across the walls. Someone, outlined in the door glass, peering inside.

The door floated open.

"Sandy?"

"Butch! Back here! Hey, man, hurry!"

Butch crept down the hall.

"It's okay, he's gone! Damn, this is great! Are we ever glad to see you!"

"Dark in here. Who's in there with you?"

"My brother Joe. Hurry, man, the keys are right there on that nail."

Butch tried them one at a time, fumbling. Victor urged him on from inside. At last a key clicked.

"That's it. Pull!"

The door scuffed across the cement. They rushed to the front of the jail.

Joseph stopped. "Did they leave their guns?"

"Never mind," Victor said. "Let's get going."

"No. Wait." Joseph searched through desk drawers and came out with a shiny chrome pistol the size of his hand.

"Joseph, come on. They'll be back!"

"And they'll come after us." Joseph filled his pocket with bullets and moved to the door. "Remember what the Boy Scouts say. Is anybody on the street?"

"Hell yes, everbody," said Butch, squinting through the glass.

"Let's go anyway." Joseph tucked the gun in his belt.

They stepped out. A pickup truck sped past. The glare from

the hardware store revealed a stream of people flowing downhill, to the bay.

"Thought I might have to cut you out, Sandy." Butch flexed a hacksaw blade between his fingers, then he tucked one end in his shoe and the other up his pants leg. His fancy dance clothes looked ravaged, as if he had spent the night fighting through thorns. The jacket was gone. One sleeve of his shirt was ripped and he had only two buttons left.

Joseph locked the door from inside. "Confuse the old guy for a minute, anyway."

"How come both you guys were in there?" said Butch.

"Long story," Joseph said. "We better get off this street."

They turned down a dark lane. "I can't believe it," Victor marveled. "Of all the luck. A jubilee."

Butch grinned. "Pretty damn swell, huh? We better step lively. It ain't gonna last long."

"How do you know? I bet they'll be out there picking up stuff all night."

Butch's grin widened out. "It's somethin what you can get folks to do just by puttin an idea in their heads."

Victor stopped. "Hey, what did you do, anyway?"

Butch cackled, danced ahead up the lane. "I got you out once and I seen you needed getting out again," he said. "I been in that jail a few times myself. I knew that old cop ain't got but about half sense. I thought now, what's one thing a fat old bastard can't resist. Food. So I went down on one of them piers and set up yelling jubilee, and before you know it the whole place was runnin wild. Like a bunch of damn ants."

"You did that? By yourself?!" Victor caught up with him.

"These folks may catch 'em a fish or two, many of them as there is, but that'll be about it," said Butch.

Victor grabbed his hand. "A fake jubilee, man, that's crazy! That's great!"

"It's the damnedest thing I ever heard," Joseph said. "Vic, I'm beginning to see what you see in this guy."

"And they went for it, too!" Victor said. "Butch, you should have seen that cop huffing and puffing. What took you so long?"

"Well, I tell you, I got distracted. Come to find out I had some new fish to fry."

"Fish?" Victor said. "Oh no, I know, don't tell me."

"You seen her. You the one known her name from the radio. Dinah. I swear to you, Sandy, that's one hell of a lot of woman to fit into such a little bitty dress."

"I saw y'all hitting it off," Victor said. "You mean she—she really liked you?"

"You bet," said Butch, strutting on with his thumb in his chest. "Gal gets lonesome on the road, you know, night after night, never sleeping in the same place twice. Lord have mercy!" He threw back his head and howled.

"Keep it down," Joseph said, with a glance down the street. "You wanna put us back in jail?"

"Relax, brother man, I just got through getting you out."

Joseph waved them through a weedy vacant lot. Victor lagged back to tell Butch the details of his mission to Glass's room, the treasure trove stashed under the bandstand, the confusion while Edgar came out of his sleep, the subtle closing jaws of the trap. "Then she said neither one of us was gonna get in their way, and she picked up the gun and she shot him."

"Yeah, I saw him dead," said Butch. "Time I got out of that bus, they was loadin him on a hospital truck. Bunch of folks watching. I looked around for Glass or the old dame, but I didn't see neither one. Figured it had to be them. They both got snaky eyes. That old fool. I told you he didn't know everything."

Joseph stopped. "Vic, where do you suppose Ellen put in with the whaler?"

"Beats me. By the pier, maybe?"

"Big crowd down there. We might run into our pal the Keystone Kop," said Joseph.

"We can cut over and walk where there's no traffic," said Victor. "Joseph. Wait up a second. Listen to me. You're free. You're out. You should go. I can get by okay. Butch'll help me. Take the whaler and get to Mobile. That man's coming for you. You can get away."

"Yeah, I know," said Joseph. "Run and keep running."

"Never mind what I said. They'll put you in prison. They'll . . ." He couldn't say it.

Joseph smiled. "Let 'em try. I only deserted the one time, Vic. I ain't deserting you now."

"That's stupid. They'll catch you."

Joseph said, "If I leave you to chase after that submarine on your own, you'll screw it up."

"But—"

"They ain't gonna catch me," Joseph said, striding ahead. "That's the beauty part. I got an idea."

Victor trotted to keep up. "What is it?"

"I'm in this thing with you," said Joseph. "If what you say is right, that thing's coming back. We can get the Coast Guard in on it. All we need is a boat."

Victor fell in step down the vine-tangled gully. "Wait. Butch said there was nobody on Edgar's boat, didn't you?"

"Righto."

"That might do it," said Joseph, almost to himself. "If I handed the Coast Guard a goddamn U-boat, that might do it. The Army'd never have the nerve to shoot me after something like that."

Butch laughed. "Yeah! I heard that!"

Victor fought down a little wave of resentment: suddenly the monster was no longer his: it was Joseph's way out of a scrape—but how silly. Victor needed all the help he could get. The danger was real. This was more than a scrape. Joseph was his brother.

"How do we steal the boat?" he said.

"Get on it, start it up," Joseph said. "Drive it off."

"But where to?"

"First we'll take a look at that map of yours," Joseph said. "Then we'll see. We can't just go to somebody with this crazy story . . . we need to know what they're up to." Victor felt an arm around his neck. He let himself be pulled in. "It'll be all right, Vic. Old Joe's here now. We'll *catch* the damn thing."

"They couldn't have come and gone last night," Victor said. "Glass was too busy putting me in jail, and she was too busy killing Edgar."

"Ah-oh," said Butch. "Looka here."

Five or six fishermen advanced up the long hill, waving their nets, arguing. Their empty ice chests scudded over the pavement.

Well who the hell blew the fire horn?

Don't look at me!

Got soaking wet and for what

Who told you it was jubilee?

I just heard

Who started it?

Probly some kids

"You know," Butch said when they'd passed, "I got to hand it to myself. This is about the best thing anybody ever did."

"Lucky we're the only ones who know it was you," Joseph said.

"Did you see the look on their face?" Butch laughed and dashed up to the head of the street for another survey of his havoc, spread out below.

"That's twice now he got me out of jail," Victor said.

"He's noisy, but he is handy to have around," his brother agreed.

Scores of the disappointed wandered away from the water, shaking their heads. The metallic aroma of rain arrived on the breeze. The tide washed up high, to the edge of the beach. Whitecaps shattered the dark glass of the bay.

"Look, Joe, there it is." The whaler, tied to a stubby dock down the beach from the municipal pier.

Victor set out running and reached it first. "The tide's gone down since she tied it," he called. "There's water in the stern."

Butch helped him dump it.

"Let me drive," Joseph said. "It's been a long time since I drove a boat."

Victor stood in the surf, holding to the whaler's transom, staring out at the waves. "Storm coming."

Butch climbed into the bow.

Victor said, "The other times, I could feel it. I'm not sure yet. I think it's still out there. I bet they'll try to bring it in if there's a storm."

"If they haven't already," said Joseph. "They might be finished and gone."

"No," Victor said, climbing in. "Don't ask me how, but I know. They're not done with us yet."

29

A L L   A L O N G the horizon to the west, veins of blue lightning shot through a wall of clouds. The storm was too far away
to make thunder, but the wind and bursts of lightning were
already here. The bay was aroused, tossing, white-capping, now
a vast dark sea, now an electric tableau of shore and pier house
and piers reaching out to the whaler as it struggled through a
frozen wave. Joseph cut at an angle to the swell. The little boat
lurched and bobbed up.

Butch clung to the crosspiece, taking waves in the face. He
screeched when the biggest ones hit. Victor crouched behind
him, holding on with both hands, remembering times he had
been sick at sea, then trying to unremember.

A flash lit the great point, the Hotel. Victor shivered all
over. Joseph labored to keep the tiller headed into the waves.
The wind wanted to push them back the way they came, as if
it knew something.

"You gonna take her right in the boat basin?" hollered Butch.
"Those sons of bitches might be waitin for us. Maybe we oughta
sneak in some way!"

"Just what I'm thinking," Joseph yelled back. He swung the
boat toward the woods on the north flank of the point. The
bow lifted and rode on the long rolling waves.

Victor was glad to have help. He knew better this time than
to go blundering in alone, without stopping to think, look,

make plans. If the three of them got their heads turned the same way, they might just be able to outsmart whoever needed outsmarting.

One great swell took them up, swept them almost to shore, dissolved hissing. The propeller dug into mud. Joseph cut the motor.

Victor leaped into the water with the bowline, dragged the boat toward trees overhanging the shore.

Joseph ducked. Butch put his foot on the prow like Washington crossing the river, and went into the trees standing up.

Victor scrambled up to tie the line around an oak stump. They emerged from the trees to a grassy field that seemed to stretch for miles. The wind washed the trees at its edge.

"This is one hell of a pasture," said Butch.

"It's a golf course," said Victor.

"A what?"

"For playing golf. Never mind. Look there."

The roof of the Hotel cut a clean line above the trees. They walked the border of the fairway.

"Sandy, you better not show your face around here," said Butch. "They'll be looking for you."

Joseph waved his hand. "Shh. Keep down."

They hunched in a grove of low trees. Victor craned ahead: a thicket of masts. The yacht basin looked peaceful as Pearl Harbor on Saturday night—sleek boats lined up flank to flank, the curve of the breakwater, low glowing lights. In the last slip before the channel, the *Constance*'s flying bridge towered over the others.

"It's still here," Victor breathed.

"No lights on board," Joseph said. "There's somebody down yonder."

"Where?"

"Look. By the shed."

Butch hunkered in beside them. "That's the boy I talked to before. The one who saw the cop grab Sandy. He's okay."

"You never know," said Victor.

"Butch, you get him talking," Joseph proposed. "Me and Vic'll slip around that way and try to get on."

"Gotcha." Butch straightened and strolled out from the trees, down the lawn. They heard him striking up conversation. He pointed out west. The boy nodded.

Ingenious. The weather.

"Vic, why's he call you Sandy?"

Victor made a face. "Little Orphant Annie's dog."

"Oh." Joseph made the same face.

"Look." Victor pointed. "You can see the cottage. It's dark."

Joseph said, "Let's get out of here." He led the way through the ring of shadows, on tiptoe across the oyster-shell drive. Victor stayed close by his heel. They ran soundlessly along a strip of soft grass, then quick down the dock to the last slip, where they hid behind a little tool bin. The *Constance* gleamed, nodded, waited for them.

"How many in the crew?" Joseph whispered.

"Three. That guy Charles, the cook, and the pilot. But I don't see a soul."

"It's too easy," said Joseph. "It might be a trap." He reached in his belt for the pistol.

"One way to find out," Victor said, darting up the gangplank.

He waved Joseph on, then stole down the starboard deck, checking in each window before advancing. Joseph worked down the port side. They met at the door that led below. Victor held his finger to his lips. They took positions on either side. He opened the door, just an inch. He heard nothing. He peered around the doorjamb. Dim lamplight down the stairs.

He put his foot on the first stair, listened, went down another, listened, and nodded at Joseph. A lone gaslight flickered in the passageway. Joseph headed back to the engine room, while Victor walked through the dining salon to the galley. The doors were all open, the rooms dark.

They met at the foot of the stairs. "Nobody home," Victor reported.

"Amazing." Joseph stuck the gun in his belt. "Anybody could walk on this thing and take it."

"And here we are," Victor said, as they bounded up the stairway. "I'll run grab the stuff and whistle for Butch on my way back. See if you can figure out how to start her up."

He had just reached the foot of the gangplank when he saw Butch headed down the dock, the boy from the boat shed dragging some kind of line or hose behind him.

Victor waited. "Jesus, Butch, way to go, tell the world," he said under his breath.

Butch winked. "Got the old folks on board?" he said in a loud voice. "This here is Waldo. He knows Edgar and Madame from way back. He's gonna give us a fill-up."

Victor caught on. "Yeah, right. They're down below. She's getting impatient," he said. "She says to get a move on. I'll bring the last of her junk from up there. You guys get us ready to go."

Waldo squinted a moment at Victor, as if trying to place him, then went on lugging the hose up the gangplank.

When Butch set out to do something, Victor had to admit, he did it with grace—whether burning a boat or fooling the whole town of Fairhope or snookering this guy out of rationed gasoline. In his way, he was as smooth an actor as Madame.

Victor strolled down the dock until he was out of their sight, then he took off running across the great lawn, past the gate in the pink wall, the darkened bungalow, around one wing of the blacked-out Hotel. No one strolling tonight. It was late, and a storm coming up.

Just hurry. He cut through a hedge of azaleas to the ballroom's main entrance. The door was unlocked.

Without the splendor of its lights, this was only a room, a big room with bare tables and a silvery ball hanging from the ceiling. Victor eased the door shut behind him. A rim of green fluorescence ran along the foot of the bar, way in back. Crepe-paper twists drooped from the rafters. His heels echoed on the hollow dance floor.

He hopped up to the stage. Tommy Fossey's seashells were gone, the instruments, the music stands, everything but the spherical microphone on its cast-iron stand. Victor stood looking out at the gloom, filling in the dancers, the audience, a big band behind him, streamers and confetti, the clamor of a crowd—

No time for little-boy games. Not now. The game is real. The game has started.

Past the curtains, down the narrow staircase to the little half-door. The crawl space was tighter than he remembered, but he squeezed between pipes and thank God, they were still there: the machine, the black folder, the camera, the deck of cards. These things would save him. He clutched them to his chest and crawled back the way he'd come.

He slipped out the stage door. The Bandits of the Beat had left tire tracks in the sand lot, but no other sign that they'd ever been here. The wind whipped the big oaks and rattled the stand of banana trees by the gazebo at the end of the point. Victor kept to the promenade, following the seawall around the rim of the lawn.

Across the yacht basin the *Constance* was mirrored in the water, a red light aglow on its flying bridge.

Victor made his way around the lagoon. The boy was detaching the hose from a nozzle in the afterdeck when he came up the gangplank. He edged by, hefting the machine. "The old lady's got a lot of letters to write," he said.

"Good for her." The boy went on coiling the hose.

Victor carried his things to the pilothouse. The deck thrummed under his feet; he smelled sweet exhaust in the air. When he opened the door, Butch and Joseph glanced up from a panel of luminous dials and lights.

"Way to go, guys!" he cheered. "You got her going already? Couple of mechanical geniuses."

"Look here." Joseph pointed to a button marked START. "I just pushed it. A moron could steal this boat."

"Got it just about figured out, Sandy." Butch's big smile reflected the glow. "Is Waldo done yet?"

"Just finished. That was some smooth talking, Butch."

"The old man's got a lifetime paid-up account with the Hotel," said Butch. "Nobody got around to telling Waldo that his lifetime is over."

"Shh, here he comes," Victor warned.

"Guys need anything else?" the boy said.

"No thanks, Waldo," said Butch. "Listen, what we was talking about. I know I can get you a quart, maybe more. I'll come find you."

"Great." Waldo went off down the gangplank.

Victor withdrew the map from the black binder and stowed the rest of his evidence in a little compartment just behind the captain's chair. He glanced over at Butch. "Little business on the side?"

"Look, Sandy, I swapped sixty gallons of gasoline for a pint of shine. You got any complaints?" Butch patted his hip pocket. "Turns out the boy knows his stuff. I shared him to a swallow."

"No wonder you're looking so happy," said Victor. "Joseph, we ready?"

"Throw off the lines."

Butch hopped over the rail and worked down the pilings, tossing ropes as fast as he could untie them. As he scampered aboard, the boat shifted back from the dock.

Victor wheeled in the gangplank. Joseph was right. This was too easy—this spectacular boat for the taking, and free gaso-line. . . .

Of course Madame and Glass thought Victor was still safe in jail. They would never dream he could mount such a swift counterattack. They'd stuck him away and forgotten about him, forgotten those who might help him. That was their biggest mistake.

The boat inched away from the dock, smoothly into the channel. The moment the *Constance* left the protection of the breakwater, the chop turned to ocean-sized waves and the yacht began to roll with such enthusiasm that Victor had to grab the rail with both hands.

The storm was here. A wall of rain swept in, half a mile to the west now, utter darkness under the pitching clouds.

A bolt of lightning split the air with a whine and struck the water.

Victor flinched and ran to the pilothouse. Joseph stood with his feet planted apart, making sense of the jumpy wheel with his hands. He looked like he'd been born to steer this boat. He should have been in the Navy, Victor thought, maybe he wouldn't have deserted the Navy. "Gonna be a whale of a storm, Joe. How you doing?"

"I'm having trouble." Joseph leaned into the wheel. "There's something not right."

"You'll get used to it. Where we headed?"

"From the look of this map, they were planning their rendezvous about a mile off Willie's island. Over the Trough."

"Yeah I noticed," said Victor. The Trough was that stretch of deep water west of Willie's island, the deepest in the bay. Willie used to claim it was a hundred miles to the bottom, and the world's biggest fish lived down there. "You think they're there now?"

"It makes sense," said Joseph. "They'd need deep water to lie in. That thing would probably draw fifteen feet. Then they've got a line straight upriver."

"Why don't we go to the Coast Guard?"

"Look at us, Vic—busted out of jail, on a stolen boat. We got to have something to show them."

"What about this machine and the other stuff? The map?"

"It'll take more than that," Joseph said. "That map could stand for last week, or next month. I say we get off the bay, head for quieter water, and find out what this other X means." When he pointed to the Magnolia River, the wheel jumped out of his hand and spun sharply, knocking his knuckles. He stuck his arm through the spokes to stop it. "Go look out there, Vic. Something's dragging. There's got to be some kind of anchor or something we didn't see."

"Come on, Butch."

Raindrops smacked the windows like BBs. Butch did not leap to his feet. He clutched the door for balance and made his way uneasily out on deck.

"You take that side," Victor shouted over the rising gale.

Butch swallowed and went to the port rail.

Victor bent over his side. Pellets of rain stung his face. He saw foam and plunging water, the wind beginning to shear the crests from the waves, but no anchor line. He leaned over the rail to make sure. He had just raised up sputtering from a faceful of spray when he heard Butch's shout.

He dashed across the deck.

"Looka here." Butch pointed to a quivering chain that ran over the rail, through a swinging steel guide arm, across to an electric winch mounted on the cabin wall.

"This isn't the anchor," Victor said. He pointed starboard to another winch, an enormous stockless anchor heaped with rope. "*There's* the anchor."

Butch gave his chain a good yank. "Well it's something, and it's heavy," he said.

They looked at each other.

Victor pulled the knob. The winch buzzed and grumbled and started to turn. The chain came up clanking and dripping, popping links, riding over itself on the reel.

The arm swung out on its pole.

"Oh my God," Victor breathed and he felt for the knob to turn it off, turn it off! but by the time he reached it the weight was full out of the water and dangling just shy of the steel arm.

A man.

He hung like a puppet, the chain looped under his arms, a big dark hole punched in his chest, hands bound at the wrists with white cord.

Vivid lightning, the crash—the *Constance* leaned and leveled herself. The man twisted slowly, slowly.

"Holy shit," said Butch.

"Get him in, bring him in!"

"*I* ain't touchin him—"

A dead man.

"Go get Joseph. Tell him I need help."

Butch fled. Victor grabbed the chain. The guide arm pivoted. The man swung toward him, feet bumping over the rail. They collided, an embrace—Victor's face came into something hard, cold, wet, smelling of fish. He stumbled back in horror, wiping his eyes.

This man had been shot, chained, dumped over the side as an anchor, and then dragged along the bottom, battered, festooned with seaweed. He still wore most of a black uniform. The only recognizable feature was his stiff little mustache, but it was enough. Victor knew him. Edgar's manservant, Charles.

The boat rolled. The body swung out like a pendulum, and *bang!* kicked the wall with its feet. Victor slid to one knee. No mercy. A hole in the chest. A chain around the middle. No mercy.

Then Joseph was there, dodging the sway of the corpse, crying "Mother of God!"

A big wave smacked the side, drenching them all.

"It—he worked for the old man," yelled Victor, groping for the winch handle.

The winch clanked and unrolled. The feet touched down. The joints would not bend. Charles toppled back in a slow, stiff arc, defying gravity, like a magician sinking out of a levitation. His head touched the deck. The chains went slack.

30

VICTOR HELD up the feet while Joseph slid the tarpaulin under. "Now let's just roll him," said Joseph. "He'll roll right on over."

Victor knelt in the slashing rain, torrents of cold summer rain and blue lightning. It would be better to do anything else, he thought, better to jump out of an airplane with no parachute at all than to have to push Charles's body over onto this slick green blanket, tuck the corner under his other side, roll him up like a rug.

What could Charles have done to reap this? Surely he hadn't been part of the plan. One handclap from Edgar and he was there, ready to serve; had he ever said anything more provocative than "yes sir"? Maybe someone caught him listening at doors. Maybe he refused to believe what he heard about the old man's sudden death.

"Damn, Joseph." Victor wiped his hands on his pants. "I never saw a dead person in my life before last week. All of a sudden they're everywhere. Did those people come here to bring spies or to kill everybody?"

"Vic, you have mixed it up with the wrong type of people."

"Something went wrong with their plan. Something bad," Victor said. "It doesn't make sense to leave bodies all over the place."

"You know what they say, the dead don't tell tales." Joseph lifted one end of the bundle. "Here, give me a hand."

Victor was surprised at how light his end seemed. He backed toward the stairway door. "You don't think they put him there as some kind of a message, do you?" he said, feeling behind him for the knob. "They didn't know we'd be the ones to pull him up."

"No," said Joseph. "You already got your message. They had him there for safekeeping. Until they could do something else with him. Like keeping a fish on a line in the water till you're done fishing."

Victor lifted the bundle shoulder-high and began picking his way backwards down the curving stairwell.

"Watch your foot now," warned Joseph, struggling to hang on.

"Got it."

The boat took a giddy roll to port. Joseph lost his balance.

Victor stumbled and crashed into the handrail. The body hit the floor with a sickening thud and rolled against the wall.

"Who's driving this thing?" Victor cried.

"Your buddy," said Joseph. "I'll run grab the wheel." He lit out up the stairs, two at a time.

Victor held onto the wall while the boat slowly found its equilibrium. A peal of thunder set the lamp crystals tinkling.

When he closed his eyes he saw an X-ray vision, but it was not Charles or Edgar or Willie or the face of the first Roy Glass, dead in the swamp. It was Victor: limp, white as Crisco, an angry red scar running from throat to navel where they'd opened him up and stitched him back together. Had he been shot? Couldn't tell. No ropes or chains. It was a premonition or a memory found by his eyes out of focus, the way he could stare himself silly in the mirror, staring and staring until his own face became terrifying and ridiculous, the way one word repeated over and over again could lose its meaning and come to seem primitive, a flapping of the tongue, as in *Willie, Willie . . .*

He had wished her to die. He had wished for the war, for the life on the radio, in the places letters come from. He had wished for the stars to lose their way through the sky. Now the stars were drowning, the bodies were real, and Victor knew he could never return to that old tiresome comfortable peace, no matter how hard he wished.

This monster would swallow him whole. It brought a kind of madness along with it, visions of death on a riverbank, sitting up waving from a dock, toppling onto a table, out under the waves, coming closer each second. Victor's adventure had become a tour of the dead, winding up at this glimpse of himself when his own turn would come. It unnerved him. The black submarine was out there looking for him. If this vision came true—

Get a grip on yourself, Vic

Come on, Sandy

Look to your heart, honey boy—

None of the voices inside him were his.

He found a book of matches, struck one, and held it up in a little doorway under the stairs, looking for a chair or the edge of a bed where he could sit for a moment and recover his own balance. . . .

Oh, no. Not again. I can't take it again, I can't, not another one. Please.

There she was, on the bed.

Victor blew out the match.

You'll go out of your mind

Get out of this room

Your eyes are deceiving you

Run do not walk do not run, run—but he found the nerve to light another match, and though she was sprawled facedown on the bed, he saw her shoulder blades rising and falling in the rhythm of profound sleep.

He touched the flame to the wick of the wall lamp. Warm light filled the little cabin.

She still wore the white satin dress, and the fabric had traveled up the rich curve of her thighs. . . . She would be furious to find him standing watching her this way, but he could not turn away, once he had seen her.

Her hair was a mess, waves and tangles of gold. Even though the pillow hid her face, Victor was afraid of her beauty. He saw himself dancing with her, and his jittery heart started racing, moisture in his palms, a powerful lawless feeling, way deep.

How could she sleep through this storm and the commotion outside her door?

He went to touch the soft of her arm. "Diana."

She did not respond.

He pressed her wrist with his fingers. "Diana. Wake up."

She breathed, undisturbed.

An improbable watercolor hung on the wall behind her: a little boy running through a vast field of flowers.

Victor lifted the pillow. She was the most beautiful creature he had ever seen, and once again his ears were roaring, and death seemed much farther away than the other side of the wall. She was a gift dropped to him from somewhere high above all this. He smoothed her hair with his finger.

He touched her shoulder, tapped her cheek with his hand, rubbed his fingers on her arm. "Diana. Wake up now. Come on."

They wanted everybody out of their way for one night.

At least she was alive. The floor tilted. Victor staggered two steps and grabbed the edge of a steamer trunk.

He had a sudden urge to kiss her.

He knew something of the manly code involving a woman when she is asleep. Until now he had never faced that temptation. It amazed him that a feeling this tender and woozy could swarm up in the midst of a war. At this moment a kiss seemed the answer to all of his questions.

A familiar alarm bell was ringing. She was dangerous. She was the bait in the trap. She had sent Victor down to the cottage to watch Edgar die. She had sent him directly to jail.

The floor came back level. Victor placed his hands on the edge of the mattress, leaned down, and kissed her cheek. She owed him that.

He held back a moment to watch.

He was not Prince Charming. She did not wake up. She would never know.

He kissed her again, on the mouth.

Her lips tasted of oranges.

He swallowed, put his hands in his pockets. The room steadied; the boat seemed to be moving into gentler water.

"Diana," he said, and then the force of his attraction caused him to turn away, to flee the hot little room, up the stairs to the rainswept deck.

The sky had opened up, filling the air with its own roar, rain falling straight down now, in darkness. The lightning diminished, and the wind, to make room for this ocean of rain blunting the waves, dousing Victor as he felt his way along the handrail. He could not tell where the *Constance* was heading. Shore, clouds, and rain were all the same color of night.

A circle was polished in the foggy glass of the pilothouse. Victor opened the door.

Joseph tipped back in the captain's chair, his shoe on the wheel. He was steering this boat with his toe. Joseph the deserter was gone. This man looked never to have run in shame from anything. He turned with a triumphant smile. "Brother, we got this thing under control!"

"What we got is a stowaway," Victor announced.

"What?" The foot came down from the wheel.

"Diana. You remember, the girl. She's down there asleep on one of the beds."

"The blonde? You bet I remember. How the hell—I thought we looked in all the rooms!"

Victor said, "There's a cabin we didn't notice under the stairs."

Butch slammed in the other door, his hair streaming. "It'll work good," he said to Joseph, then: "Hey, Sandy, brother man here told me who that was on that chain. These people are nuts, killing their own slaves like that."

"Yeah, but listen what else we got," Joseph said. "Vic found a passenger down there. His girlfriend. The blonde."

"No kiddin," said Butch. "Alive and kicking?"

"That's what I wondered at first," Victor said. "She's asleep. They gave her something, I think. Like they knocked Edgar out until they were ready to shoot him."

"Naw, Sandy. She just couldn't bear to be away from you."

"Shut up, Butch." Victor rummaged in the cabinet where he'd stowed the code machine; he remembered a white metal box with a red cross, and sure enough, inside he found a row of glass capsules stapled to a card labeled SPIRITS OF AMMONIA. "I'm gonna try to bring her around. Where are we, anyway?"

"We just passed Willie's island," said Joseph.

"How can you see in this rain?"

Joseph rubbed the circle with the cuff of his sleeve. "I could run this river blind. See? There's old Murphy's boathouse." He put his toe on the wheel, and grinned. "Got it under control. We got what they want, Vic. This boat. That stuff you found. And that girl. You go wake her up."

"Don't do nothin I wouldn't do," Butch put in.

Victor stepped into the rain.

31

VICTOR SNAPPED the capsule under her nose, hovering so close that the fumes filled his head before Diana ever drew a breath. He turned away, dropping the halves of the vial, stumbling and coughing and holding his eyes.

Ammonia was too melodious a name for the stench that swallowed the room. How could anyone sleep through that?

He pried another capsule from the card. This time he turned his face away and held his breath when he broke it. Vapors swam up her nose. Her eyes fluttered open. She choked, gasping for air.

"Here, sit up," he said, raising her by one arm, "come on, I know, it's terrible." Her hair fell in her face; she leaned over the edge of the bed, racked by a coughing fit. Victor pounded between her shoulder blades, just the way he did for one of his mother's morning cigarette seizures. "It's okay. Just take a deep breath."

"Stop." She shook his hand off and rested her face on her knees. "God, what did—you do—to me?"

"Smelling salts." Victor sat on the end of the steamer trunk. He could not see past her tangle of hair. That's how she hides, he thought. "You were pretty well gone. I've been trying to wake you up a long time."

"Water," she croaked.

Victor stepped into the passageway, over the body of Charles, through the dining salon to the galley.

By the time he returned, Diana was sitting up on the narrow bed. She took the mug from his hands and drank it straight down, eyeing him over the rim. The pillow had left a subtle pattern of ripples on her left cheek. Her gaze was suspicious. "Where is Grandmother? What time is it?"

"Almost midnight," he said.

"What—what do you mean? It was after two when I came down from the dance." She seemed for the first time to notice the rocking floor. She turned her ear to the rumble of engines. "Are we going somewhere?"

"We're already gone," Victor said. "The dance was last night. It's Wednesday. It may be Thursday by now. Have you been asleep all this time?"

"Grandmother didn't say you were going with us." Diana

shrank against the wall. "She said it would be just the three of us and the staff. Where is she?"

"She's not here." Victor folded his arms to show he did not mean to touch her. "There was nobody on the boat except you. And I didn't find you till now." He exulted at the memory of his kiss.

"I've got a terrific headache," Diana said. "Have I really been asleep that long?"

"I think they gave you a drug," Victor said.

Diana pressed her hand to her eyes. "I waited the longest time after the dance. Grandmother came down. She was awfully nervous. Mr. Glass made us hot toddies. She said Grandfather didn't feel well and the project was called off. Maybe she—I remember I got so sleepy, and she said we were leaving at dawn, so I should just sleep down here . . ." She sat up, squeezing her temples. "What's wrong? What's happened? You know something."

"She was lying to you," Victor said evenly. Watch her eyes. Watch the look in her eyes. Then you'll know. "Glass put something in your drink. That's just one of their tricks."

Her face flushed. "What are you talking about?"

Victor rose from the trunk to face her. "You knew they were going to get rid of me, didn't you. You helped set the trap. You sent me to that bungalow when you knew."

"Listen, Victor"—he felt a trivial welling of pride that she remembered his name—"I told you what Glass told me. He wanted to see you. That's all he said." She looked away, and then fiercely at him. "What's going on!"

"Edgar found out about your grandma and Mr. Roy Glass," Victor said. "He threatened to blow the whistle. So they shot him."

Her mouth fell open. The shock was too sudden to be an act. "Shot who? Grandfather? You're lying!"

"I'm not. She did it herself. Madame. He was dead before he realized she was going to do it."

Diana sprang to her feet. "No! Oh, no!" Her eyes darted like a rabbit caught in oncoming headlights, then it hit her. "They were—oh God, you're lying!"

"I got no reason to lie," Victor said. "They had me thrown in jail for it. He died quick. She shot him three times. Right here." He thumped his chest. "That's how much she loved him."

Diana sank to the bed. "I don't believe you."

"Go look in the hall right there, go on, look," Victor said. "You remember Charles, your handy butler? He's out there wrapped in a tarp. We found him dragging off the side of this boat. Seems to me you're pretty lucky. Your granny's a vicious lady. She's got blood on her hands. You think I'm lying? Go see for yourself."

Her voice was faint. "But why? Why would they do that?"

"I think the old man turned on them," said Victor. "At the dance, remember? He wasn't the least bit drunk. He figured it out too late. They're on the wrong side, Diana. They're bringing in spies. Roy Glass is an agent for the Germans."

"That's impossible," she said. "Grandfather said he works for the FBI. He said those people were refugees!"

"Don't you see?" Victor cried. "They had him buffaloed! They used his boat, spent his money, and killed him. They're double-crossing everybody in sight!" He saw she was not convinced, and he could not think of a single reason he was so hellbent on convincing her, except that he knew she couldn't be on their side, and he wanted her on his side, and he wanted to touch her again. . . .

"Grandmother may not have loved him," she said, "but she could never hurt him—"

Victor grabbed her arm, forced her to look at him. "She

didn't *hurt* him," he said. "She shot to kill. Maybe they were going to come back for you. Maybe not. Maybe they meant to kill you too. I think they're trying to get away. We're going to stop them. You've got to tell me anything you know."

She knocked his hand away. "Don't touch me."

That infuriated him. Did it always take force to make someone believe? He seized her by the shoulders and forced her up from the bed just as roughly as his daddy had ever forced him, pushed her five steps to the door, stepped around her and rolled the green canvas bundle over, twice, with his foot. A bruised white arm flopped out.

Diana took a sharp breath. Victor felt the satisfaction of hearing her disbelief shattered, but also sudden shame at the way he'd done it. Why did it give him such pleasure? He should cut off his hands before ever using them to make somebody do something.

"I'm sorry," he said, folding them behind his back. "I promise. I won't do that again."

She had barely noticed; she stared down, transfixed. "Charles loved Grandfather more than anyone else in the world. He never hurt anybody. Why would they do this?" She blinked up, eyes shining. "I knew something was wrong. I'd never seen Grandfather act so awful to her, and that look on her face . . . I told you. Like she wanted to kill him." She retreated to the doorway. "It's Roy Glass. It's his fault. He talked her into it. I've been watching. He—he's got some kind of spell over her. He flatters her. I've seen them. They go off for long walks when Grandfather's taking his nap. When you said he'd found out about them, I thought you meant some . . . scandal."

Victor stooped to cover the body. "Isn't she a little old for Glass?"

"He's young and nice-looking and she can't resist him," said Diana, groping for details. "He makes her feel beautiful. He gives her presents. She showed me. A diamond ring. She said he was a pest, that was her exact word, but she laughed about it. She doesn't know what she's doing."

"She knows," Victor said. "She handled that gun like she'd known a long time."

Diana spoke into her fist. "She's lost her mind. It's happened before. I never thought she could . . . hurt someone else. Especially him. He loved her so much."

Rising, she began to pace the little cabin. Victor thought of an animal locked in a cage. He remembered himself in the cage.

"She tried to kill herself twice, when I was a little girl. I found a scrapbook of newspaper cuttings. She'd saved them. She loved the publicity." Diana's face crumpled. "She listens to me. I could have stopped her. I never thought she—oh, I could have warned him!"

She burst into tears.

Victor sat where he was. He could tell by the way she held herself apart that she did not want his comfort.

Something Madame said: *I did it for love.*

"Will you help us?" he said.

"Nothing—I can do." She shook her head, fighting the tumult in her voice. "I'm sorry. I'll be—okay in a minute."

She had no trouble believing the truth. She must have suspected something. How long had she waited for Madame's evil to show itself? How long had she lived knowing the evil was there?

Her parents are dead, Victor thought. Her grandmother has murdered her grandfather. Have pity. Everyone has a disaster coming down in the blood.

She did not seem beautiful now, at least not in that perfect untouchable way. Her face was bent by sorrow, and the shame she must feel—the way Victor felt when his father went off on a tyrant display: humiliated not by the punishment, but by the disgrace of the giant, the man who once filled up the world, shriveled down to an imitation man.

"You're better than she is," he said suddenly. "They've done wrong. They've got to pay."

Diana wiped her eyes on her sleeve. "Why do you need me? You're so sure of yourself. Go on and find them."

"We'll find out as much as we can, then we're going to the Coast Guard. You can help us convince them."

"You just took off with Grandfather's boat?"

"Joseph's driving. My brother. And Butch is helping."

"A bunch of boys," she said, "boys playing at make-believe games. You won't be able to stop them."

"Maybe not. They've killed everybody who tried." Victor stood up. "It's us or nobody. They're not going to get us this time. We'll be ready for them."

"Victor."

He turned.

"I had a dream that you kissed me."

Wildly he tried to think of some way to deny it, but there it was: she ought to know who had kissed her. He might be embarrassed but he wouldn't be sorry.

"Well?" he said, after a while. "I didn't think it would hurt anything."

"No. Really. If you'd known, would you still have kissed me?"

"I don't guess so." He blushed in spite of himself. "I didn't think you'd let me."

"It's a good thing I was asleep," she said.

"But you're wide awake now."

She nodded. Her gaze opened inside him like a flower.

Victor grasped her shoulders for balance, and kissed her—a gentler touch, and his eyes drifted shut so the moment was a soft vibration, a touch, a fleeting conjunction. She drew in a breath and moved back.

"That was very sweet," she said, dropping her gaze.

"I'll be upstairs." Victor ducked out the door. On his way up, he thought about how much he wanted to throw rocks at the world and jump in the air and be bold. To win. To show her he wasn't as sweet as she thought. Blind her to his homeliness and his river-boy ways. Get this war over with. Kiss her every minute.

It was only a dream. He came out to the darkness, the steady downpour on the river, spouts of water spilling off the flying bridge. Rain hung like fog in the air. No way to tell where they were—on the river somewhere. Time had stopped with Diana. Now it started again with a jolt.

Victor followed the sound of clinking glass to the afterdeck.

Butch had fashioned a lean-to of oilskin sheets supported against the stern by a variety of wooden stakes and broken-off timbers, so the rain ran down and puddled on the deck.

"Hey Sandy, that you?" He stuck out his head. "Come in out of the mess. But don't strike a match."

Not around *you* I won't, pal, Victor said to himself, crouching into the tent. The air was alive with volatile fumes. Butch had rigged a siphon from the fuel nozzle, and was guiding its stream into a wine bottle between his knees. Gasoline pooled around his shoes.

"You're putting gas in wine bottles?"

"Naw, I'm pissin in 'em, what do you think?" said Butch, his thumb on the siphon, setting the bottle aside. In the sweaty half-light, Victor could see crates of bottles stacked against the rail, already filled. "Hand me another one, Sandy. That old man, I tell you, he drank him some wine. Old stuff. You should have seen all I poured out."

Victor moved to the open side for air. "What in the world are you gonna do with all these?"

"I was talkin it over with brother man," Butch said, chugging liquid into the bottle. "We ain't got much firepower. These people are *tough*. You plan on catchin 'em with that one popgun, or what?"

"I didn't think we would do it ourselves," Victor said.

When he opened the door Joseph looked up and smiled. Victor realized that nearly everybody who mattered to him was on this boat now—like old Noah's ark, it would carry them to some kind of safety, some land at the end. The old world was drowning forever.

"Hey, Vic, did you have any luck?"

"She's awake. It took her a while to believe me, but she already knew something was up," Victor said. "Madame was stepping out on the old man. With Roy Glass. He gave her a diamond ring."

Joseph whistled. "There's more to these rats than just a sinking ship," he said. "What is our girl gonna do?"

"I think she'll help us," said Victor. "She hasn't got much choice. We're not taking her back, are we?"

"No way. Look here." Joseph rattled the map. "They drew three bends in the river, and we've gone past two. Whatever it is, this is it right over here." He opened the door. "The rain's letting up. Can you come out and watch me starboard?"

Victor slipped out behind him, and cupped his hands over his eyes.

Joseph eased off on the throttle, so the engine murmur was all but consumed by the steady drizzle.

A wall of dark woods, a broad carpet of marsh, then the view opened to a clearing in trees on the right bank, a sprawling log cabin with lights in the rooms, lights fixed to the gutters, lights on the porches running around three sides. No one in all that light. The old Johnson place. The rooms appeared empty, no curtains or pictures. There were automobiles everywhere in the yard—shiny Chevrolets and old A-Model Fords on blocks, pickup trucks, junked Plymouths.

"X marks the spot," Joseph called from the wheel. "You reckon all those cars belong to old man Johnson?"

"No, you remember, he fell in the river and drowned," said Victor. "New Year's Eve, a long time ago. They've been renting it out."

"To Henry Ford, it looks like," Joseph said.

The *Constance* slid by, purring engines, so close that Victor could have shattered a window with a stone. He remembered this cabin aglow: the night he first heard the sound in the bay, when he set out upriver to fetch his gasoline stash and witnessed these lights, the hubbub of a party floating over this very stretch of river.

Butch brought the aroma of gasoline up from the stern. "We lived there once," he said, "me and the old lady. It belongs to Noltie now. He found somebody to pay him fifty dollars a month and throwed us out."

"I think there's something up with that place," said Victor. "Could we sneak up and get a good look?"

"Easy. Back her into the mouth of the creek. Get off on the other side of the point."

"Will you come with me?" said Victor.

"Hell, why not." Butch leaned in the pilothouse door. "Brother man, turn her around right up here. See the point? Plenty deep right there. You can put us off yonder."

Victor ran to retrieve Edgar's flare pistols and a pair of green ponchos from one of the porpoise-faced cabinets. Diana and his dizzy visions would just have to wait. Be careful. Don't step in a hole.

He pulled the musty poncho down over his head, and returned to the bow. "Here, Butch, put this on. Camouflage."

"What are you gonna do?" Joseph said. "Let's get our signals straight."

"I bet something's happening," said Victor. "They don't leave those lights on all the time. Butch knows the way. We'll see what's up and come back."

"You sure you can handle it? I'll go with you."

"Everything's on this boat, Joe. The stuff. Diana. You've got to stay hidden and keep it running. We might need to get out of here quick." Victor handed him one of the awkward pistols with its cone-shaped flare, and stuck the other down his pants. "If something goes wrong, shoot this thing. Keep an eye out for somebody coming."

Down the deck a door opened. Diana stepped out, wrapped in a man's black raincoat.

"Hey hey," said Butch. "Here's somebody."

She came to the bow, her face pale and strained. "Does anyone know where we are?"

"Sure," said Victor. "Not far from Magnolia Springs. Where I live."

"Hello, Diana," said Joseph. "Vic tells me you're going to help us." His tone, Victor noticed, was more respectful than the first time they met.

"I'll do what I can." Diana stared at Victor and Butch in their ponchos and smiled wanly. "You boys look like seals in a zoo."

That word *boy* again. Victor hated it. After he'd kissed her, after she had confessed it out loud. *Want me to prove it? Watch this.* He turned on his heel. "Ready, Joseph. Stop us right here."

Joseph reversed the engines. The *Constance* nudged as near to the point as the river would allow. "Okay, Vic," he called. "Hurry up and come back."

"Roger." Victor brushed past Diana, striding down the deck

as if he truly did own this boat. Beside Butch's lean-to was the same ladder they'd used to rescue survivors, the night Joseph appeared. Victor tossed it over the side, and pulled off his shoes. "Come on, Butch." Climbing up on the rail, he found the first rung with his foot and quickly descended to the bottom, where he paused a moment to consider how deep the water might be.

He glanced up to find Butch, Joseph, and Diana peering at him over the side, wondering the same thing.

He closed his eyes, said a prayer, and jumped. He splashed down on two feet. The water came just to his thighs.

Thank you, Willie.

He waded to shore, squishing his socks in the ooze.

Butch tumbled from the ladder to the river and came up spluttering, flapping his poncho wings.

The *Constance* loomed above them, so much larger than it seemed from on board, long sleek and dark, a mirage settling down in the mouth of this creek with its lights out, angles and edges darker than the night.

32

BUTCH CRASHED ahead through the jungle, following what he swore was a path, but was not. Limbs slapped Victor's face. Little rainshowers persisted under the dense high ceiling of branches, stirred by a breeze. The air was alive with night sounds: leaves whispering against leaves, a wild thing plummeting off in a burst of snapping, birds twittering drowsily, and the river lapping its bank, far away to the rear. Needly vines and wild yucca swords pierced Victor's poncho and ripped it.

"Butch, keep it down," he called in a hoarse whisper. "You sound like a herd of cattle."

Butch stopped. "You wanna go first?"

"No."

"Then shut up and keep up," he said, resuming his plunge.

From the water, it hadn't looked this far across the point to the Johnson cabin, but Butch led a roundabout way through a low swampy place where the muck closed around their ankles. "This is where they burned out my first kettle," he said, stopping for breath. "See? The trees are still charred."

"Maybe it wasn't Noltie after all," said Victor. "Maybe whoever's in that cabin didn't like having neighbors so close."

Scaling a barbed-wire fence, they hiked across a pasture and into another jungle, working and sweating through nets of vines. At last lights glimmered on something shiny, ahead through the trees. Butch snuggled low to the ground. "There we are, Sandy. That's the back of it."

Victor crouched beside him. Through a parting of limbs he saw lights reflected in the hoods and trunks of scattered vehicles, and beyond them a log kitchen, a ladder propped against the roof, a broad sandy yard.

The flare gun was poking Victor in the wrong place. He shifted it to his hip pocket. "I don't see a soul," he whispered. "Like they're expecting a whole bunch of people, but nobody's here yet."

Butch drew the branches aside and took off running. Victor stayed close behind. They ran all the way to the shelter of a little pump house at the edge of the light, just yards from the cabin's back porch. They paused there, listening for sounds from the house.

Victor scuttled out of the darkness, across a stretch of bright sand, up under a window.

He raised his head over the sill, stood all the way, and waved Butch on. They stole up the steps. The screen door was hooked. Victor punched his fist through the screen and unhooked it.

There was nothing in the kitchen but a cold wood stove, the pine-plank floor, the big logs in the walls. Victor crept into the central hall. Electric lights blazed. Dark fireplace. No furniture.

He approached each door expecting an ambush, a dead body, or at least a table or chair—but the house was as empty as if a wave had washed through it.

There were seven rooms opening into each other. On the long porch facing the river, Victor discovered a wall tacked over with maps and charts: Baldwin County Geologic Survey. Coastal Alabama Navigational Chart. Highway Map of the State of Alabama. National Highway Map, U.S.

"Never looked so empty when we lived here," said Butch, coming in from the kitchen. "Where you reckon they sleep?"

"I don't think they do." Victor's words bounced from the walls. "Take a look at these maps."

"Yeah, I saw 'em, so what?" Butch craned to see out the window behind him.

"I don't know. Anybody from here doesn't need a map to know where they are. But I thought we'd find more than this."

"Get down!" Butch cried, diving for Victor's legs, a long sailing tackle that landed them hard on the floor under the window.

"What! What is it—"

"Boat at the dock," Butch gasped. "Get the hell out of here!"

Victor scrambled on all fours, quick to the back hall and into the kitchen, Butch skittering behind him. But he held up a moment at the back door. "Wait. We've got to see who it is. Come on. Don't slam it."

He darted down the steps, around the corner of the house to the skinny ladder propped against the eave, up in a flash, grabbing the gutter, pulling himself onto the slippery roof. "Come on!"

Butch looked around in desperation, as if someone might whisper in his ear a sensible order to flee, but then he shrugged and shinnied to the top of the ladder.

Victor hoisted him up by one arm.

They crawled up the slick incline, clinging like bugs, loosing little cascades of twigs and green acorns with their feet. They hung on to the ridge by the chimney to survey the river, the boathouse, a sizable boat lit with dim amber lights nestled at the dock.

Stooped figures came through the yard, among the cars, toward the cabin. *Don't look up. Keep walking. Go into the house.*

There were five men in long gray overcoats, woolen caps pulled low on their faces as if the moist breeze were a blistery winter wind. They all had ragged beards. One fingered the leaves on a low-hanging magnolia; another stooped to press his hands to the ground.

Go in the house.

Victor felt an elbow in his side. Butch pointed—Roy Glass striding up from the dock, tapping his hat in his hand. His hair looked white and his spectacles winked in the glare.

"Come in the house," he said loudly.

One of the men muttered something.

"We will speak only English from this point," said Glass. The screen door squealed.

Victor pressed his face to the edge of the roof, smelling the tarpaper shingles, examining each man approaching the door.

They were older than he'd thought, their beards shot with gray, eyes shadowed. Some carried guns, others green duffel bags.

This is the bravest thing you've ever done, Victor chanted to himself. The bravest thing.

Don't look up.

Below there was banging and walking around. Doors slammed. Deep voices blurred together.

Concentrating on how light and silent he was, like an Indian made of air, Victor picked his way down the slope to the very lip of the front porch. Butch slithered down on his belly, a few inches at a time.

Hanging their heads over the edge, they looked down into the azalea bushes and heard nearly every word.

Glass was speaking—". . .to change to civilian clothes. You will bury your uniforms out in the back. You must leave no trace here. This is strictly a transit station. You will be here no longer than it takes to change."

Victor shot a look at Butch, who tilted his ear.

"Our order of operations has been compromised," said Glass. "This station is closed. CATALOGUE is terminated. You will have no contact in this district."

A buzz sprang up among the men. Glass clapped his hands like a schoolteacher.

"This is not for discussion. Events have made this location unsafe. I wish I had time to brief you, but I don't, so listen to what I have to say. Your orders are the same except that you will proceed without further orientation. I will give each of you a set of keys to an automobile outside. The make of your vehicle is on the white tag. I want you to examine these maps closely, and decide your routes in advance. No two men on the same road tonight. You will go to your assigned locations, establish yourselves, and send the signal that you are in place. Then you will receive further instructions."

The men shuffled around this news. One said, "Sir, what if we find ourselves lost?"

"There are maps in each car," said Glass. "Remember to drive on the right. Speak only English. And be very careful whom you ask for directions. These people are more suspicious than any of us have been told."

At that moment, Butch made a subtle move forward to hear better: his knees lost traction: he started to slide and kept sliding and slid all the way off the roof, crashing face first into the azaleas.

"What was that!"

Victor raised up on the edge and sailed out wide, landing down on one knee, staggering up just as Butch freed himself from the bushes.

Victor dragged him by the arm around the house, up over bumpers and hoods and the tops of cars, to the bed of a truck, to the ground. He jerked open the trunk of a battered Hudson. "In here!" He flung himself in on Butch, pulled the lid down over them, shut out the light.

"Sh—" a breath.

Someone running by

Keep quiet

Oh boy it's done now

The footsteps circled back, coming close. Victor had the monstrous urge to shout and give them away, and he remembered it came from hide-and-seek when he was a boy. He could never stand to stay hidden. When the seeker came near his hiding place, the secret became unbearable and he squealed or took off running. He was always It.

He controlled himself now, but the footsteps stopped at the bumper. The lid flew open.

A light in his eyes. Victor held up his hand. Roy Glass pointed a long black pistol.

33

ONE AT A TIME. Get out of the car."

Victor went first. Two bearded men stood behind Glass, holding lights.

Glass waved the gun at Butch. "Now you. Get out. Both of you turn around." He slammed the trunk. "Put your hands on the car. Spread your feet."

Help me Willie, Victor began, but he knew it was too much to ask. He was over his head.

Rough hands felt down his sides, down one leg, up the other, snatched the flare gun from his pocket. The poncho was jerked over his head, his left wrist bent back and locked in cold steel. Glass put a boot in his back and sprawled him flat.

Victor spit sand from his mouth. "You can't kill us," he cried. "We've got something you want. We've got proof. I gave your code machine to the police."

Victor saw the shadowplay as Roy Glass shoved Butch to the sand. "If you've already given over the machine, I have no reason to keep you alive," Glass said. "We are leaving the country."

"We've got Diana—"

"Fine. Keep her."

Four shadows gathered around Glass. Victor turned his head. Could these men be spies? They were ghosts. They were thin and too white. Some of them held pistols.

"These boys have been quite a thorn to us," Glass said, "two thorns in our sides. We must pluck them out. George. Ernest. Bring them along."

Hands gripped Victor and lifted him up. Butch cussed and tried to wrench free of the man who wrestled him to his feet.

All at once Victor felt giddy, light-headed, as if the whole thing were a demented joke and he should run, let Glass shoot him in the back and have his belly laugh. Fear. Is this trip necessary? Don't you know there's a war on? Now you do. In the hands of real actual Germans, just like in your fantasies, only this time it's real, it's real, Victor, they speak English, their guns poke your spine as they march you down the slope to a dock, a boathouse. Is there a cage inside? Will they beat you? Is it that time all over again? Where is Daddy, oh Daddy if you could see me. Victor tripped and was jerked to his feet.

Walking ahead to the end of the dock, Glass aimed the flare pistol at the sky. "I presume this is to alert your friends that you are in trouble." The rocket streaked up, a fiery red arc in the fog. "That should bring them out."

Stay away, Joe. Victor would not let himself look upriver while Glass watched his eyes. The fog advanced. Victor hoped it was enough to hide the *Constance*.

The lights in the cabin flicked off, room by room, then the lights at the corners, along the roof line. Automobiles roared to life, headlights sweeping the trees.

"Put them in the launch," said Glass. "I want them down on the floor. I don't want to hear a sound out of them. Do you understand?"

"Yes sir."

Victor sneaked a glance. The mouth of the creek was invisible; this was not smoke from an Agent X-9 bomb, this was somber, pillowy, river-creeping white fog, moving in dense blankets. Joseph and Diana might be hovering just beyond the point, or passing on the river's far side. *Run. Get away while you can. Run for help.*

Butch's captor put one hand on his neck and the other on his shirt and hustled him into the green-camouflaged launch with the U.S. Coast Marshal insignia, bench seats back to back, a big open floor at the stern.

Victor's captor tugged his wrists so he had to bend over to keep from falling. "You're a mighty careless spy, Mr. Glass," he hissed. "I thought spies were supposed to be smart. I keep finding your dirty work everywhere."

"The gag, Ernest," said Glass, peering through field glasses into the murk.

The big German forced Victor down to the seat. Butch rolled on the floor, kicking at the one who was tying his feet.

"Thataboy, Butch!"

A fist slammed Victor's ear.

He sank to his knees. He saw little white fireflies dancing and heard a high whistle, a flute. A cloth came around his face, through his teeth like a bit, tied so tight that his tongue flopped back on itself and he could hardly breathe. The man tightened the knot. Victor felt someone moving his feet, and he knew if he tried to move them himself he could do it, but he had the odd sensation of peering down a tunnel at the men tying him, while the fireflies danced all around in a cloud. A rope bound his ankles. Not the rope and the trip out on water, not me, oh no, boy, but Victor's feet would not do what he told them. He could not feel the side of his face. He lay in the bottom of the boat and listened.

The other German had his hands on a wildcat. Butch struggled and hollered and spat until the gag came into his mouth, and kept struggling. Roy Glass jumped him. The wiry man seized the cuffs, ran a rope to his feet, and cinched it tight. Butch bowed out in the middle and lay trussed like a deer.

Victor lay very still and decided he wasn't dead yet, so maybe they weren't ready to kill him. He had to chase the fireflies away and stop hearing the flute. He would be very still. No one would know he was there. He heard Butch's labored breathing, the deep muffle-hum of the inboards, the men hurrying away.

Glass walked the dock, sweeping the fog with his binoculars. At last he said, "Well, that's enough," climbed in, and turned to Victor's baleful stare. "I could kill you now, leave you here," he said, "but you were right. We have been careless on this job. I don't know how you managed to get out of jail, but it was a mistake.

"If you'd thought about it," he went on, coiling the line and pushing off with both hands, "you would have realized that was the safest place for you until we were gone. We should have finished you off with Edgar. But we needed time and— it all fit so neatly. Too neatly. Madame couldn't resist." Glass goosed the throttle, steering down the fog-heavy river, talking over his shoulder. "The charge would not hold up a week, but once we're gone, what would it matter? Edgar is dead. You'd go free. We thought we could bring it off."

You can do better, Roy Glass: a charge of murder as a personal favor? Thanks a lot. Victor worked his jaw to relax the gag. He saw streamers of fog passing over the dark tops of trees. They were flying downriver.

"This is where your grandmother lived, isn't it." Glass pointed. "You can hardly see in the fog."

Don't you talk about her, you bastard. You didn't know her. You're not fit to speak her name.

"It is a shame she died," Glass went on. "She was a nice lady, very helpful."

Victor writhed against the ropes.

"Oh, this makes you angry? I know more about her than you

know. It is my business. We determined to use this river, and she happened to live at the mouth of it. What could I do? Make her my friend. She couldn't tell the difference between me and the first Roy Glass. I brought her cakes and red licorice, just as he did. She always had a little story to tell. At first we used her harbor to make exchanges. Told her we were fishermen coming in from our boats. Then she helped us find the cabin. She came out to wave whenever we went by."

Victor was powerless to stop his lies. This could not be so. Willie. It's not so.

The trees vanished. The launch passed into the bay and began beating hard on the waves. Glass's words jounced like stones to the floor of the boat. "You are thoughtless, Victor. You should know what your actions have earned you. When you told me what had washed up on shore, I came down here at once. This time I used stronger rope and more weight. I put Glass back in the cove, where we had him. Your Willie came down to the dock to wave. I did not see her until she saw what I had done. She sat down on the dock. That was it."

Glass whirled around. "*You* are the source of this trouble. If you hadn't stumbled in, the whole thing would have gone off as planned. Every one of these people would still be alive. As it is, you've spread suspicions all over the place. You think you are a pair of smart kids. We'll take you to deep water. No one will find you."

He faced the wind. Spray dashed over the prow.

Go on and kill me, as Willie would say. You can go on and kill me, because a thing like this only happens to you in your life once. It wasn't enough that he was bound hand and foot on the floor of a launch, headed for the open water—the monster had reached back in time, seized Willie, dragged her down to the dock, and killed her all over again.

Of course she had helped them. She'd help anyone who would

give her a kind word. It was not in her blood to see enemies behind friendly faces.

She spent her whole life trusting people. She fed raggedy children and shrimpers just in from the sea. She bought whiskey from Butch. She believed this smooth man with his candy and his phony lectures about her blackout curtains. She never dreamed anybody could do such evil as she saw him doing, out from her dock that Sunday. The sight must have stopped her old heart.

All because she happened to live at the mouth of the river, where everything comes in from the bay.

34

BUTCH PRESSED Victor's leg with his toes.

Victor pressed back. *Hang on, buddy.* He rolled over against the transom.

The engines dropped their pitch. The launch slowed to a crawl, lifting and falling in waves. Glass polished his spectacles and squinted into the fog. The bay was engulfed by great clouds of whiteness drifting like icebergs, like ships.

Victor became aware of the humming, the rumble: vast engines idling somewhere ahead. He smelled diesel fumes on the air.

A shrill bell—like school . . .

Then it stopped.

Waves gulped and splashed under the hull. Roy Glass stood up, blinking red and green bowlights with a switch on the dash.

The hum reverberated deep in the fog.

Then a long black sculptured flank emerged, directly and lengthwise ahead, a blade of black steel rising sheer from the water, stretching forever into the distance. It rested still on the water, rumbling deep in its throat. Waves washed around its nose and over the deck. As the launch drew near, the bay seemed to flatten out, almost calm under the flowing mist. At last Victor saw the entire dark length of the thing, the black curves of the pulpit, the stark pivoting guns, spires and pipes, the conning tower reared up midway like a suspicious head, to see who was approaching. A cable ran from the pulpit to the stern, and another from the tallest pipe to the tip of the bow. White foam bubbled up where its body met the water. A white eye blinked on and then off.

No wonder this was the enemy. It was made of smooth and invisible darkness, designed to slip under waves and move in for the kill, strike swiftly, at night, and then glide away, blinking its eye, hiding to kill again. Everywhere was the anonymous hand that had shaped it more surely for stealth than any creature of the sea.

With inboards at idle, the launch bobbed along the waterline in the stream of exhaust. Glass gathered a loop of rope in his hand. Victor saw three—no, four—heads bobbing up, then the bridge spilled over with dark figures, eight or nine men lickety-split down a ladder and crowding out onto the deck. They danced and grabbed the cable overhead for balance.

Glass tossed the rope. Two men came into the launch, then two more. *"Schnell!"* shouted Glass; someone jabbered back in that indecipherable tongue. Four hands grabbed Victor and lofted him like a baby over the side into four waiting hands. He heard Butch hit the deck beside him.

A crowd surrounded them, murmuring. Victor was hoisted to his feet, propelled across the slippery boards to a ladder, passed up hand-to-hand and across the dark open bridge to a corner. An iron hatch stood on a hinge over a circle of red light: a room below. Hands on him, dozens of hands, hard and gentle, handing him down through the hole. Victor's feet never touched the ladder. The smell enveloped him down in the red oval room, a doctor's antiseptic and the breathing odors of men, the tang of machines, sharp hot oil, rust, cigarettes, paint, filtered air. The men stank of smoke and something else. They walked him around a hanging steel column with handles and an eyepiece (the periscope!) toward another hatch.

Butch came down like a mummy lowered into a tomb.

None of the men spoke to Victor, or looked at him directly; he had an impression of great weariness, from their untrimmed beards and hollow cheeks. They wore woolen trousers and open-necked shirts or dirty sweaters with the sleeves pushed up. Their faces were pale in red light. How could they breathe this air? They passed Victor along like a fragile object they had been ordered not to break.

He floated over a second yawning hatch. Anxious faces turned up to see him. There must be fifty men in this ship! From the outside, it seemed a black inhuman creature, but inside it seethed red as a picture of hell—gauges, pipes, dials, map tables, banks of switches encrusting every surface, and all these men wading through a lake of red light.

Victor was borne gently down the ladder, to the heart of the ship. There were men for each set of wheels mounted on the wall; red, green, blue flashing lights, brass levers set in the floor, men speaking into tubes poking from the ceiling; one man gazing like a fortuneteller into a blue glowing pool of light; everywhere the writhing pipes, the exposed organs of the creature, and these ragged men feeling and feeding and touching, adjusting. They glanced up at Victor, then back to their dials. They were not ghosts or dreams or the damned, but real men, alive, in the belly of this living thing. They were not old men, but something had made them old.

Hands placed him over a shoulder. This man was not gentle. He stooped to make sure Victor's head banged a hatchway, lugged him down a narrow passage with bunks set into the walls, through a curtain, past a room where three men looked up in surprise from their radios.

"*Amerikaner*," the one hauling Victor announced, and kept going.

"*Wo ist der Kapitän?*" came a shout. The man shouted something Victor could not understand, and slid him off his shoulder to the floor of a tiny bathroom.

The door slammed and flew open again.

It had taken two men to carry Butch; they wasted no ceremony dumping him on top of Victor. They shouted in German.

The bell shrilled, and now the siren was whooping, feet pounding past the tiny cubicle. The door slammed. A hand turned the lock. Victor rolled out from under his friend.

A cage enclosed a dim red light bulb. A tiny electric fan droned in the ceiling. The mirrors, the sink, the shower stall, the junior-sized toilet were all of stainless steel, whorled with endless polishing. Just beyond the door, a loudspeaker popped and played a lady crooning a slow tune: *That old black magic has me*—boom—*in its spell . . .*

Of course it was the Mobile station; for some reason Victor had expected "Lili Marlene."

Rubbing his face on his shoulder, he worked the gag over his head. He would always taste these fibers on his tongue. "Butch," he said. "Turn around here. Maybe I can—"

Those icy fingers up and down my spine . . .

"Hold still." He fidgeted around to face Butch's back, took the end of the knot in his teeth, tugged like a terrier until he saw some slack, then pulled on the other end. The knot fell apart.

Butch spat the gag from his mouth. "Jesus God, thank you Sandy, at least I can breathe."

"Well they got us," said Victor, "they got us this time. Was there any way you could have kept from falling off that roof, Butch?" He pulled up against the door. "I mean, we all make mistakes, but all you had to do was stay where you were."

Butch wiggled onto his side. "Whose bright idea was it to climb up there in the first place?" His eyes flashed. "Who spotted 'em comin and told you to run?"

"We aced it," said Victor, "between us, we aced it. Look at us. Look where we are." He thumped his head on the door. "I wish this was a dream and you'd just wake me up."

"Sandy, did you get a look at this thing? It's the—the—it's about the *blackest* thing I ever saw."

"I hope Joseph gets the Army and the Navy and the Marines," Victor said. "I hope he blows this thing to hell and us with it."

"Aw Sandy, talk about a boat worth stealin! Did you get a load of their guns? You and me and brother man ought to get hold of this here, couldn't we have a time?"

"Fat chance," said Victor. "They just want us to think about it awhile before they kill us."

Butch's eyes shone with a thrill, as if he'd been the one doing the capturing. "Nobody's gonna believe this," he said.

"You're forgetting something, Butch. We're not gonna get a chance to swap this story around. You hadn't got a knife or anything?"

"Nope. I guess we'll just have to wait on brother man."

"Joe and Diana on that boat, against this ship and those guns?" Victor shook his head. "We can't wait. We got to figure out something."

"I'd put on another jubilee," said Butch, "only I don't think these boys'd know what it was."

"At least you had some bright ideas," Victor said. "All I do is get us in tight places. I always think I've got it figured out, you know, when I start into something. But people never do the way I think. They do the other way around. Does it seem like that to you?"

"Maybe you're the one that's backwards," said Butch. "I don't look to what other folks do. I just look out for myself."

Victor stared at his feet. "You got me out of jail twice, and got yourself in deeper both times. You didn't have to do that."

"A man's got to look out for his dog," Butch said with a crooked grin.

"I'm not your dog."

"Sure you are. A man's dog is his best friend," Butch said, slinging hair from his eyes.

Victor had to smile.

"I heard what that son of a bitch said about the old lady," Butch said. "You forget about that. You can't help what she did. I got old lady problems myself. They got minds of their own."

"Willie did what she wanted, all right," said Victor. "I tell you what makes me happy. We screwed up his plan, but good."

"He is a son of a bitch, though, ain't he," said Butch. "I never would thought you could run a spy house out of that old cabin. I had my kettle *that close* to their place. Jesus. The Nazis. They're not like I thought. They ain't even *wearin* helmets."

The bell started shrilling, men running fast past the door. The red light blinked off three times. A shudder ran through the air. Victor's ears popped. "Did you feel that? They shut the hatch."

Butch's eyes widened. "What does that mean?"

"We're going down."

"You mean like down under the water?" said Butch.

"You got it. That's why they call it a submarine." Victor closed his eyes and leaned against the bulkhead. The floor began urgently vibrating. The room sank like the elevator in the Admiral Semmes Hotel in Mobile. The sound of water swallowed the walls, then the waves ceased—a breath withheld—the churning diesels.

How deep could they go? This was the Trough. A million miles down through the dark. Light never comes here. The fishes are blind. They blunder into one another and open their mouths and swallow what they cannot see. Victor imagined the monster sinking through layer after layer of his troubles, until the weight of them all would cave in its sides and he would surely drown. Roy Glass was right. And the cop. And his father, and Willie, and the nagging voice inside him that kept up the count of his uncountable faults. This was what Victor earned by his actions. This was where his quest brought him—to a stainless steel bathroom on the floor of Mobile Bay, the weight of all that water pressing down.

The men shouted to each other, running by. The air began thinning, sucked out by a draft.

"Sandy?"

"Uh huh."

"You think this is it?" Butch's grin had faded. His throat scratched his voice. "Are they gonna dump us and get away with it?"

"They may not get away with it."

"I got somethin to say, and I better say it now so I won't go to hell. I'm sorry I burned that boat out from under you. I wouldn't have done it if I'd known you."

Victor sat back, amazed. "Are you really afraid of going to hell?"

"Hell, yeah, Sandy, ain't you?"

"Not really," said Victor. "I know a lot of people who'll get there ahead of me. Besides. I bet it's not so bad."

"You think?"

"I bet it's no worse than anywhere else."

"Well then everybody'd want to go," said Butch.

"They do. Look around you."

"Not me," said Butch. "I'm goin to heaven and tear up the place."

Victor laughed. Butch could make him laugh at the bottom of his troubles. Butch had no respect for fear, but he got scared, and here he was more scared of what God might do to him for his sins than of what the Germans had in mind. His wildness had taken him out to the edge, but not over. Victor felt a sudden wash of love for him. "I'm sorry too," he said. "I got you into this thing."

"At least I got to see it," said Butch. "Some folks never see one thing their whole lives. Listen. I got an idea. If we ever get out, maybe we could go into business. There's big money out in the swamps."

Victor said, "I don't think I'd make much of a moonshiner."

"I don't know, you're pretty sparky," said Butch. "Think it over."

The door opened out and Victor fell backwards into the passageway—two looming Germans and Glass, upside down. Glass said something about the *Kommandant*, and turned on his heel.

"Here we go again," said Butch. The sailor stooped to lift him, but instead flashed a knife and cut the cords binding his hands to his legs, then the cord at Victor's ankles.

"Thanks, Adolf," said Butch, as the big silent man helped him up. They were shuffled up the dim passageway to a room cluttered with tables, chairs, and more silent men. Everyone looked to one corner, where Madame stood smiling at a bearded

submariner. Another sailor crouched in front of them. A flashbulb popped. The first sailor beamed, kissed Madame's hand,
and melted back into the huddle.

Victor realized that the men had arranged themselves in a
line, each one waiting his turn to pose with Madame.

The engines were silent; the pop! of the flashbulb the only
prominent sound in the murmur. Victor pictured the submarine
hovering over the bottom.

Madame spotted them in the door. "Ah, *bringe sie hier*." The
crewmen parted to let the boys through.

She wore black, under a tweed raincoat, and a sizable glittering diamond on one finger. The red light was kind to her
face. She smiled, a seamless ironical smile. "Victor, don't look
so shocked," she said. "These men all know me. I'm a legend
to them. They want to have their picture made with me. Don't
you? Come here."

"No thanks." Victor squared his shoulders. "I've got a picture
of you that'll last me for good."

She laughed, hooking her arm through the arm of the nearest
crewman. "I'll bet you do. As you can see these boys are starved
for new faces. I'll be treated like royalty."

For the first time Victor realized he was at least ten inches
taller than Madame. He straightened up, so it would show.
"Where are you going?"

"Home," she said. "My new home. My new life. I plan to
be very happy."

"Germany?"

"France, actually. It's all the same now. One Europe. They
love me there."

Victor felt like the little dog in the movie, yanking the curtain
aside to expose the wizard as a frowsy old man. "You had to
kill Edgar and the others to get to France?"

Madame took a moment to pose with a dark-haired sailor too

young to have started a beard. "*Vielen Dank*, Madame," he said eagerly, backing away.

"*Bitte*. Boys, *das reicht*."

The men grumbled, but an officer said something authoritative and they filed out through the hatches.

That left the pair guarding Victor and Butch—and Madame.

"I guess you're rich, aren't you," said Victor.

"I didn't have a nickel in my name as long as Edgar was alive," she said. "The cables went this morning. His accounts in Zurich are mine. And then poor Charles divined what had happened, and stood there and shook like a leaf and threatened us. Roy took care of him. I didn't have the heart." Her eyes flashed as she poised her fingernails on a steel table. "I had the heart for Edgar, though—silly old fool! He double-crossed *us*. He didn't care a thing about me, at the end. He ruined himself."

"He didn't *kill* himself," Victor put in. "You did that."

"Tell her, Sandy!"

"I did," Madame said. "And I'd gladly do it again. There's a better life ahead of me. I had to go beyond Edgar to find it."

"That's great," Victor said. "I bet he was glad to help you out. Remember Diana? She knows what you did. She's with us now."

Madame shook her head as if trying to make herself understood in a foreign language. "No, no. Listen to me. Diana has nothing to do with it. She and Edgar were a phase in my life, and that's over. She can fly on her own. I've taught her well." She clenched her hands and went on in an agitated whisper. "I'm going to have a better life. I have something waiting for me. They want me to be the voice of the New Europe. Imagine. My voice broadcast through the air to millions."

"You mean you're a traitor," said Victor. "Like Tokyo Rose."

"Not a traitor. A heroine. You can be one or the other, you know, depending on whose side you're on, and when. You can be both." She resumed her smile. "The newspapers will love the story. I'll be the talk of the Reich."

"What happens to me and Butch?"

Madame said, "I suppose you'll live or die. I don't care."

"Maybe so," said Victor, "but we won't rot in hell, will we, Butch?"

"Not a chance." Butch stuck out his chin.

Roy Glass came through the forward hatch. "There's some radio traffic," he said. "We may have trouble getting out of the bay. Henkel intends to surface and go full speed through the pass. The fog is very heavy. We have a good chance."

"I'll just stay here out of everyone's way," said Madame, backing into a little cubicle. "This is so exciting. A submarine." She pulled the curtain over the door.

"We'll dispose of our other problems now," said Glass, with a meaningful wave of his hand. He rattled keys, unlocking handcuffs. The Germans took their captives by the arms.

"Do not make one step out of line," said Glass, nudging the base of Victor's neck with the long black pistol.

The red lights pulsed. The hissing swelled suddenly to a roar, and the rush of water through the walls. The floor tilted. They went down to the heart of the ship.

35

FROM THE DEEP darkness, the submarine rose and kept rising, trembling the surface before it broke with the vast subterranean roar that had shattered Victor's dream the very first night. Huddled against the wall of the conning tower, he felt the water shuddering past the skin. The cold mouth of the gun pressed his neck. Men shouted over the bell.

A sailor scampered up the ladder and threw open the hatch. Sweet cool air flooded in. The submariners laid back their heads and took big hungry breaths.

Glass barked instructions. The men took Victor first up the ladder and out to the bridge, then Butch, who cursed and lashed out. Still the dark night. The fog smelled so clean.

You know how. You know how to be brave.

But the gun was too close on his neck. He was marched down a perilous stairway to the deck, rolling and pitching in the fog. Roy Glass stayed on the bridge. The rest of them tiptoed out the slippery catwalk, past the machine gun.

A big sideways swell struck the submarine. One sailor went down on his knee; the others grabbed for the cable. Victor turned in slow time to see the conning tower, the mist swirling, the sleek prow materializing in one eyeblink, sweeping out of the fog at a terrible speed, bearing directly for the submarine.

The men on deck saw it too and started to run. There was no time.

The great prow closed the distance and struck the submarine with a mammoth concussion, flinging everyone off the deck into the air.

Victor tumbled a cartwheel and landed whump! on his back. As a wave closed over his face he knew he was okay and Joseph had come to save him. Get your head up and swim and find Butch and get around the stern somehow, get to the boat. He fought up to the spectacle of the submarine on its side, impaled on the *Constance*'s nose, then slowly righting itself and pushing the intruder away. The siren screamed. One man clung to the deck. Someone—Glass?—staggered down from the bridge.

A flicker of light in the bow of the yacht, then a flame sailed over and exploded against the forward machine gun, spreading a pool of fire.

Butch thrashed and hollered. Victor shouted, "We've got to swim!"

Two more gasoline bombs skimmed across and burst on the deck guns, sending men who had managed to climb back aboard fleeing up the ladder to the bridge. Another bomb erupted at their feet. Victor witnessed the horrified rush for the hatch.

He put his face down and swam blindly, lunging up to let his lungs explode and make sure Butch was still behind him, then kicking off again. Now a machine gun rattled, the fires were dimming on deck, the *Constance* seemed to draw closer. Victor kept swimming. The water was black and running on past, pitching him up and down. He opened his eyes under water. He discovered the waves around him were thick with flounder, floating, silky brown bodies, strange double eyes staring up at him. How could he see in the dark?

He flung his head up. A line of raindrops marched across the top of a wave and spattered past. Then a large darkness came between Victor and the submarine—the stern of the *Constance*. Diana beckoned from the top of the ladder.

His hand reached the first rung. Butch flailed up behind him. Victor hung to one side, heaving for air. "You—go first!"

Butch dragged himself up.

Come on, Victor. Live up to your name.

The waves full of fish . . .

He scaled the ladder, accepting Diana's strong hand, landing on both feet, shaking water from his hair.

"They're still shootin!" yelled Butch.

A dot of stuttering light—bullets raced down the cabin toward them, tossing up splinters, whanging past. They ran for the shelter of the port rail.

Diana cried, "You've got to stop him!"

Victor looked forward. Joseph crouched at the bow on one knee. The flaming end of a rag drooped from his hand. He gave a wild jungle scream and slung the bottle with his best overhand fastball throw. He was possessed. He was fighting his war. He had forgotten all about driving the boat for the pleasure of throwing fire at the thing.

"He's out of his mind," said Diana. "He pointed us straight at that thing and pushed down on the throttle."

Butch ducked by the rail. "Sure got us out of a scrape."

Victor crept up the deck. "Joseph! We're okay! Let's get out of here!"

Joseph swung around, hair tangled with sweat, his eyes strange, glinting wild. "They came into my trap."

A line of bullets sang past. The glass in the pilothouse shattered, pouring in a sheet like water to the floor.

"You got 'em, Joe, you got 'em! Let's go!"

Joseph stood to hurl the bomb. It ruptured, a bright flash on the afterdeck gun. The last gunner raced for the hatch. The clang carried over the water. The deck would not burn, but fire pools licked and ran down it. The submarine grunted aloud, whooped its siren, and began to move.

"They're getting away," Joseph shouted, shaking his fist. The submarine showed its whole flank and glided by in a determined line, shrugging out the flames on its back, not at all like a wounded beast. The fog closed around it.

"Come on!" Joseph ran to the pilothouse. He sent them all dancing back two steps with the acceleration.

Victor collided with Diana. "She's on there," he said, "with Glass. They're getting away."

Diana gave him a curious look. "Do you think you can stop them yourself? No one believed your brother on the radio."

"They might believe you," Victor said. "Do you know how to run that thing?"

"Sure . . . but what should I say?"

"Just tell 'em what happened. Make them believe you."

"Okay, okay." Diana held up her hands, backing to the stairs. "You talk to Captain Marvel up there." She disappeared.

Victor went to the pilothouse, where Joseph was spinning the wheel through his hands. "They had you on that thing, Vic, I knew it!" He wiped sweat from his face. "What did they do to you? How the hell'd you get out!"

Victor leaned on the door to catch his breath. "Man, your timing was perfect. They brought us up to shoot us. Two more seconds and you'd been too late."

"That girl's pretty handy." Joseph stuck his head through the shattered window to scan the horizon. "After you went under she kept us running a circle, while I tried to raise somebody on that damn radio."

Butch came to the door, his eyes wide. "Looks like our bombs worked out, hey, brother man?"

"Made 'em think twice about hanging around," Joseph said. "Go bring up some more."

"Sure thing." Butch hurried off.

Joseph stretched out his hand. "Look, Vic. The fog's thinning out. There they are. You can see 'em. They're trying to get to the pass. Look at 'em run. You son of a *bitches!*"

Victor stepped out on deck. The wind was dividing the fog into great drifting clouds and canyons of clear air. The long shadow broke clear of one wall and slipped into another, vanishing, reappearing, changing shape. The *Constance* ceased to be a stately thing and rose up on her hull, throwing a high plume of spray.

He rushed down the stairs to find Diana in her grandfather's chair, bent over the microphone, her eyes shining with excitement. "I've got them. They need to know our heading."

"South, to the pass," Victor said. "Fort Morgan. They're trying to get out of the bay."

"Unknown transmitter please report over," said the loudspeaker.

Diana pressed the trigger. "We don't know where we are in the bay, but we're heading south. They're trying to get out through the pass. Help us, please! Over!"

A long peal of static, and then the flat voice said, "Ah, roger, unknown transmitter, we'll get someone there to meet them, you get out of there. Over."

She turned to Victor. "They thought Joe was a kid playing pranks. I guess it just takes a girl's touch." Then she lost her smile. "You saw Grandmother. What did she say? Did you talk to her?"

Victor leaned on the door. "Oh, sure. She said it was time for you to fly on your own. Since she taught you everything you know."

Diana's mouth tightened. "She said that?"

"She's going to France. She wants to be the next Tokyo Rose. You were right. She's nuts. But they loved her, those men. They were taking each other's picture with her. The last thing I expected, let me tell you."

They climbed the stairs. They could hear Joseph shouting as he revved the engines. They came out on deck just as *Constance* broke through the last veil of fog to the glittering bay, deep blue in the haze of the setting moon. A sandy peninsula stretched away east, where the sky showed the first gray of morning. The darkness out west was unbroken.

Half a mile directly south the long shadow made foam, driving fast for a distant cluster of lights—the fort. The pass. The open road to the Gulf.

Now the *Constance* was closing the distance. Victor made out the black tower, the pulpit, the deserted bridge. If they turned their periscope this way, the Germans could not miss the big gleaming yacht pursuing them under this moon. The bell must be ringing, men running through passageways. Victor wondered if any of those shiny torpedoes were aimed out the stern.

Butch came up from behind, hauling a crate of bombs. "What do you think, folks? Brother man's gonna catch the damn thing!"

From the towers on the sandy point came slender fingers of light, probing the mouth of the bay, feeling this way and stopping, reversing, touching every scrap of driftwood floating in from the Gulf.

The submarine faltered. The *Constance* bore down, skimming over the waves.

"Get your heads down!" cried Joseph, pulling the *Constance* about, setting a direct course for the nose of the thing. This time he meant to shear it off.

Butch dashed up the deck.

Victor pulled Diana down beside him.

The black wall flew by. The *Constance* struck a glancing blow, jarring every splinter. Victor reeled to the stern. The submarine was veering off the wrong way, away from the pass, into the shallow water in the lee of the point.

The light fingers felt over and found it and played on its length. A siren croaked a low throaty note, rising, then another, rising, crying alarm, more lights blazing.

The submarine plummeted full speed and blind for the beach. Victor stared in awe as it bellied into the sandy bottom and plowed on, rising out of the water like a massive black whale, exposing its hugeness, grinding to a halt in shallow water not a hundred yards from shore.

Guns erupted along the beach, a white flash then *boom!* and a massive upheaval of surf. A shell struck just forward of the conning tower.

Victor heard Joseph's rebel yell; the yacht's prow swung around for another run; pounding guns, water geysers erupting everywhere around the submarine, and too close to the *Constance*.

Victor ran for the pilothouse. "They're shooting at us, Joe! Don't go in there!"

But Joseph glowed with rage and the unfinished battle. He gripped the wheel. Giant columns of water shot up on both sides, but Joseph drove through as if they were greetings. He would strike the last blow.

The black beast lay on its side, spilling smoke. Men popped out of three hatches and threw themselves into the bay. Victor yelled, "Get down!" The *Constance* drove into the submarine's side.

Then Victor was down on his hands in the broken glass. His ears rang. He pulled himself up on the door. Blood ran into his eye.

In the cabinet. The code machine. He stumbled on deck.

The two ships were joined forever, shivering at every shell. Butch knelt in the yacht's blasted bow, lighting fuses, chucking the bottles into a ragged hole in the wall of black steel. Gasoline pooled at his feet.

Flares shot up from the shore, filling the sky with pink light.

A rag touched the deck. "Butch, watch out!" Victor cried. Fire sprang up. Butch danced back, gaping at the flaming bottles in his hands, sent them soaring over his head and took off down the deck. The crate exploded—flying glass and a white-yellow fireball that arose like the sun and knocked him out flat.

Victor dragged him away from the flames. He saw Joseph helping Diana over the stern rail. A rocket screamed over. Diana screamed, too, and leaped for the water.

Butch sat stunned. "Hey Sandy," he said, with a sideways grin.

Victor shook him hard and got him on his feet, one leg over the rail. "Come on, Butch, swim like hell for shore," he shouted, and pushed.

Butch plunged under and came up thrashing.

Victor grabbed the machine, teetered on the rail, and jumped.

The water seemed warmer now. He towed the machine behind him. It was ruined, but it was still proof.

Diana was walking on the water twenty yards away.

Not on the water. Up to her knees. A sandbar. A shallow path to the shore. She hid her face from the shrapnel.

Victor's feet found sand. He stood up and turned to see. The guns hammered jets of white fire and loud streaking shells. The *Constance* sagged at the stern, her flying bridge tottering, big gaping holes in her hull, fire raging through the forward cabin. The searchlights ignored her to wander the length of the beached submarine.

The shore was lined with soldiers and jeeps and guns barking into the air. The first wave of survivors waded ashore, inspected by white beams of light.

Butch reeled up. "We're all right!" he cried. "We're all right! Sandy? Where's brother man?"

Victor searched all around in the water, then at last spotted Joseph—on the wreck of the *Constance*, at the stern, where the waves washed over the rail. He stood with his arms folded, watching the catastrophe.

You won, Victor said. You beat them now get off that thing. And just as he said it, in the moment he saw his brother and his mind whispered danger, a gun thumped and a shrieking white fire tail shot over the conning tower and plunged into the burning cabin.

The detonation rumbled like a wind, then a roar, then the

Constance blasted open with the force of its fuel igniting, a fire cloud touching off a bomb inside the submarine, and then another, and then the whole world blew up. The air filled with black smoke, obliterating the moon.

This was the dark burning stench of it. War. This ringing in Victor's ears. This bleeding. This hollow inside. Diana waded toward shore. Victor stumbled in the dark. "Joseph!"

"Come on," Butch hollered, coughing, "this way!"

Victor went to the sound of his voice. The sandbar gave way and he toppled into the water. Wherever his hand came down he touched fish. The water was bursting with them. Flat brown flounders and groupers and stingarees, millions of tiny silvery mackerel, dancing shrimp, snappers and redfish and catfish and trash fish had all left their depths and come to these shallows to wash up on sand, to stare at the moon, and to die.

This was the real jubilee. Nothing could stay under this bay.

36

RETURNING YOU now to our studios in New York, this is Carl Phillips for the Mutual Broadcasting System. Good evening." The radio man held his breath, raised his hands, and broke out in a smile. "That's all, folks."

Moore's Store erupted with applause. The ladies of Magnolia Springs surrounded the announcer, pinning him against the produce bin. Everyone else mobbed Victor and Butch, shaking hands, ruffling hair, squeezing shoulders, giving out loud bursts of enthusiasm. Everyone told them how brave they were, and touched them as if some of the bravery might rub off.

The front door jingled as families made their way out. The newspapermen shot pictures of the code machine in its honored place beside Mr. Jesse's cash register. Four women hugged Victor and said they were friends of his mother. Mrs. Wagner leaned in to say she always knew one of her students would go on to great things. The Methodist minister asked if the boys would speak to the Youth Union about their experiences. (Butch lolled his head to one side and stuck out his tongue.) Mr. Jesse pumped Victor's hand and said this would have been the greatest day in the history of Moore's Store if only the slick-haired fellow had remembered to mention the name on the radio.

Victor stood in an embarrassed daze and said the same polite sentences over and over. He'd never imagined there were so many people in all of Magnolia Springs. Girls who wouldn't speak to him at school brought their parents up to meet him. Boys with whom he'd sneaked cigarettes hung back, then stuck out their hands and mumbled congratulations. A group of grown men huddled at the back of the store, awaiting their turn.

This was all Victor could have dreamed, the town at his feet, the old ladies marveling "coast-to-coast radio" and clicking their tongues. Butch was there to share in the glory, but Joseph was gone, and nobody mentioned his name. Maybe that was why he felt so empty.

Then he saw his father among the men waiting in back. His emptiness turned to cold fear. He had known that fear too many times not to feel it as a reflex.

He straightened. Stand up and look in his eye. You're not sorry. Or guilty. Remember. You won. You're not his little boy. Show him.

Daniel came up at the rear of a gang of shrimpers who pounded Victor on the back and said "Goddamn!" and "Nazi hunter!" and "You sure this your boy, Dan?"

"I'm sure," came that colorless rumble. "Hello, son." He held out a hand.

Victor shook it.

The other men backed away.

His father was shaggy, unshaven; he looked as if he hadn't slept in a month. His eyes were the same old hard line. "What did you do to your face?"

"When we ran into it," Victor said. "I hit my head on a door."

"You didn't tell your mother you were hurt, when you called," said the old man. "They get a doctor to look at that?"

"Sure," Victor said. "It's nothing. Don't worry about it. How is she?"

"She's asleep now. I've talked to that FBI fellow, Roberts. Come on." He put an arm around Victor's shoulder and led him to the front of the store.

The radio man intercepted them. "I guess this is your dad, say, Victor? Mr. Sylvester, my pleasure. I bet you're proud of this young man."

Okay, what will you say to that you old—

"We surely are," said his father.

The announcer beamed. "You boys were terrific. Real human stuff. They'll love it."

"Thanks," Victor said, then his father caught his eye and he said, "thank you, sir. Listen, Daddy—I got to talk to somebody a second." He waded back through the perfumes and print dresses, and spoke in Butch's ear. "The whaler's tied to a dock right out back. You give me five minutes and meet me. We'll get out of here."

Butch looked around from the sea of admiring faces. "Okay, Sandy. Take your time."

Victor went to the door. His father was already halfway up the street to the house. He followed. People came out of the store to watch him go.

The bug light cast the porch in an unhealthy yellow. Moths swirled around it. The blue star was gone from the window. His father climbed to the porch, leaned against the rail, and waited.

Victor came to the foot of the steps. "Where is everybody?"

"Your sister took the children to John and Rose's. Your mother's upset. I didn't want them around."

The night roared with crickets and frogs. Victor looked up at his father, outlined in the light.

"All that down at the store. You know they was going to do that?"

"They told me this morning," said Victor. "I didn't know there would be so many people."

"I guess that makes you feel pretty important," his father said. "The radio. All those people patting you on the back."

"No, Daddy." Victor did not want to be here.

His father folded his arms. "I took the boat down to the fort this morning," he said, "see if there was anything left. The tide took it all away."

Victor swatted a bug from his ear.

"I don't understand what happened to Joe," said his father. "I guess I didn't know him."

Victor said, "He was brave, no matter what they told you. He could have got away. He had plenty of chances. It was like he had something to prove." He shifted back into shadow. "I know how he felt."

His father eased down to the top step. "Come sit here."

"I'll just stay where I am," Victor said. "I'm not sure I belong here anymore."

His father sighed. "I know what you're thinking," he said. "You been through a lot. I put you through some. But that's life. You got to learn to be tough."

"Oh, I'm tough. You don't know how tough I am." Victor swallowed.

His father said, "You could have come to me with some of that. I could have helped you."

"You never would have believed me," said Victor.

"You might have tried."

Victor steeled his heart. "I never even thought about it."

The old man put his hands together. "I done plenty of things I'm not proud of."

Victor waited.

That was all.

They stayed quiet a while, listening to the night sounds, and then Victor said, "I have to go."

His father pushed up off the step with a groan. "Come on inside, your mother will want to see you."

"I can't. I can't stay here. I'll come back. I'm not the same. I need to go somewhere. I got to think about things."

"Son, come inside and let's get some supper. A good night's sleep is what you need." He opened the screen door and waited, the harsh yellow light in his face.

Victor stood in the yard looking up. A moment of truth arrived, and went by.

He turned and took off running toward the river. His father called his name, but that made him run harder. He flung up his hand and waved over his shoulder and ran.

37

THEY RODE the whaler down the river in darkness.

After a while Butch said, "What did he tell you?"

"Not much." Victor steered with one hand. "It was like I hardly knew him."

Butch stretched out in the bow. "My old lady hadn't known where I was since the first time I got away from her."

"When you run off like that," Victor said, "where do you go?"

"To the woods," said Butch. "You can get along fine in the woods. There's plenty to do."

Victor steered into the wide lower river, lightless woods on both shores. "I thought I might stay at Willie's for a while," he said. "It's not too bad. There's plenty of room."

"Being inside makes me squirrely," said Butch.

They puttered on a while, then the shore opened out for the mouth of Noltie Creek.

"I tell you," said Butch, "I love the idea of the dragon lady and old Glass settin in jail in Mobile."

"I hope Diana's not in there with them," Victor said.

"You think she'll come lookin for you when she gets it all settled?"

"I haven't thought about it," Victor lied.

Butch waved at a jungly point. "Let me off yonder, Sandy. I got an idea to drop in on old Dauphine. Give her a shock. She won't believe what all I got to tell."

Victor slowed the boat. His heart sank. He didn't want to face the island alone. "Don't you want to come out there with me? I thought we were going in business together."

"I'll find you," said Butch, standing up in the bow. "Weren't we fine, though, you and me, talkin on the radio? You reckon anybody heard us?"

"Everybody in the world," Victor said. "They say we might have to testify at the trial."

Butch grabbed for a vine and swung up to a low-hanging branch. "They hadn't heard everything yet," he said, grinning down. "You just stay out of trouble."

Victor brought the boat around to keep the propeller out of the mud. When he looked up, the branch was swaying. Butch was gone.

The river slept.

Victor felt the first uneasy twinge of loneliness. He set the tiller for the middle of the channel. Faint light from the stars showed the way. A mullet jumped clean over his bow.

THE AIR in Willie's house was unbreathed. He expected a ghost or a fragrance, some sign. She had to be here. She kept calling him. He kept thinking: if he could stretch out on his cot on the porch, let the bugs hit the screen, close his eyes and clear out his mind, he might be the boy he used to be, and hear what she was trying to say.

He wandered through the kitchen to check her hiding place behind the loose board.

He sat down in her chair and lifted his feet to the ottoman. The silence was overwhelming. He looked at the room from her chair. Without moving he could touch her jar of cold cream, her red leather Bible, a glass bowl of buttons and pennies and safety pins, the dials on the Silvertone radio, a box of perfumed notepaper, and an orange juice tin full of stubby pencils.

He knelt to plug in the radio. A bouncy swing tune burst out, all brass and syncopation. Victor sat on his heels and listened.

It brought Diana back to his arms, silken, dancing, warm breath on his cheek. That memory glowed and melted into the taste of that gentle kiss, while she pretended to sleep.

Strange, how people disappear on you.

Victor went to the screen door and pushed through, down the steps. A deep night breeze washed through the yard. Squirrels clicked and raced along the arms of a live oak. A boat rumbled through the mouth, into the bay.

Victor started out trotting along the white sand rut, then he lost his fear and went faster and ran over the top of the hill. It felt good and dangerous to run in the dark. With a powerful energy he sailed along the old familiar path, over roots, sending alarms through the brush. Nothing could slow him down.

He plunged off through vines to a ditch, through the stream, to the base of the oyster-shell mountain.

It reached to the sky.

Each step sank him in to his knees. Little landslides of shells skittered off down the sides.

With his legs buried, Victor imagined all the people who built this mountain hidden inside it, sending vibrations through his feet. He picked up an oyster shell to run his fingers over the scars on its back.

The marsh stretched out under the stars. Water carried the light to the western horizon. There was nothing but peace as far as Victor could see.

A NOTE ON THE TYPE

The text of this book was set, via computer-driven cathode-ray tube, in Garamond No. 3, a modern rendering of the type first cut by Claude Garamond (1510–1561). Garamond was a pupil of Geoffroy Troy and is believed to have based his letters on Venetian models, although he introduced a number of important differences, and it is to him we owe the letter which we know as old style. He gave to his letters a certain elegance and a feeling of movement that won for their creator an immediate reputation and the patronage of Francis I of France.

Composed by Crane Typesetting Service, Inc.,
Barnstable, Massachusetts
Printed and bound by The Haddon Craftsmen, Inc.,
Scranton, Pennsylvania
Typography and binding design by
Iris Weinstein

F
CHI

Childress, Mark

V for Victor

$18.95

DATE DUE
